THE SUMMER WE SKIPPED WOODSTOCK

WOODSTOCK

Jack Atherton

www.BOROUGHSPUBLISHINGGROUP.com

PUBLISHER'S NOTE: This is a work of fiction. Names, characters, places and incidents either are the product of the author's imagination or are used fictitiously. Any resemblance to actual events, locales, business establishments or persons, living or dead, is coincidental. Boroughs Publishing Group does not have any control over and does not assume responsibility for author or third-party websites, blogs or critiques or their content.

ISBN 978-1-953810-13-7

For my wife, Aymsley, who deserves better
And with thanks to Hugh

THE SUMMER WE SKIPPED WOODSTOCK

1

Leon

I have no hope. They stuck me in short center field, whatever that is. Phillip Fiedler somehow hit a ball straight up in the air and everyone's shouting, "*Heads up, Leon.*" Okay. My head is up. The ball is blocking the sun and the effect is dazzling. Worthy of *Aida*.

That's the opera I'm listening to through an earphone in my transistor radio. While it's 1969, a bunch of Egyptians from around 1969 BCE are singing a hymn to their goddess. I've been looking toward the bleachers at my goddess, Alyssa Lawrence, and smiling. Until now, when the ball is plummeting. They call it a softball. Before the game I tried squeezing it and it's not soft. Spaldings are soft. You know, the pink rubber balls. Instead of playing paddleball, at which I'm not bad, or even tennis, I agreed to fill out the staff softball team so I could spend an hour gazing at Alyssa.

Now I'll never behold my goddess again because the ball is about to kill me. Defying fate, and hoping Alyssa will see that even if I'm ridiculous, I'm at least courageous, I spread my arms wide and stare up at the missile hurtling toward my head.

The last thing I remember is hearing the roar of the Egyptians and the spectators here at Salzman's Hotel.

***

Alyssa

"Is he crazy?"
    "Is he dead?"

"Is he a complete idiot?"

I'm asking myself all that too, but the girls and their parents are the ones yelling. The question about idiocy came from Ardis Greenberg, a six-year-old who's as hard-boiled as the eggs they serve here at Salzman's, even when you order them loosely scrambled.

I'm worried that the outfielder's brains may be scrambled because that ball hit him smack in the head. I want to run out to see if he's all right, but I've got to stay here with my group. What was his name? Leonard? Something formal like that. He was sweet the other night when we all went bowling. What was he thinking staring at the ball and not sticking out his glove?

Oh, look at that. Hank is kneeling next to him, looking like a doctor. More a burly Ben Casey than a slim Dr. Kildare. Still. No, don't lift his head, sweetheart. Leonard may be in shock. Is he conscious? Oh, there's Dad. He's telling Hank, nicely I hope, not to move Leonard.

"Leon, I'm getting your mother," Sammy Ginzburg calls out. *Leon.* Yes, that's his name. Mr. Ginzburg is a guest who's been umpiring the game in a Hawaiian-style floral shirt, Bermuda shorts that reach down to his ankles, and pitch-black sunglasses, which explain most of his awful calls. Now Mr. Ginzburg is shuffling as fast as he can across the road to the lobby, even though he's about eighty and ate a gargantuan lunch, which caused him to complain he could barely move. Sweet man.

"Should we call an ambulance?" I ask from the stands.

"Does this town even have an ambulance?" Meaning Mount Freedom, New Jersey. That's Seth asking. He's a waiter. Seth thinks anyplace outside "the City"—meaning Manhattan—has only home remedies, like bleeding people with leeches.

"Run to the lobby and call nine-one-one," I order Seth. He's my friend so it's okay. Normally, Seth hates taking orders, which makes it hard to be a waiter.

"If he could run, he'd be in the game," Phillip jeers. Phillip's a busboy, and we're all the same age. Sixteen. He's the one who made the hit, which I never would've thought possible since Phillip was swatting at pitches like they were mosquitos.

Now we hear Donna Salzman's voice booming over the loudspeakers everywhere. Her family owns the hotel. Mrs. Salzman clips each syllable, but like pretty much all of us, she still sounds like a *Noo Yawka*.

I've tried working on my own voice. It's not easy without sounding affected.

"May I have your attention," Mrs. Salzman echoes through the speakers. It's not a question. "Magda Kraus. Paging Magda Kraus. Your son has been hit in the head on the softball field. Hit…*in the head*. Please go to the softball field. Also, Connie will be conducting calisthenics at the pool in exactly fifteen minutes. Thank you."

More than a hundred campers and adult guests are watching the annual game that pits Salzman waiters and busboys against the rest of the staff, including counselors like Hank. I'm a counselor too, but the game is restricted to male staff, even though my hits would have sailed way over Leon's head. I'm not brawny, but I'm lethal. Ask my dad. He's also on the hotel staff. He's the band's male singer and our team's left fielder. Dad's probably blaming himself for not having snagged that ball before it brained Leon.

Seth takes off for the lobby at a fast clip. Most people here don't know Seth is a dancer, and he can *move*. He can't play ball since he's almost albino and his skin is too sensitive to be exposed to the sun. Seth's been sitting in the stands with us with a towel over his head. My campers love him, including Ardis, whose favorite word is idiot.

My body sensitivity is my derrière. Not all the time, but today, thanks to these bleacher planks, which are about ten inches wide, and the lumber hasn't been sanded since it left the forest. It helps a little that I'm wearing sturdy plaid shorts. My outfit is completed by a white t-shirt with the name Salzman's in green above the silhouette of a muscleman diving off a board. The muscleman looks like my boyfriend, Hank.

Sandi, my co-counselor, has on sheer white short-shorts. Our little girl campers don't notice her underwear, but it's a good thing Sandi's not sitting with Hank's teenage boys, or with Hank, who pretends not to notice. It doesn't help my derrière that Ardis keeps squirming on my lap. She's a fidgety freckleface with frizzy red hair and glasses like goggles. She's a tiny child except for her mouth. I'd like to sit on top of Ardis, but her great-grandfather never takes his eyes off her.

Oh good. Leon's moved his legs. He's bending his knees and his fingers.

Leon can't be a complete idiot because Hank told me he plays classical piano. Although there are idiot savants who can do that and most anything else.

I hope he's going to be okay. We all do. Almost.

"When are you going to start the game again?" Ardis hollers.

2

Leon

My head is bound with a bandage. Alyssa has not visited me at the hospital, so I console myself, as always, with a fantasy. I imagine that when the ball assaulted me, Alyssa sprang up from the rickety bleachers, lunged to my aid, and tripped over one of her loud-mouthed campers. Then the ambulance brought her here to the emergency room, to a curtained cubicle next to mine. She's murmuring my name as doctors try restoring her to consciousness.

But, as always, the fantasy's interrupted, this time by Phillip. Unlike Alyssa, he has come to visit and he feels bad. As well he should. We agreed before the game that as my best friend this summer he would hit only ground balls nowhere near me. I didn't count on Phillip having even less control of a bat than I do.

Phillip is my age, sixteen. Like me he's tall and skinny, but with a much bigger nose, wire-rimmed glasses, and a cinnamon afro H. Rap Brown would envy. I think Phillip acts more like a nerd than I do, though I feel compelled to tell you that the word "nerd" was coined by Dr. Seuss in his 1951 story "If I Ran the Zoo," and Phillip would keep quiet about that. Perhaps I'm more of a nerd.

Or, as Phillip points out, "You're a moron." He adds, considerately, "Are you feeling well enough to discuss this?"

"Yeah," I exhale. Like he's one to talk.

Phillip showed up for the game in a shirt with a picture of Albert Einstein sticking out his tongue. Actually, Einstein was a down-to-earth guy. He would have worn a baseball jersey. Maybe the Yankees, or the Mets if he lived near Shea Stadium in Queens like I do, even though I've never been to a game. At least I have a cap.

"You're a moron," Phillip repeats slowly in his adenoidal drone. "I can't believe you thought looking like a moron would impress that girl."

"Goddess."

"That's sacrilege." Unlike me, Phillip goes to Temple.

He and I met two weeks before this softball game at Salzman's Hotel. We became friends because everyone thinks we're both morons, however many grades we've skipped. Actually, there's a guy at the hotel who makes us really look like morons. Hank Einhorn is not only older, he goes to Cornell, and he goes out with Alyssa.

He's my nemesis.

What's humiliating is that Hank doesn't know he's my nemesis and wouldn't give a rip if he did. He was the first person to reach me spread-eagle in short center field—which Phillip tells me isn't a real position, just the place where they stick an extra player who can't play.

Now look at this. Hank's come to the hospital. Probably because he's not only the teen counselor, but also captain of our staff softball team. He must figure with power comes responsibility. Hank loves power, if not responsibility.

Okay, maybe I'm being unfair. Hank's made the hospital bearable by bringing my transistor radio and the earphone in time for the final scene of *Aida*. It's hard to resent a guy like that, even if Hank can't resist joking, "I didn't bring your baseball glove because you wouldn't know what to do with it."

The thing about that glove is that it means a lot to me, although I make better use of it as a doorstop. My dad bought it along with the cap because everyone says 1969 is finally going to be the year for the sorry Mets.

Trouble is, being a refugee, Dad doesn't know a lot about baseball. Marilyn Monroe marrying and then divorcing Joe DiMaggio pretty much covers it. So the glove isn't the kind the other guys have—cowhide with intricate webbing, emblazoned with the name of a star like Mickey Mantle or Willie Mays. That's what Hank has, an old three-fingered Stan Musial glove. Hank oils it as lovingly as a girlfriend's back. Then he ties the glove up around a beat-up baseball to form a "pocket."

Hank let me try his relic on. But he's a lefty, and we're not sure what I am. While both my hands have to work equally well to play the piano, neither of them can do anything with a baseball, much less a glove or a bat.

Before we left Queens, Dad got me a glossy synthetic leather glove with a pre-formed pocket. We both thought it looked spiffy because it wasn't brown, like the leather ones, but red, white, and blue. Dad's all about fashion, being in the business.

Hank shut up a waiter when he called my glove a toy. That's why, when Hank now jokes about leaving my glove behind, I smile good-naturedly. Though not as wide as the candy striper wearing a pink pinafore. Cindy laughs out loud, squeezes Hank's arm, and whispers to him, not me, "I'll be right back. Have to check on another patient."

"I'll be patient," Hank quips. Which sends the cutie into gales of laughter.

When she leaves, I ask Hank, "Hey, aren't you already going out with someone?" I can't bring myself to say Alyssa.

"Yeah," Hank admits, lacing his hands behind his head and displaying his muscular arms like a trophy. "But Alyssa's…frustrating."

Which is the first thing I've heard at the hospital that makes me feel better.

***

Alyssa

Funny how when he was kneeling next to Leon on the softball field, Hank looked like a TV doctor. Though not mine. When *Dr. Kildare* starring Richard Chamberlain debuted in 1961, I was nine. When the series ended five years later, I was heartbroken. Richard was my first boyfriend. Blond and graceful, with gracious manners and a beautiful voice, speaking and singing. Yes, Richard sang love songs on an album I played next to my bed every night.

His rival on another TV show was Dr. Ben Casey. I don't remember the name of the actor, he meant so little to me, but Ben

Casey was dark and beefy and could have been a linebacker or a cop. Don't get me wrong. I respect cops and cheered with my dad for the Giants linebacker Sam Huff, 'til he went to the Redskins. Speaking of Dad, he's dark and beefy and everyone thinks he's extremely handsome, even when he's not on stage. Of course he sings beautifully. But he's no Richard Chamberlain.

When I was twelve I had my first real life boyfriend, Brian Cooper. We'd bicycle up and down the Long Beach boardwalk, our teeth rattling over every plank as we inhaled buckets of sea air. Long Beach, New York, not California. It's off the easternmost South Shore of Long Island, on the ocean. Brian and I did homework together. Brian helped me with math, and I helped him with English. Mom helped us both, since she's an English teacher. Knowing about my crush on Richard Chamberlain, Mom even gave me books about doctors. My favorite was *Arrowsmith* by Sinclair Lewis, although that doctor winds up abandoning his wife and baby and is kind of a creep. Brian and I also went to movies. We snuck into *Dr. No* because Brian had heard about James Bond and I thought it was a medical movie. No one warned me that this doctor wanted to blow up the world.

Mom, who is the gentlest person you ever met, hit the ceiling when she heard about me sitting in the dark with a boy who was getting "ideas" while ogling Ursula Andress in a bikini. You can imagine what Mom would've thought about my first party at home the next weekend, for both girls and boys. We watched TV and listened to Beatles and Dave Clark Five records in the basement, sprawled out on shag carpeting so tall you needed a machete to walk through it. And then—da-da-da-*daaa*—we played spin the bottle. It scared me to death. This was my house, my parents were right upstairs, and my rat fink little sister, Vanessa, was spying from the stairway until we spotted her and kicked her out, making her swear on pain of torture she wouldn't tell Mom and Dad.

Brian had mixed feelings too. He knew that he'd probably have Mom for English at Long Beach High and Dad for history. That's my father's full-time job, teaching history. He sings at Salzman's, and before that in the Catskills, but only during the summer. Dad also coaches baseball and football, and Brian wanted to go out for both—he had to stay on my father's good side. Also, Brian idolized my older brother, Johnny, Long Beach High's greased lightning wide receiver. Johnny was the only player expected to win a full ride to a top college. On the other hand, Brian was aching to make out behind the sofa where everyone the bottle pointed to went to kiss. Especially because committed couples, like Brian and myself, didn't have to kiss anyone else.

How was it? Okay. My braces made French kissing perilous. Brian had already wolfed down a dozen of Mom's pigs in blankets, which she made with Italian sausage since Dad is Italian. I nearly swooned, and not in a good way. Brian sensed this but chalked it up, not to his garlicky breath, but to my lunch box.

Sixth grade was the height of my Dr. Kildare fixation. It wasn't cool, but I still carried a tin lunch box everywhere stuffed with sandwiches, pencils, and kid lipstick, because the box showed Richard Chamberlain in his hospital scrubs. This ticked off Brian to no end. He finally had enough and said Dr. Kildare was—well, I won't repeat what he said, but let's say "a wimp."

I told Brian his ears made him look like Alfred E. Neuman from *Mad* magazine, which was cruel, but true. Brian's older sister told me that he slept for the next week wearing earmuffs. She made me apologize, which I did with maximum sincerity, but we broke up anyway. Brian was my last boyfriend for years because of something that happened that summer that I don't want to get into. The point is that now, in the summer of '69, I have a boyfriend who looks like James Bond and Ben Casey rolled into one: Hank Einhorn.

Eat your heart out, Brian Cooper.

And Dr. Kildare.

3

Leon

How did I wind up on a softball field listening to opera and daydreaming about my roommate's girlfriend? Because my parents decided to spend this summer in the country. Well, one of them did. Dad said his job selling women's sportswear would keep him in the City at least until August, when sewing machines briefly stop whirring and pushcarts quit clattering across Manhattan's Garment District. That means for the month of July, like a lot of husbands here at Salzman's, Dad is visiting only on weekends.

Let me clarify about him selling women's sportswear. Dad doesn't sell clothes in a store. He sells *to* stores from a factory. My mother got him the job years ago when she was a Garment District model, displaying clothes to national buyers. She and Dad met when he was studying fashion at the Parsons School of Design in Greenwich Village. Dad hoped to be a designer. He hoped even more that Parsons would send him to their Paris *atelier* so he could get back to Europe now that the Nazis were gone. None of that worked out, but at a Parsons cocktail party, debonair, elegantly tailored Fredi Kraus met the dazzling Magda Bentzinger, another refugee. She found him a job selling clothes instead of designing them, they got married, and two years later, on a snowy December night in 1952, I made my debut.

Now, sixteen-and-a-half years later, Mother seems to have accepted Dad's story about being too busy to visit us except on weekends. This is the first time we've ever escaped from Queens during the summer, except for visits to my mother's brother, Uncle Max, at his place in Connecticut. It was Uncle Max who lent us a car to drive to New Jersey. The chief appeal of Mount Freedom is that it's cooler than our apartment, which doesn't have air conditioning.

Uncle Max's Oldsmobile doesn't have air conditioning either, but—always pretending to be prosperous—Dad kept the windows rolled up so people would think the car was keeping us cool. Until they peeked in and saw us sweating.

The Olds quickly became a rolling, groaning Turkish bath. Yet heatstroke was the least of my worries. I doubt Uncle Max knew Dad was going to lash a half-ton steamer trunk to the top of the car. For the whole two-hour crawl through traffic from Queens to Mount Freedom, I feared the car's roof would cave in and we'd be crushed under my mother's cocktail dresses, my father's blazers, and my piano scores. Luckily, all the suitcases stacked on the back seat next to me propped up the roof.

To get out of Queens we had to pass the Calvary Cemetery. What a send-off. Three million people are buried there. We saw miles and miles of tombstones that at night must be terrifying. At 8 a.m. they were just depressing. Going anywhere in New York you can never be alone. Eight million people above ground and three million buried below. And I'm not including subways.

Soon, however, came the thrill of crossing the East River to enter Manhattan. And not by subway. For the first time in my life, over the Queensboro Bridge. We could see everything.

"*Look*." I pointed. "That's the UN isn't it?" Even with all the other buildings bristling around it, the United Nations tower seemed sleeker than the rest.

Dad asked, "Didn't your school ever take you?"

"No. Not yet."

"I don't know what the hell they do at the UN," Dad sniffed. "For all their yapping you'll still wind up fighting in Vietnam."

Mother said nothing, but I could see her neck stiffening.

Viewing Manhattan wasn't much of a thrill for my parents. For Dad, the City means work. My mother must have been thinking of all the Fifth Avenue stores where she can't afford to shop. But for me, Manhattan means success, acclaim, maybe even fame.

To complete this fantasy, I asked, "Dad, can we drive by Carnegie Hall?"

"Why? Your practice is going so good they're waiting for you?"

"C'mon."

"Fifty-Seventh Street is too crowded. I've got a faster way to get to the tunnel." The Lincoln Tunnel. Oh well. The kick when driving through that tunnel is spotting a line painted down the middle showing where, deep below the surface of the Hudson River, you leave New York and cross into New Jersey. But as we emerged from the tunnel and I gazed for the first time at the Garden State, my eyes glazed over.

For the next bumper-to-bumper hour on Route 46 we endured an endless succession of diners, strip malls, and billboards advertising yet more diners and strip malls. One sign did catch my eye. Painted to look like an old Dodge City wanted poster, it beckoned us to a place called Wild West City. Cowboys aren't my thing. I like swords more than guns. Still I figured, if we're this far west, somewhere in New Jersey there must be a tree.

Sure enough, at last Dad exited the highway and we arrived in Mount Freedom. This tiny town seemed a million miles from the City. Instead of strip malls we saw a wooden general store that hadn't been painted since Dodge City was in the planning stage. Mount Freedom also boasts a miniature golf course with obstacles that include a pygmy Eiffel Tower and a giant pig. We passed small but snug detached houses with front and back yards and thickets of trees. They had a cemetery for a few hundred people, not millions. Like a little kid, I pressed my face against the back window until Dad finally let me roll it down. We smelled cut grass instead of exhaust fumes. I beamed and Dad inhaled a bushel of fresh air. Mother, however, maintained her glacial reserve. She looked straight ahead and said nothing, apart from insisting we stop at a gas station so she could freshen her makeup before making an entrance. Then, a hundred yards ahead of us, the photo from the brochure I'd taped on my bedroom wall came to life.

"Is that the hotel?" I asked, amazed.

"Well, the sign says Salzman's," my father joked, ever unfazed. "So it's either the hotel or some guy named Salzman has a hell of a big house."

That guy was Izzy Salzman. He bought this summer resort right after World War Two, when his sons returned from the service and could run it. As a young man, Izzy and his wife Sadie had immigrated to the Bronx from a Russian *shtetl*. That's a Jewish village. Cossacks never got around to bashing their heads. Still, as Sadie sternly recalled after seeing *Fiddler on the Roof*, "There was no singing and dancing." Starting out with nothing, Izzy did well enough as a furrier during the Depression to move his family from the City to Mount Freedom. Then this shambling bear and his equally massive wife retired and played host and hostess.

Salzman's isn't the Ritz or even Grossinger's in New York's Catskill Mountains. Like Izzy, it's a little shabby, but cheaper than the competition. Originally, the old man purchased a scattering of cabins up the hill from a tree-lined pond. The hotel his boys built is more ambitious. Their modern main building boasts a vast laminate-paneled lobby with orange Naugahyde sofas and plastic plants. Two-story wings off each side of the lobby house dozens of guest rooms.

Shabby or not, as we approached the hotel my first glimpse of the main building gave me a jolt. Why? I've seen more beautiful places, even in Queens. It wasn't that the long building was slathered in swirls of white stucco. It wasn't the half-circular driveway filled with newer cars than Uncle Max's. It wasn't even the elation everyone feels when they arrive someplace for a vacation.

I think it was a premonition. A sense that in this building I'd find real romance, and that I'd find it because this is where I would change. I'd open up and become the kind of guy I've always wanted to be.

4

Alyssa

"May I help you unload?"

Those were the first words we heard this summer at Salzman's Hotel, and they impressed Mom. There was no question that the strapping young guy *could* help because—all right, I'm not going to keep going on about how he looks or you'll think I'm shallow. The question was whether Mom would allow him to help us empty the small U-Haul trailer hitched to our Buick Riviera. So "may" was the correct word. Sorry to keep going on about grammar, but I want to be a writer. Or at least graduate from high school.

Anyhow, Mom knew that hers was not the permission required. Unassuming as she is, Mom makes most of the decisions around the house. But not about packing and unpacking trailers. Dad has this down to a science, and he's warned us for years that if anyone removes a single item incorrectly, all our belongings will tumble out of the vehicle and down to perdition.

"That's kind of you," Mom said to the young man, "but my husband will be back in a minute."

Dad was in the main building saying hello to Cully Salzman. As head of the business end of the hotel, including entertainment, Cully is Dad's boss—although Marion at the front desk once told me that Cully is in awe of Dad. This is our second year at Salzman's. We used to go to Brown's in the Catskills until Dad had a fight with the bandleader there. Here, he's the leader. It's not that Dad is domineering. However, as Mom says, he can be "needlessly combative."

"Well, if your husband would like some help, I'd be happy to oblige. My name is Hank Einhorn. I'm the teen counselor." He smiled and I've got to believe Mom was dazzled too. Yet Hank didn't glance at me once.

"I'm a teenager," my sister announced.

"No, really?" Hank raised his black, beautifully arched eyebrows. Vanessa was sticking her head out of our bungalow's front window. Right after we arrived, she'd run from the car to avoid any work.

"Yes. I guess I'll be in your group." Vanessa gulped. "*Hank.*" My fourteen-year-old sister is no Southern belle, but she drawled his name so it sounded more like "hyacinth." Or, "Hello, sailor." I'm sure our mother planned to put a lock on that window.

To change the subject, Mom said, "This is my other daughter. My older daughter, Alyssa."

Hank glanced down at my outstretched hand, extended his own, and at last looked into my eyes. He smiled. Not wolfishly. More like inviting me into the joke. Exerting a slight but steady pressure on my tingling fingers, he said, "How do you do?"

I couldn't think of the answer, so Mom noted, "Alyssa is going to be a counselor too."

"Then we're colleagues." Hank grinned. "You'll have to give me tips about how to handle your sister," who, by now, was out of the bungalow and attaching herself to Hank like his Siamese twin.

I suggested, "Holding up a chair sometimes helps."

"Vanessa, as long as you've rejoined us, why not bring this inside?" Mom handed her a hat box that had been on her lap since we left Long Beach.

I wondered if Mom had reservations about Hank Einhorn. Was he too chiseled? Too charming? Having been brought up in an orphanage by nuns, and having taught high school for almost twenty years, Mom can spot troublemakers a mile away. As for me, standing almost as close as Vanessa, I didn't see any chinks in this guy's armor.

***

Leon

When we arrived at the hotel Dad pulled Uncle Max's car up under a thrusting canopy, Salzman's bid for Miami Beach glamour. A Black man greeted us. He identified himself as Sonny the head bellhop.

"Oh yes?" My mother swiveled her head and purred, "Thees is my boy, Leon. He iss going to be vurking fur you." That was Mother's Bavarian accent. Henceforth, I'll forego the phonetics.

Sonny turned his smile on me. I couldn't tell if it was menacing or I was simply scared about starting my first real job.

"By Labor Day we're going to grow some muscles on those bones," Sonny threatened.

"Let's start right now," my father said. He has a Viennese accent, lighter than Mother's, and a tighter smile. "Leon can carry our bags." We had enough bags to last Elizabeth Taylor through this eight-week vacation, but Dad was looking to save a tip.

Sonny understood and smirked. His smoky voice sounded like the singer Billy Eckstine, and he sported Mr. B's pencil-thin mustache. "No, no, can't have that. Leon's out of uniform. We must uphold the dignity of the establishment." No guests were checking in that day other than the parents of staff members like me, but Sonny was wearing sharply creased slacks, a bowtie, and a scarlet bellhop jacket with one shiny brass button. He seemed not to notice my mother's blatant appraisal.

I wound up lugging the luggage. As supervisor, Sonny still got his tip. My mother insisted. At least there were no stairs, because my parents' room wasn't in the main building but in a budget bungalow across the street. I never complain about economizing. It beats hearing them fight about money.

In fairness, a lot of guests get Dad's "special deal." Parents receive a discount when their kids work. If you're at least sixteen, you live in the staff quarters, Sadie Hall. That's why my family arrived three days before the July Fourth weekend rush. I was going to be a bellhop or die trying.

Leaning against the Oldsmobile, Sonny quizzed me between each run I made with my folks' baggage. After dropping their big trunk with a thud in the bungalow, I returned to the car to hear, "So, your mom tells me you're a musician. What kind of music you like?"

"Classical mostly, and what I guess what they call 'The Great American Songbook.'"

Four overstuffed suitcases later, "Sung by who?"

"Oh," I huffed, already exhausted. "A lot of people. Sinatra. Not so much the way he sings now. Back in the forties and fifties."

"Sinatra." Sonny snorted. "You know Frank Sinatra waited 'til nineteen sixty-seven—nineteen freaking sixty-seven—to record his first song by Duke Ellington? Does Duke Ellington rate a page in your 'Great American Songbook?'"

"Sure. Tony Bennett always sang Ellington."

"And Ella Fitzgerald. You like Ella?"

By this time Sonny had loaded me up like a donkey with garment bags, carpet bags, Val-a-Paks and purses.

"Ella's great," I wheezed. "Ellington's great."

"Now how did a white-as-a-sheet teenybopper like you figure that out?"

Well, since Sonny asked, I'll tell you.

While Phillip is undoubtedly right and I'm a moron, it seems I'm a moron with an official designation.

Last year Mr. Comras, my high school guidance counselor, furrowed his brow and told me, "Leon, let's face it. The reason you're an oddball is that you're an extreme introvert. Hello. Are you listening to me?" He called my mother in for a conference. Afterward, Mother put it differently. "*Du lebst in deiner eigenen Welt.*" You live in your own world.

Mother looks and sounds like the old German movie star Marlene Dietrich, substituting "w" for "r." Although when she's annoyed, Mother doesn't call me a "wotten" kid. She manages to say rotten.

I didn't inherit her looks. That's good, because what kind of guy wants to look like Marlene Dietrich? I did inherit my mother's thin frame, blond hair, and nearsighted blue eyes. While she refuses to wear glasses, as a little kid I picked out the thickest black frames we could find, hoping they made me look like…*Zorro.*

Zorro was the perfect alter ego for an introvert, the hero who fooled everyone into thinking he was a weakling. Every night I dreamt of rescuing the only girl I ever dreamt about up to that point, Marcy Pinto. In the dream, Marcy was tied to a tree. Nobody was bothering her, but for some reason, she was tied to a tree. "Go away, Leon, I'm fine," Marcy told me. I had to go away in my own dream. Later I figured the tree was a phallic symbol. But when I was eight,

Marcy and that recurring dream were blissfully innocent. In the dream I was wearing a real Zorro mask, not glasses.

The lenses were as thick as the frames. This came from reading a lot, although that took a while. Because my birthday is in December, my parents had me skip kindergarten and start first grade without knowing any of the letters of the alphabet. That meant during recess, our grandmotherly teacher, Mrs. Stonehill, had to lead me to a special room. She smiled and her cheeks grew even plumper. "These blocks are going to help you read, Leon."

"I'm too old to play with blocks."

"These are magic blocks. It's true." They were bigger than regular ones, and the raised letters were covered with sandpaper. "Look what happens when you rub your finger over the letters. Close your eyes and try it, dear."

I loved that she called me "dear." Still, "Why do I have to close my eyes?" I was a whiny kid.

"A wonderful blind girl named Helen Keller rubbed her finger over letters," Mrs. Stonehill said. Her voice caught a little. "Rubbing helped Helen remember."

I tried it. Then I heard Joan Caffiero laughing. Joan was the smartest girl in the class and she'd pried open the door. Soon everyone knew I was rubbing blocks. Tommy Sefcik closed his eyes and rubbed his fingers over my face. Joan's parents had to come in for a conference with the principal, my mother, and me. "Joanie felt so bad about telling the other children about Leon," Mrs. Caffiero said. "She cried all night." Joan apologized and Mrs. Caffiero gave me cannoli from their bakery.

What really makes me an introvert started long before that. For the first five years of my life I slept in my parents' bedroom. It must've felt crowded for them too, but my parents did have time for intimacy, assuming they still wanted some, because each morning before dawn my father lifted me out of my cot and sat me in front of the small black and white TV in the living room, the only other room in our apartment except for the kitchen and bath.

I know the time because at 5:00 a.m. the TV came alive. The geometric test pattern you saw after midnight in the '50s changed to a shot of the American flag. They played "The Star-Spangled Banner." Then came the first show of the day, *Modern Farmer*. A less useful show for someone living in Queens I can't imagine, but there it was, as sure as the rooster crows.

Then I watched *Captain Kangaroo, Mighty Mouse, Howdy Doody* and other kid fare, all of which almost drowned out my parents' fighting.

"They were on sale," my mother screamed, waving a green dress. I'm translating the German. It sounded worse in German. "Sherry arranged to get them for nothing."

"You wouldn't need three new dresses if you weren't inviting men for a pickup." My father spoke softly, with a chuckle in his voice, a thin smile drawing his thin nose down even lower. Dad was always chuckling. He knew it drove my mother crazy.

Yet I sensed he was right. The day before, when Mother was taking me on the subway to a piano lesson, we saw a scruffy teenager with slick wavy hair. He was listening to a transistor radio, a big one, without an earphone. Out of the loudspeaker a guy was howling, "You ain't nothin' but a hound dog…" I asked Mother why the singer was allowed to say "ain't." Then I saw the teen giving her a look that made me angry. I wanted to kick him but said nothing. Instead I turned away and looked forward to getting home in time to see my favorite TV show, *Million Dollar Movie*.

Channel 9 in New York was owned by RKO, the movie studio. Since original TV programming was more expensive, *Million Dollar Movie* played RKO classics constantly. Katherine Hepburn, Cary Grant, and my favorites, Fred Astaire and Ginger Rogers. Even if I didn't know the alphabet, those movies made me precocious about two things: music and romance.

Ginger was funny and cuddly, nothing like Mother. Fred was as debonair as Fredi, my continental father. But unlike Dad, who spent hardly any time at home, Fred Astaire was there for me—twice a day, since *Million Dollar Movie* played the same film twice a day. Fred sang the best music I knew as a little kid: Gershwin, Irving Berlin, Cole Porter, Jerome Kern. I sang his songs too, in a piping voice like Fred's, and played them by ear on our upright piano.

This old Bösendorfer was one of the few possessions Dad's wealthy parents smuggled out of Vienna, one step ahead of the Nazis. It had a rich mahogany finish that I learned to polish long before my playing was polished. Generous Uncle Max, a man with a big mustache and even bigger cigars, was so impressed by my noodling that he paid for piano lessons. Mother told me that was a sacrifice. So *Gott hilf mir*—God help me—if I didn't practice at least five hours a day, mostly before school, with blankets muffling the sound. I soon wanted to skip school to keep playing.

It was impossible to imagine ever doing it myself, but the best moment watching those movies was seeing Fred woo Ginger beneath the moon in a seaside gazebo. She'd been evading him. He refused to give up. He joked about how dull it would be to rejoin the crowd. Then Fred sang about being obsessed with the girl of his dreams, how she was the only one he longed for, in the sunshine and the moonlight. He was singing Cole Porter's "Night and Day."

While they danced Ginger still played at pushing Fred away. He limped back humbly, entreatingly. She then entered into their reverie, lyrical, jazzy, and fun. Too soon, the music reached a crescendo, subsided and unwound. Fred held Ginger like a pearl beyond price, leading her to a white deco banquette where she looked at him adoringly.

As a child, and here at Salzman's Hotel, I wondered if any girl would ever look like that at me?

"*Ahem.*"

What? Oh, that was Sonny harrumphing. We were back at my parents' bungalow. I was hauling the last piece of luggage, along with a mahjong set and a makeup case.

"I'm going to keep my eye on you, Lee-on." He shoved me, not too hard.

"How 'bout a little help with the door?" I asked.

"What are you going to do when I'm not here?"

"I'll get tipped."

"Oh yeah, Lee-on. I'm going to keep my eye on you."

5

Alyssa

My first day of work started as they all would. A hundred or so campers in their Salzman's t-shirts and some kind of shorts gathered at the base of the hill that leads to a pond. That's where Salzman's has a playset for the little ones, although bigger kids often commandeer it and swing high enough to touch the clouds. Then they jump off, whooping or screaming, and mark the landing spots to see who flew the farthest. The six and seven-year-olds get so excited seeing this that it's all Sandi and I can do to keep the girls from grabbing the big kids' ankles so they can go along for the ride.

The dell is dominated by a giant flagpole. At a blast from a trumpet the children run over, gather in age groups, and we salute at the beginning and the end of each day. A counselor for the junior boys, Neil Esposito, plays "Taps." My dad, the musician, says it should be "To the Colors," but at least "Taps" is more appropriate than Neil's theme song, "Tijuana Taxi."

Eugene Goldman and his wife Ellie are the day camp directors. Ellie covers her ears when Eugene bellows special announcements through his megaphone: "Bring permission slips signed by your parents for the field trip to Bertram's Island," a local amusement park. Or, "Stay away from the tall grass next to the campfire clearing. It's crawling with poison ivy. We don't want to have to slather you with calamine lotion." The Goldmans, who are middle-aged teachers like my parents, could make a fortune off a calamine lotion concession.

Next comes breakfast. Hank's teenagers take their meals at the back of the main dining room. The rest of the camp eat in the children's dining room. Its long tables invite food fights. Sandi may be all fluttering eyelashes and breathy small talk when male staff are hovering, but Hell hath no fury like Sandi after she takes a banana peel in the kisser.

The first and last time that happened I had to pry her hot pink fingernails off Stacy Aaron's throat. Stacy, a seven-year-old from Staten Island, is happy to fling fruits and vegetables and most of the rest of the menu because she's a picky eater, confining herself to macaroni and cheese. Ardis Greenberg can't understand Stacy. She encourages her friend to order plenty more than pasta, so Ardis can feast off two plates.

After breakfast our fourteen girls, along with Sandi and I, play dodge ball, or hula hoops, or doggy, doggy, where is your bone? That last is about guessing who's holding a rubber bone behind her back.

If it's raining we go to the arts and crafts room in the basement of the main building. Stacy, the food flinger, makes lanyard bracelets and necklaces with plastic thread that's every color of the rainbow. We stopped sculpting with Play-Doh because the girls weren't content to smell it, they also couldn't stop eating Play-Doh, even picky Stacy.

After a lunch of potato pancakes, or maybe kosher hot dogs, and of course, mac and cheese, the girls change into their bathing suits and we troop through the lobby to what Salzman's proudly advertises as its Olympic-sized pool.

***

Leon

Patrolling the lobby in my red jacket and black bowtie, a smile for everyone, and a hernia from schlepping bags for two hundred families that first weekend alone, I got my first glimpse of Alyssa Lawrence.

Now let's stick to the facts. No rosy exaggerations. The plain truth is that Alyssa is Botticelli's Venus come to life. He painted his goddess's hair with real gold. Someone did that to Alyssa's hair too. Her neck makes a swan's look stumpy. Tiny lines around her eyes crinkle when she laughs. Then they open and no Renaissance painting, no medieval stained glass—only the sky over Mount Olympus—can match the blue of her eyes. The one difference between Alyssa Lawrence and Botticelli's Venus was that Alyssa wore flip-flops and a bathing suit, covered by a long Salzman's t-shirt.

Ladies, please don't jump all over me—although that's never been my problem—yes, the first thing I noticed about Alyssa was her looks. Sue me. I'm sixteen. The first thing I notice about a fire hydrant is that it looks like a woman's breast. We're talking hormones, and not just for boys. My best friend back in the City—all right, my only friend—Joanie Caffiero says most girls at this age are the same way. You remember Joan, the girl in first grade who told everyone about my using Helen Keller blocks and then crying about it. Joanie has since moved to Manhattan's Upper West Side where her parents took over a cousin's bakery. They enrolled Joan in a Catholic high school, but we're still close.

"You know what the nuns tried to teach me?" Joanie once asked over the phone. "That teenage boys glom onto girls' looks, while God made girls get all gooey over faith, integrity, and self-discipline. Well forgive me, Sister Mary Gabriel, but that's a crock. Take it from me, Leon. Most girls get hot over a guy's looks too. Some may marry funny-looking rich guys, but they don't stop looking."

Where does that leave me? I'm not good-looking or rich. But I'm still free to look. Even that first time, I saw more than Alyssa's beauty. I saw that she was making sure her younger sister, a pretty pre-teen, rubbed on suntan lotion. I saw that Alyssa was carrying a paperback of a Jane Austen novel I hadn't read, *Northanger Abbey*. I saw Alyssa managed to maintain her poise despite getting tackled by more than a dozen little girls. They were hanging on her like Christmas tree ornaments. Except for a couple of tots whose heads popped out from beneath Alyssa's arms. As she throttled them in the crook of her elbows, all you could see were the kids' heads.

Everyone, including Alyssa, was laughing their heads off while she sneered with a tough guy snarl, "Hey, why don't you pick on someone yer own size?"

Two days after Salzman's day camp started, those girls already adored her.

***

Alyssa

Why Salzman's lets us traipse through the lobby on our way to the pool is beyond me, but I guess there isn't much choice. The alternative would be making an end run around the back of the kitchen, which is piled with garbage. Or we could march through the softball field. That would require crossing the road twice. This country road is hardly a highway, but the girls wear sandals and flip-flops on their way to the pool, and at least half their shoes always slip off after they've taken two steps. Which you don't want happening in the middle of even the pokiest road. Therefore, we soldier through the lobby.

The second afternoon we did that, I noticed something peculiar. A young bellhop, tall and weedy as a reed, was staring at me. He had blond hair, which is unusual at Salzman's, at least among men. Many of the women have varying shades of light hair, from ash to platinum, thanks to Clairol: *"If I've only one life, let me live it as a blonde."* My own hair could have gone either way, since Mom is fair Irish and Dad's swarthy Italian. It went blonde, a lackluster blonde with no help from Clairol, although being out in the sun so much adds a few glints.

The skinny guy stared at me through heavy black glasses that framed his blue eyes. He wore a short red jacket and a bowtie, and it occurred to me that he must be one of Hank's roommates in that hellhole where they make the male staff sleep. I hadn't visited yet, but Sandi told me it was awful.

Under my Salzman's tee I was wearing a two-piece bathing suit, pink with big white polka dots, that reveals about six inches of midriff—all my mother will allow. Was she raised by nuns, or had she taken vows herself? Sometimes I wonder. Besides carrying enough sunblock to protect not only my girls but also my sister, who never remembers to wear any, I also had to haul towels, life jackets for the girls who hadn't yet passed their swimming tests, and a book that always makes me smile. Jane Austen's *Northanger Abbey* is a scream, literally. Its heroine, Catherine Morland, is my age and, unlike Lizzy Bennet in *Pride and Prejudice*, Catherine is dumb as a stump. Her favorite pastime is rolling down hills. Also reading Gothic novels. They make her fear that behind every locked door she's about to find an unhappy wife who's been imprisoned or better yet, *murdered.* Catherine's a delightful goof. I, of course, can't read her adventures when my girls are swimming, but at the end of our pool session their parents bundle the kids back to their rooms, and I have a chance to swim, lounge, and laugh over Catherine 'til it's time to dress for dinner.

On that second day though, before we reached the pool—right in the middle of the lobby—my little demons thought it would be funny to jump me. I had to drop everything, fight for my life, and on top of everything else, contend with Hank's roommate staring at me with such a slack jaw, I could see he still had tonsils.

***

Leon

My first glimpse of Alyssa ended with everyone staring at me, thanks to my least favorite guest, Tilly Mintz. Tilly's husband, Ronny, is a big tipper. He slipped me ten bucks when I checked them in three days before. Then his wife, a harridan with a beehive hairdo, accused me of stealing an electric fan she'd brought from Flatbush. Sonny was going to fire me until we found the fan hidden in the spare tire well of her car. Tilly claimed she forgot it was there. No apology, and I didn't expect one. Still, Tilly must have been embarrassed because every time she's spotted me since then, she's complained to Izzy Salzman that I use my master key to sneak into her room, open her drawers, and paw her lingerie.

The Mintzes are forty-year-old fashion plates. Like most of the husbands, including my dad, Ronny is able to pay for his wife's eight-week summer holiday by working in the City Monday through Friday. Ronny is an accountant, and at his office he probably dresses like one. But when he returns to Salzman's every Friday night, Ronny festoons himself with a Beatles wig, a fake Zapata mustache, a Nehru jacket, and an amber amulet. Everyone applauds his flair. Tilly still has the legs for miniskirts. Well, they're skinny. But baking in the sun makes Tilly look seventy. Refusing to smile makes her look mean. Even though Mrs. Mintz probably has nice lingerie, Izzy isn't buying my alleged panty raids.

Still, that first day I saw Alyssa, Tilly had her revenge. Seeing me gape in the lobby, Tilly rasped within earshot of everyone, "Close your mouth kid. You look like a goldfish with glasses." Alyssa's campers giggled, maybe because my mouth opened as wide as a shark's trying to take a bite out of Mrs. Mintz. "Besides," Tilly consoled with mock sympathy, "she's out of your league."

Which, of course, was true. I prayed the lobby floor would open so I could disappear. Alyssa blushed furiously. I like to think she'd have said something comforting to me or cutting to Tilly, but those little girls, curse them, were pulling Alyssa out toward the pool.

For the next couple weeks, I continued watching Alyssa whenever I could. Not like a peeping Tom. Mostly I saw her playing soccer with her campers on the ball field across from my post in the lobby. This was hilarious. The six-year-olds converged on the ball from every angle and kicked it viciously. When the trapped ball didn't budge they kept on kicking. Then when Alyssa moved in to break up the melee, the kids kicked her too. She and her co-counselor, Sandi Lerner, calmed them down by handing out juice boxes. Have you ever read *Lord of the Flies*? Those savages were boys. They're angels compared to these little girls.

The first time I actually spoke to Alyssa was during my introduction to bowling. This was on a Friday, when I didn't have to work late servicing poker games in the card room. Sunday through Thursday, regular players keep at it 'til two in the morning. I earn hefty tips—fifty bucks or more—bringing them fresh decks, drinks, cigars, and cigarettes. But on Friday and Saturday nights all the guests go to the headliner shows in the playhouse, leaving me free to go out.

Not that I have anywhere to go. Listening to records or curling up with a book is my idea of a hot date. Anyway, it's the only kind I can get. But on this Friday night, two days before the staff softball game where I got brained, Hank rounded up the other five guys he bunks with, including me, as well as Alyssa, Sandi Lerner, and Sheryl Meyers, the switchboard operator. Then he steered Alyssa and Sheryl into his red Peugeot convertible while the rest of us followed in the Lerners' bigger car. Our destination: Creamo's Bowling Alley.

There must be a bowling alley in Queens, but I've never gone, despite bowling being huge in the last few years. Predicting it's going to be as upscale as golf or tennis, developers are building space-age alleys. Creamo's is seedier than those, but it has lots of lanes with automatic ball returners. Also, a bar and a pizzeria.

Somehow I wound up in the same lane as Sandi, Hank, and Alyssa. Hank, of course, was fluid and smooth. Sandi was good too. Surprisingly good, because her shorts were so tight she could barely take three baby steps before releasing her ball.

Still, Hank only had eyes for Alyssa. She wore black slacks, not too tight, and a black shirt with pink panels, I guess you'd call them, from her shoulders down to her hips, with her name embroidered on the front. A genuine bowling shirt. She also brought her own leather bowling bag. She took out shiny two-toned shoes and a ball with the pattern of a swirling pink hurricane.

Hank marveled at that. He didn't have his own ball, which made his near-perfect score that much more impressive. Hank also didn't have his own shoes. The grumpy woman at the counter was ready to pounce when he refused to rent beat-up red and green shoes that Rip Van Winkle may have worn when he went bowling. Then Hank flashed the woman a grin, showed her that his own shoes had rubber soles, and won a wink and a nod. I grinned at her, and glowering, she gave me a pair of clown shoes.

Picking out a ball threatened even more humiliation. Hank effortlessly heaved the first one at hand. I tried grabbing the next ball on the rack and almost dislocated my shoulder. It wouldn't budge.

"Ally, you know your way around here," Hank said to Alyssa. He called her Ally. No one else did so I guess it was an endearment. "Help Leon find a ball or we'll be here all night." With that ego booster, Hank made a practice throw. A strike.

Alyssa smiled at me. I couldn't move. To keep standing I had to grab the back of the plastic seat behind the scoring table, and since the seat swiveled, I almost fell over anyway.

For the first time my gaze latched onto hers.

Alyssa looked at me as if she knew this was my first time bowling. Hank had insisted I join them, maybe to be friendly, but I suspect to have someone to laugh at. Alyssa seemed to sense that too.

"I think you'll like the ones over here." She led me to a bottom rack along Creamo's back wall. The much lighter balls there were a muddy red. Parents lifted them out for children. Alyssa lifted one out for me.

"I'm glad you're choosing this," she said, "because Hank told me you're a pianist and I think the heavy balls might be hard on your hand."

"What did you say?"

The bombardment of balls hitting lanes and knocking down pins drowned out her voice. Alyssa got up on her toes and tilted her mouth next to my ear. I stood paralyzed for a moment—I hope it was only a moment.

What I thought was that Alyssa was considerate to think of my hands. That I loved her. That I wanted to take her away from all this thudding and crashing and live with her forever among monks who've taken a vow of silence.

What I actually said into her delicate shell of an ear was, "Hank told you I play the piano?" Who would've thought he discussed me with his girlfriend?

"Yes. He calls you Beethoven. Has Hank heard you play? I'd love to hear you. Meantime, let's work up an appetite and then grab some pizza."

"I don't really like pizza."

"Bite your tongue. I'm half Italian."

"I mean I love pizza."

"I'll listen to Beethoven and you'll learn to love pizza. Try this one."

The kiddie ball Alyssa chose was almost weightless. The downside was that its holes were so tight, I couldn't stick my fingers in all the way, so I grasped the ball like an entomologist lifting a scorpion. Feeling a lot more relaxed now that I had a manageable ball, I bantered suavely, "You, you—you must be great. At bowling."

"Oh, now I have to live up to all this stuff my father bought me." Alyssa did a fashion turn in her professional bowling outfit. "We're in a league back home, in Long Beach, but I'm not very good."

That brought us back to our lane and the end of our conversation. Our only conversation. Hank monopolized Alyssa for the rest of the time we were bowling. Alyssa's high score was 133. Mine was 87.

Hank also monopolized Alyssa while the nine of us shared pizza pies with mushrooms, sausage, and pepperoni. I pretended to like it. Hank had only Alyssa in his car for the drive back to the hotel. I sat in the front seat of Sandi's Pontiac. Ahead of us, I watched the red Peugeot with its top down and Hank draping his arm around not only the prettiest, but also the kindest girl I'd ever met.

6

Leon

Our paths crossed a few times after we went bowling, but the next time I spoke with Alyssa—and it was momentous—was in my own room, my own *bedroom*, while I was lying in bed recovering from the softball game.

As I told you, my parents rented a bungalow across from the main building, but along with the rest of the bellhops, waiters, busboys and male counselors, I sleep down the road in Sadie Hall, sharing one of the bedrooms there with five other guys.

Having finally gotten my own bedroom at the age of five, the thought of sharing one with five strangers appalled me. We had to clear out cobwebs, wash the sticky floor, and scrape rust off the bunk beds' iron frames—until we realized that rust was protecting us from ten layers of poisonous lead paint.

There were actually two rooms allotted to the six of us, a small one for one bunk bed and a somewhat larger room for two more. Instead, we crammed all three bunks together so the spare room could be kept free for sex. We're not talking about a boudoir. Not only do these Romeos refuse to change their sheets, they leave a communal sleeping bag on the floor of the "sex room" for whenever someone gets lucky.

There's always so much to do at the hotel that our bedroom is pretty much only for sleeping. Well, also sitting up in bed and talking. Most every night is a bull session that always ends up with another chapter of *The Amorous Adventures of Hank Einhorn*. To be fair, the other guys egg Hank on. Phillip finds his confessions more exciting than letters to *Penthouse*.

I never read those letters. I look at the pictures. Phillip owns every issue ever published of *Penthouse* and *Playboy*. He keeps them stacked at the foot of his bed, not so he can get to them easily, but so Hugh McMahon won't wake us all up.

Hugh is a busboy, like Phillip, and the only local guy in our room. We admire his mop-top of straight brown hair because the rest of us have wavy, curly, or even frizzy hair, like Phillip, and you can never comb it down like the Beatles.

I'm not saying it has anything to do with being Catholic, but Hugh is ashamed to look at Phillip's centerfolds during the daytime. The choir boy loosens up after midnight. Then, when Hugh thinks everyone is sleeping, he trains a miniature flashlight on the Playmates. The light doesn't wake us, but it's attached to Hugh's keychain. This is creepy as hell. Night after night I hear it jangling like the chains on Marley's ghost. Still, we don't want to embarrass Hugh—who's a good kid, if somewhat repressed—so we let it go. Especially since Hank snores through Hugh's explorations.

Hank doesn't have to slobber over nudie magazines because he's everything Hugh, Phillip, and I are not. You know how some guys look like adults by the time they're teenagers? I've seen old photos, and Clark Gable was like that. Sean Connery was like that. Hank looks like James Bond. Seams in his cheeks, a sardonic air that on most nineteen-year-olds would seem asinine, and the kind of muscles Sonny Jones wants to strap on me. I'm gone by the time he wakes up, but the other guys tell me that Hank springs out of his bunk every morning and launches into a routine of push-ups, sit-ups, and squats that make the TV fitness guy Jack LaLanne look like a bump on a log.

I'm reporting the facts as I know them. It's possible to accept and even appreciate that guys like Sean Connery and Hank Einhorn look good. The way Joanie says girls want guys to look. Still, don't you think it's kind of a sick joke that God made women want to sleep with men? That He made women find our private parts attractive? Even in sex ed we don't say private parts, but I'm keeping this clean because my mother might read it.

Speaking of sex ed, morons I know—I don't mean bookworm morons like me and Phillip, but bona fide morons—used to joke about dreaming to be tampons. Sorry girls, but tampons actually seemed sexy to them. Until sex ed.

My sophomore sex ed class in Queens was taught by Mr. Zanconato, a health instructor born to be an undertaker. Mr.

Zanconato quizzed us on the scrotum, the ejaculatory duct, and everyone's favorite, the bulbourethral gland. Male anatomy was bad enough. Then he ruined female anatomy by making us memorize the ovaries, the greater vestibular gland, and, for crying out loud, the rectouterine pouch. With cross-section diagrams.

Couple that with a novel I snuck out of the public library by Bernard Malamud called *The Fixer*, where a Russian Jew's about to have sex with a girl until he realizes he'll go to Hell because—*oy vey*—he sees that she's *menstruating*, and I decided to become a Benedictine monk.

After sex ed there was no need to teach abstinence. For a few weeks, anyway. Anticipating sex ed, God keeps the human race going by giving us hormones, which, in teenage boys, make us find even cross-section diagrams of girls mouth-watering.

But it's not only women who find Hank attractive. Now I have to tell you about Seth Perlman. Seth drools over Hank's calisthenics the way Hugh and I drool over Miss July. Seth doesn't even try to hide it.

Along with Vietnam and the coming moon shot, the summer of 1969 is shaping up to be about gay rights.

Gay is a new term for most of us. Before now, everyone said homosexual or fag or queer. "Gayer than laughter" was a compliment for a girl in a song in *South Pacific* called "Younger than Springtime." Then last month, right before my family left for Mount Freedom, a crowd rioted when police raided a gay club in Greenwich Village called The Stonewall Inn.

Now get this. Late one night last week, Seth told us his father and a friend own The Stonewall Inn. Phillip didn't buy it. "The papers say that place is owned by the Mafia."

Seth lowered his eyelids and pursed his lips.

"So?" Phillip pressed. "You're saying your father's in the Mafia?"

Seth shared a slow Cheshire Cat grin. Everything he does is slinky and slow. Which doesn't endear him to Salzman's guests, since he's allegedly a waiter. The Flash couldn't serve food fast enough for our guests.

Seth smoothed back his blond peekaboo bangs like he was surfacing from the pool. He's not handsome but acts like he is. I can't imagine having that much self-confidence, so much that you don't care if people consider you a jerk.

"I call Dad's partner Uncle Tony," Seth purred. "Which he prefers to what the newspapers call him."

"What's that?" I asked.

"Fat Tony," Phillip interjected. He's a news junkie. Also, he's a coward like me. *The Mafia*. We flipped over on our bunk beds faster than pancakes, hoping to drop the subject. But Hank, as always, picked up the ball.

"If Fat Tony Brindisi is your uncle, does that mean your father's in the Mob too? 'Don' Perlman?" Hank chortled, but Seth refused to be offended.

"His name is Si Perlman. And Tony is my honorary uncle."

"That's some honor," Hank observed.

"My dad's involved in a lot of businesses," Seth said, unruffled. "Legitimate businesses. Including this hotel. That's why I'm here."

"The Mafia placed you here as a waiter?" Hank was now howling, while Phillip and I were sweating bullets.

"I'm keeping my eye on things," Seth pouted. "My dad's the money man. His loans keep this place afloat."

"Well," Hank said, "I knew it couldn't be the hundred a week people pay for three meals a day, shows, day camp, and all the towels you can stuff into a suitcase. Are you kidding with this?"

"No," Seth said, looking steadily at Hank, thrilled that he'd finally snared his idol's interest. Because this was a rare occasion. Usually Hank talked only about himself.

Hank is the teen head counselor. Campers as old as fourteen are in his group, boys and girls. Including Alyssa's sister. Hank came to the hotel as a friend of Joel Salzman, one of Izzy's grandsons. They met at Cornell. Working here is a step down for Hank. His father is a big-shot lawyer in Washington who wanted Hank to clerk with his firm this summer, or apprentice or whatever they call it. But Hank says it's an old-line Republican firm, stuffy, reactionary and—even with a partner named Einhorn—anti-Semitic. So Hank is teeing off his old man by spending this summer at a second-rate Jewish resort. That's the least of it.

Hank's become famous at Cornell for being a radical agitator, a top guy with SDS—Students for a Democratic Society. They lead anti-war protests, black power protests—they drive conservative professors off campus. For crying out loud, they managed to shut down the whole school and cancel final exams.

But that's not what interests us. Night after night we want to hear what it's like to live in college. An Ivy League college, no less.

"Do you stay in a dorm, like this?" Phillip asked our second night together.

"Nothing like this," Hank said. We all agree Sadie Hall is a dump. "Next semester I get to move into my fraternity."

"Which one?" Normally I hang back. But I was curious if Hank meant the Jewish fraternity a guy I know about joined at Cornell.

"Sigma Chi."

"Wow," I couldn't help mouthing. "As in 'The Sweetheart of Sigma Chi?'"

Hank hit me with a pillow. On the head, which hurt more than you'd think if you're not used to it. "Only you would know that song, Leon. Tell us when it was written, and who made it famous."

I knew he was busting me, but I couldn't help answering, "It was written before World War One. Bing Crosby sang it later. What?"

They were all cracking up, even Phillip. I wanted to hit him with the pillow, but who knew where that would lead.

"Dean Martin sang it too," I protested, like that would shut them up. I felt especially bad that Hank found me pathetic. It's not lost on me that I may know the Sigma Chi song, but Hank is a member.

"They let radicals join a fraternity like that?" I asked. "I mean, you're pretty radical, right?"

"I'm radical *left*." Hank hitched his thumb at a poster next to his bunk of Che Guevara.

Phillip pointed to a pinup above his bunk of Barbi Benton. "Can we cut the politics and talk girls? Yeah, I know Hugh is listening. This is the other Hugh's girlfriend. Hugh Hefner," he explained with mock patience to our shy guy. "I want to know if they have sweethearts like this at Cornell."

Hank blew out a breath but placated us. "You schmucks aren't going to get into community college if all you think about is girls. I'm trying to keep Nixon from drafting your fat asses and getting them shot off in some rice paddy. I'm trying to keep oppressed people in slums from rioting, and tearing up your lily-white neighborhoods in Brooklyn, and Queens, and—McMahon, where are you from?"

"Succasunna."

"What?"

"It's about ten miles from here."

"What the hell is that, an Indian name?" Hank asked it like he was Custer at Little Bighorn.

"I guess."

Hank shook his head. Then he got back to orating. "Look, wherever the hell you're all from—"

"I'm from Great Neck." This was Andrew Harris, chiming in from the top bunk above mine. Andrew is another busboy, a big boy who weighs maybe two hundred-fifty pounds. How he climbed onto that top bunk the first day so he could claim it, I don't know. But now, every time he goes to bed, we have to hoist Andrew. Between Hugh McMahon on his midnight hunt for Playmates, and Andrew Harris teetering overhead like a giant boulder, I don't get much sleep.

Andrew continued spewing in one breath, as he always does once he gets started, "That's why my parents haven't come back here this summer. They moved to the Island." Meaning they moved from Brooklyn to Long Island. "I'm telling you, that's what more and more families are doing. I don't know how hotels like this are going to survive."

The long-term survival of Salzman's not being one of Hank's top priorities, he stared balefully as Andrew ran out of breath, like Ahab sizing up Moby Dick. Then Hank resumed. "Wherever the hell the rest of you are from, I'm fighting to prevent the next race riots, and all you want to hear about is pussy."

"Not me," Seth smiled. "I want to hear about Succasunna."

Even Hank laughed. Then he said, "You think college is nothing but football and food trucks and banging local girls?"

"You bang girls?" Phil choked this out, hitting a high C.

"I heard they have food trucks." Fat Andrew heaved a sigh. "All night."

"I'll tell you what woke me up in the middle of the night last April," Hank said darkly. "And it wasn't a food run. Three in the morning. I'm sound asleep. Suddenly, my roommate—not Joel Salzman, our other roommate—pulls off the covers so I almost fall out of bed, and he says, there's a cross burning outside Wari House."

"What's Wari House?" Phillip shuddered.

"It's the Black women's co-op."

"A cross burning?" I asked. "The Ku Klux Klan?"

"Worse. This wasn't inbred Southerners. This was set by students. It gets even worse. Kwami—my roommate—Kwami goes with the Afro-American Society to the student union. That's what they call the place where students hang out. Clubs and crap like that. And parents. It was Parents Weekend and some of them were staying there. I go along even though it's cold as a witch's tit. What the hell, I've already gotten into the paper, the school paper, for a shouting match with one of the fascists. Not a student. A philosophy professor named Allan Joyce. He wants the world to be run by philosopher kings. We're demanding that Cornell kick out all the fascists and racists, and guys who hate queers." Hank looked at Seth, who looked back at him like he was Oscar Wilde, Sal Mineo, and Divine all rolled into one. Hank went on, "We're also going after the warmongers. The ROTC cretins, the gung-ho schmucks—everyone who's trying to get you little schmeckles killed."

There was a pause while this soaked in.

Hugh said softly as always, not looking anyone in the eye, "I've got a friend. Not a close friend, but a guy I knew forever. He got killed."

"Where?" Hank asked.

"I don't know where. I wish I'd known him better."

"In Vietnam?"

"Yeah, Vietnam. I don't mind telling you, I'm scared they're going to send me too 'cause I don't get much of a deferment. I'm going to community college."

"We should all be scared," Hank said, punctuating each word by staring at each of our faces one by one. "This isn't World War Two. You're not fighting to save democracy from Hitler and Tojo."

"Who's Tojo?" Andrew asked. Seth sniggered. We all looked at him.

"What?" Seth spread his hands. "You don't know? Japan. He was, what, the emperor of Japan."

"The top general," Hank said, not dismissively.

"Right," Seth agreed.

"Also the prime minister," Hank added.

"Who was the emperor?" Seth asked, like it slipped his mind and he really wanted to know.

"Hirohito," Hank said. He likes to teach. "He's still the emperor."

"So what was the point?" Hugh asked. "Of fighting?"

"We fought," Hank answered, "and we dropped two atomic bombs on Japan and they surrendered. The point was, that because we won, the emperor is now only a puppet and Japan is an ally with a democratic government. But Vietnam is not Japan. Vietnam never attacked us like—"

"At Pearl Harbor," Seth volunteered.

"Pearl Harbor," Hank continued, looking at Hugh. "Ho Chi Minh fought the French because they used to run Vietnam. It was a colony. Now Ho Chi Minh has to fight us because America took over. He's fighting guys like your friend, and maybe all of us before too long, because Nixon is propping up gangsters in Saigon. Why? For Vietnam's oil. That's the truth. That's what this war is all about. That's what wars are *always* about. Professor Allan Joyce won't teach you that at Cornell, but that's the dirty stinking truth. I may get kicked out of Cornell, but I'm going to keep shouting at the top of my lungs about fascist warmongers, profiteers, and bigots. I may be taking a bullet even before they try shipping me off to Saigon, because you know who showed up when we took over the Straight, the student union?"

"Who?" we all asked.

"Cretins from another fraternity. Neanderthals. They started fighting with Kwami and the other guys. Including me. They were mad as hell at me."

"Because you're white?" Phillip asked.

"Damn right. But we were the ones with the guns."

"*Guns*?" That was me.

"I didn't have one. I hate guns. The Second Amendment is a crock. It's about militias. But another Black guy, all dressed up like a guerilla, with a headband and everything, he shoved a rifle at Kwami. It was a freaking gun show. That calmed down the fascist frat boys...and the cops. They stayed outside, but they were circling like sharks. Then—and this was the next night, the standoff went on all day—guys I know from SDS lined up all around Willard Straight Hall."

"SD—?" Hugh again.

"Students for a Democratic Society," I answered. Then to Hank, "You've got pretty militant friends."

"If it wasn't for them, who knows what the pigs might've done. I bet they were about to storm the place."

"So, were you arrested?" I asked.

"They wound up *negotiating* with us." Hank grinned. "The freaking pussy president of the school resigned. Didn't any of you hear about this?" He sounded offended. I had, but I didn't say anything.

"Were the girls all right?" Hugh asked.

We all looked blank.

"The Afro-American girls. Did the fire burn anyone?" Hugh is a nice guy.

"No," Hank said. "If it had, the whole school would have gone up."

We sat and digested all this for a minute or two. Then Phillip said, "I'm sorry, but you can't just throw that out. Do you really bang girls?"

Hank could only laugh. Phillip is a putz. But we all drew a little closer, including me.

"It's late," Hank yawned. "Beethoven has to be up in a couple of hours." Meaning me. "Nobody makes the girls do it," Hank said. Not defensive. Not apologetic. Smug. "Look," he went on, sliding under the covers. "I'm not discussing this. That's all I need is you jerks on the top bunks jacking off. Read Hugh's magazines." Hugh turned red as a fire engine. Hank felt bad right away for embarrassing him. "I mean Phil's magazines." Then Hank sat up. "Here's what I will tell you, that'll help you more than hearing about banging. That'll maybe help you get a girl of your own one day. You don't look at a girl like she's got a staple through the middle. Like she's in a magazine. You make her think she's special. That she has taste, and a brain."

"Maybe she does," I said to the guy who was going out with Alyssa.

"Maybe she does. Maybe she doesn't. But you look in her eyes, you don't look at her boobs. You laugh at her jokes and make her think she's as witty as, I don't know. Dorothy Parker. Beethoven knows who that is. Since she's dead."

I took the bait. "'You can lead a whore to culture, but you can't make her think.'"

"What?" Hugh asked.

"Dorothy Parker was a writer." I said, ashamed to be lecturing. "She was playing a game where you had to come up with a sentence with the word 'horticulture.'"

We all absorbed this and then the bunk above me rumbled. "'You can lead a whore to culture.' That's good." Andrew guffawed.

"The problem is," Hank said, stifling the laughter, "most girls aren't that good, but you have to make them think they are."

Hank did mean good. As in decent. Moral.

Phillip likes to think he's Hank's confidante. He isn't. I don't think anyone is, not even his friend from Cornell, Joel Salzman. But a couple of days after that long bull session, Phillip told me something shocking.

We knew Hank despised his father, but he never talked about his mother until Hank got a letter from her and called his mother a four-letter word in front of Phillip that I'm not going to repeat. Phillip must have looked shocked because Hank defended himself by saying his mother was on her third lucrative marriage, and was now on the make for husband number four.

Hank despises his mother too, and he apparently doesn't have much respect for women in general.

This is the guy who's going out with Alyssa.

7

Alyssa

Hank Einhorn never formally asked me out. Salzman's is not high school. He didn't pass me a note in class, or have his best friend tell my best friend that he kind of sort of liked me. After we met while unpacking the trailer, Hank strode over when the children assembled outside the kitchen the first night of camp to get their half-pint of chocolate milk. This is a nightly ritual. He helped them open their school-size milk boxes and extracted a plastic straw from Ardis Greenberg's nose. Ardis may be only six, but she seems as smitten with Hank as every other female. Is it a scent he emits? A gleam in his eyes? All I know is that after two weeks Ardis hasn't once called Hank an idiot.

When their parents picked up the kids and put them to bed that first night, Hank asked if he could walk me to the coffee shop. This is part of what we call the casino, a building next to the pool that also includes the playhouse, the bar, an elevated outdoor patio with tables and umbrellas, and down in the basement, the hotel laundry— a giant steam bath where staff clean and iron all the linens for the guest rooms and dining room.

I continued toting around *Northanger Abbey*, having planned to read a chapter or two on a bench near the paddleball courts. Tall outdoor lights there provide more illumination than the fireflies boys were chasing with jars. Hank took the paperback out of my hand and glanced at it.

"Did you ever read any of the Gothic novels Austen is parodying?" he asked.

Wow. Hank Einhorn knows his *Northanger Abbey*, which isn't one of Jane's more popular books. I said, "Catherine—you know, the heroine—mentions *The Mysteries of Udolpho*. That must be pretty lurid. But no. Have you?"

"The author of that stupid novel, Ann Radcliffe—they called her Mrs. Radcliffe back then—was assigned to us last semester in an English lit course. The professor thought it's important to read things that Jane Austen and her contemporaries enjoyed. Even if it made them look stupid."

"You think Jane Austen is stupid?" I love her almost as much as my mother does.

"No, I didn't mean Austen," Hank said quickly. "But, well, she is a little frivolous."

That hurt. Still, I was enthralled to talk with someone who knows literature so well. It reminded me of the summer literature camp my parents sent me to a few years ago. That ended badly, but not because of the books.

"You go to Cornell."

Hank looked at me. I explained, "Sandi, my co-counselor, told me."

Hank smiled. "Sandi of the visible panty line?"

"You notice more than books."

"But I'd rather discuss Jane Austen with you."

I stumbled on one of the concrete steps leading up to the casino's patio. Hank caught and turned me so that my chest was resting hard against his. In the twilight the first thing I saw were his teeth. He was grinning and seemed about to kiss me. I would've let him. He held off and moved my book between us.

"No bodice ripping, I promise." He laughed disarmingly.

We hung out at the crowded coffee shop, sharing a chocolate malt and playing the pinball machine that lights up like the Las Vegas strip unless you jiggle it too hard, trying to control the ball, and the machine goes tilt. The coffee shop sells candy and sundries, including calamine lotion. You can also order mouthwatering burgers and fries, which Salzman's doesn't serve in the dining room.

We're too young to enter the bar, but since this wasn't a formal night we could have looked in at the playhouse. Hank made fun of the music the band was playing. On this Stump the Band night Dad sang any song the guests requested. Most of those people are middle-aged at best, so the songs are old too. Hank called them "sentimental sludge." Instead he invited me back to Sadie Hall, where we could borrow his roommate's portable record player, lie on a blanket outside and listen to The Who's new rock opera, *Tommy*. Nothing sentimental about that. *Tommy* is apparently about pinball and drugs. I don't do drugs, not even pot, much less LSD. Hank said he doesn't either.

Sensing I was uncomfortable, he took our malt outside to a table on the patio and Hank talked to me again about books. He said his favorites are *The Catcher in the Rye*, *Ariel*—a collection of poems by Sylvia Plath—and *The Autobiography of Malcolm X*. I haven't read any of those. My mother refuses to teach J.D. Salinger to her English classes, although another teacher did and caused a stink.

I know Sylvia Plath committed suicide. I have to read more poetry. It's been two years, I think, since Malcolm X was assassinated. My father respected Martin Luther King more than Malcolm X, but he's appalled by all these assassinations—including, of course, Bobby Kennedy. Dad thinks the victims all gave their lives for our country. The way my brother did.

I steer clear of talking about Johnny because Hank is vehemently opposed to the Vietnam War. He sees fascism behind every problem with the country. Hank jumped down my throat when I admitted to reading Ayn Rand's *The Fountainhead*.

"The only thing worse than her sophomoric writing is Ayn Rand's stupid, selfish, sophomoric message. She's a capitalist tool. I don't know how you can plow through that crap." As with Mrs. Radcliffe, I didn't pursue it.

Since that first night we've played miniature golf down the road from Salzman's, we've gone bowling, and to the movies. Often Hank returns to talking, more calmly, about books. But our relationship's less about books than baseball: first base, second base, and now, Hank thinks, rounding third and heading for home. I'm not going to give you details. I don't know how I feel. My parents would be furious. Sometimes I'm furious. Hank can be truly kind. Considerate. Brilliant. Gorgeous. He seems to respect me. For the first time in four years—*four years*—I've been opening up.

Then I freak out fearing that it's all going to happen again.

<u>8</u>

Leon

It's now the night after the softball game. I spent most of yesterday in the hospital. Donna Salzman drove me and my mother back to the hotel since my father is still in the City and we don't have Uncle Max's car. My mother thought about having me recuperate in her bungalow, but to make room we'd have to hold a garage sale, so I'm back at Sadie Hall.

For the first time this morning I'm sleeping in and get to watch Hank's exercise routine along with Seth, who's more thrilled than I am. The other guys have better things to do. By 7:30 everyone is gone. I listen to music on my portable record player—Artur Schnabel playing Beethoven's "Tempest" piano sonata, which I'm preparing for a competition in August. My head hurts too much to follow along with the score. I feel well enough to devour the bananas and cream that Hugh kindly brings. I take a shower at the end of the hall, but then feel woozy, so I have a nap.

The next thing I know, something's awakened me. I blink, reach for my glasses, and a t-shirt comes into focus. It's on a slender back. A girl's back. She turns around.

I say, "Oh." Meaning: *Am I dreaming, or is this actually happening?*

"Hello."

"What—?"

"I'm sorry we woke you." Alyssa looks sorry. She looks beautiful. "You're still wearing a bandage."

"Yes." I gulp, then smile feebly, touching my forehead. "It's a good look for me. Keeps me out of ball games."

She smiles. I'm now grateful our room is as cramped as a prison cell because it means I can touch Alyssa. Not that I ever would.

Instead, I marvel at her satin complexion. Her long eyelashes that are real, not the centipedes a lot of girls glue on. Her voice, like the humming of a kazoo you make with cellophane, the way it tickles your ears and makes you grin.

Alyssa only half laughs when she asks, "Why didn't you at least try to catch the ball? Why didn't you try to protect yourself?"

"Hard to explain."

"Is it true you were listening to the radio out there?"

"That wasn't the problem. I'm not good at softball."

"Well, maybe if you practiced." Apologetically, she glances down. Someone left underwear on the floor. Maybe me. "I'm sorry. I have no right to criticize you."

"You do."

Alyssa looks up, puzzled. "Why?"

"You, you know," I stammer. "I let down our team."

"Oh. We'll crush those waiters next time."

Now my heart is sinking, not because of the game but because Hank's appeared. He slides out from beneath his bunk clutching a record album.

"I hide this," he cracks, "fearing Leon's going to freak out one night and scream, 'Screw you, Beethoven, I'm tripping with The Who.'" Hank smugly displays an album cover with a lot of rectangles cut into a curved blue grid. Clouds and birds float by. I guess it's supposed to be psychedelic. "Leon, mind if I borrow your record player?" Hank's already lifted it. "Don't worry," he winks at me. "We're going next door."

"To the sex room?" I blurt out, anguished and in an almost falsetto.

***

Alyssa

"*What?*" I aim my stare at Hank. He's glaring at Leon. "What is the sex room?"

Hank forces a laugh. "That's Leon's name for the spare room. Even with a concussion he obsesses about—"

I cut Hank off. "Since when do you need a special room? We could be kneeling in church and you'd be all over me."

I'm not kidding. The proportion of book talk to groping has become miniscule. Hank now hangs on me like a barnacle.

***

Leon

I've seen the way he forces himself on Alyssa.

Last Monday a bunch of us drove into Morristown to see *Easy Rider*. Phillip talked me into it.

"This is an important film."

"Important for who?" I asked. "You're afraid to ride a bicycle."

"Why do you always have to go for the dig?"

"Sorry," I said, and I was. I knew Hank would be at the theater with Alyssa. There they were, standing up in the balcony of the Community Theater. They waited for the rest of us to take our seats: Seth, Andrew and me, along with Phillip and Sandi, who seemed teetering on the verge of pairing off.

We all sat in the front of the balcony with me at the end. Andrew spilled over into half my space. Popcorn he couldn't fit into his mouth cascaded onto my lap. When the rest of our group was settled, Hank and Alyssa climbed two rows behind us, all alone. The theater wasn't crowded. Morristown is not Berkeley or even Brooklyn, and, apparently, the locals weren't eager to spend two hours with dope-dealing "non-conformists."

Have you seen *Easy Rider*? Peter Fonda and Dennis Hopper act all spiritual as they ride motorcycles cross-country and run into small-town bigots. At one point they pick up Jack Nicholson. I think this is his first movie. He's excellent playing a lawyer who gets Peter Fonda and Dennis Hopper's characters out of jail. Then rednecks with baseball bats and a machete attack the three of them while they're sleeping, and they kill Nicholson.

At this point the only other people in the balcony, a surprisingly old couple, quietly picked up their popcorn box and left. We stayed to watch Fonda and Hopper reach New Orleans for Mardi Gras.

They meet hookers, take LSD in a cemetery, freak out, and finally decide the trip—the road trip, not just tripping on LSD—was a bust. *You think?* That's the revelation. They make a ton of money selling drugs but fail to achieve nirvana. Even with the hookers.

If this didn't strike me as great cinema, maybe it's because I wasn't paying much attention. I kept glancing back in the dark at Hank and Alyssa. Luckily, Sandi was looking back even more than I did, and Seth did too.

Hank didn't mind the spectators. First he was kissing Alyssa. I suppose she was kissing him back. Then I saw Hank's hand on her breast. Sandi gasped, no doubt wishing she was the one being mauled since Phillip didn't have the nerve. I turned away 'til I couldn't stand it anymore. Then I turned back and saw Hank sliding his hand under Alyssa's blouse, a stretchy emerald blouse that made it easy.

I'd seen him like this even before the movie. Hank went almost as far right next to the pool, in broad daylight. Well, not daylight. There's a shed where the hotel stores cushions for its wooden chaise lounges. Last week on pool duty I had to grab an extra cushion for Tilly Mintz's bony behind. Stepping inside the dark shed I saw Hank and Alyssa lying in a corner on a stack of cushions. I heard Alyssa saying, "Now, as soon as I say anything, I see your eyes rolling."

"That's not true," said Hank. "Hey, who's that?"

"Getting a cushion," I said loud, so they wouldn't think I was sneaking.

"Get the hell out of here," Hank hissed. Alyssa was fumbling with something. I hoped to God it wasn't her clothes.

Now at the Community Theater, I caught them going at it again. Until, unlike Peter Fonda, I found nirvana. Because here was Hank, snaking his hand half-way up Alyssa's top, and there was Alyssa dumping her popcorn over the top of his head.

"What the—?" Before Hank could spit out the rest—along with a mouthful of popcorn—Alyssa grabbed her purse and raced sideways down the aisle like a crab scooting away from boiling water.

Hank sat for a minute brushing off kernels.

For the first time, Fat Andrew looked back, ogling Hank's popcorn the way Hugh ogles centerfolds. Seth went to Hank's aid, but his hero angrily followed Alyssa out.

We had Sandi's car, so the rest of us watched the end of the movie. It was sad. A redneck in a truck shoots Dennis Hopper dead and then blows up Peter Fonda's bike. Nevertheless, *Easy Rider* is now one of my favorite films.

***

Alyssa

We're back in Hank's room with Leon lying in bed. He's heard me accuse Hank of being a sex maniac. I don't care. I'm glad someone else knows.

"Let's listen to *Tommy*," Hank sniffs petulantly. "Next door or wherever. I only wanted to make sure our Beethoven doesn't have to hear any music written in this century."

"You want to know the truth?" My voice is shaky but under control. "I'd rather listen to Beethoven. The real Beethoven." I look at Leon. He's put on his massive black glasses that make his blue eyes even bigger. I tell him, "That's actually one of the goals I set for this summer. To learn something about classical music."

"Because," Hank smirks, "Beethoven—'the real Beethoven'—is a poster boy for fascism. It appears our lovely Ally is a neo-fascist."

I survey Hank like I've never seen him before and say, calmly, "I told you, I don't like to be called Ally. If you can't say Alyssa, stick to Miss Lawrence."

"Oh, come on," Hank rolls his eyes, including Leon in his joke.

"Also," I find the courage to lecture this brilliant guy, "if I recall correctly, you consider Hubert Humphrey, Lyndon Johnson, and John F. Kennedy all to be fascists."

"Neo-fascists. But they're not adorable like you." Hank chuckles. The chuckle dies in mid-air. He gets defensive. "Well, they all got us into Vietnam. As for Tricky Dick Nixon—"

I interrupt, thinking of his politics and his almost rabid pawing. "Who hired you to supervise teenagers?"

"You're a teenager."

"Maybe we all better grow up."

9

Leon

I've returned to bellhopping. On weekends that means checking in a fresh round of guests. They were mailed brochures during the winter and spring, but I'm the first one to show them their actual rooms.

Those rooms in the main building can be a pleasant surprise—Spartan but spacious, especially the walk-in closets, since families stay on average six to eight weeks.

It's harder taking guests to the older rooms. The original lodge and the cottages Izzy bought might have been charming once. Now they're small, dank, and frowzy. My challenge is to slip in fast enough to find spiders and stamp on them like a flamenco dancer before the newcomers notice. When rooms are arachnid-free, guests still vent their disappointment. "This is nothing like the brochure." "I left a showplace at home to live in a shoebox?" "I demand to see Cully Salzman."

Now we skip into the land of Oz. Because no one has ever seen the hotel's manager. Many doubt that Cully Salzman exists. There's a voice on the phone that identifies itself as Cully when you call from Brooklyn or the Bronx to make a reservation. That jovial voice assures you that your room will be the last word in luxury and you'll never want to return home. When you arrive, Cully makes like the Wizard and you can't see him. Malcontents wind up camping outside the door to Cully's office, figuring he has to come out eventually to eat or use the bathroom. But Cully defies nature as well as the guests.

Cully is one of three Salzman sons. He runs the business end. Al heads maintenance. Since everything is always breaking down, Al is harassed but stoical. The fearsome one is Sol, a hulking man who keeps a gun on his hip and a German Shepherd at his side that makes the Hound of the Baskervilles look like a Chihuahua. His daughter Phyllis assures me her father is a teddy bear, but Sol strikes terror in the kitchen staff, from busboys like Phillip, Hugh and Andrew, to the lowliest dishwashers. In fairness, it requires terror to feed a thousand people three meals a day. Actually, there are only five hundred guests, but they eat like double that number thanks to the "Full American Plan."

Whoever came up with this plan wanted to drive a business into bankruptcy. It allows guests to eat as much as they like at every meal, and if they insist, also between meals. Back home these children of refugees tell their own children, "Eat everything on your plate. Remember there are children starving in Europe." Not so at Salzman's. Here the philosophy is, "Let me taste this and if I don't like it, I'll order something else." Often guests taste the whole dish and still order something else—everything on the menu. Then gourmands who've remained conscious complain about the food. They complain to the waiters and busboys, but not to Sol Salzman. He has that gun and that dog.

On weekdays, when few new guests check in, my job is to bring people extra soap and towels and hangers. The Salzmans dole these out like the last drops of water in a desert canteen. As mentioned, I also service card games. In the afternoon guests play gin or mahjong in the card room and at the pool. At night it's poker.

Tilly Mintz has a regular poker game with five men who cordially dislike each other and all detest her. Besides fresh decks and drinks for the table, I bring Tilly cartons of cigarettes. I've never seen Tilly without a cigarette dangling from one side of her mouth, while out of the other side she demands Scotch and accuses her fellow players of cheating.

***

Alyssa

"It depends on what you're going to wear," Sheryl says instructively. "Lately I've been wearing a lot of earth tones because I'm tired of looking like Doris Day, all pastel. Earth tones are, I don't know.

They show you care. Not that anyone cares what my fingers and toes look like. I'm stuck all day at the switchboard."

As a child Sheryl whiled away summers in Salzman's day camp. Now she's joined the workers of the world and might as well have stayed in Brooklyn. Still, there are summer nights.

Sheryl and I are sitting on the long, covered porch of Salzman's old lodge, where her family has stayed for longer than she can remember. My girls are dressing for dinner, Sheryl's shift is over, and we're painting our nails. To maintain earth tones, I'm dabbing her toes with polish that looks like pebbles.

"How about you?"

"Let's see," I consider. "Mostly I wear a white t-shirt with the name Salzman's on it and a green man diving off a board. Which polish goes with that?"

"C'mon." Sheryl is no-nonsense.

"It doesn't really matter. The kids are constantly trying to pull out my fingernails."

Sheryl smiles wistfully, probably recalling what a terror she was as a six-year-old. She asks, "What's the nicest dress you brought here?"

"It's blue. I guess a royal blue with a full skirt. I don't know when I'll ever wear it. Hank doesn't like to dress and go to any of the shows. Whatever I'm wearing, all he wants to do is get me out of it." I haven't told anyone Hank and I may be on the outs. For good.

Sheryl says nothing. I've finished her toes and she's ready to start on mine if we can agree on a color from her mother's treasure trove. "You know you complain about Hank a lot. If Sandi could get Hank Einhorn to look at her, she'd wait on him hand and foot."

"I have you for that," I smile, wiggling my toes.

"Pick a color. You don't mind looking like Doris Day, and this pearly pink would go well with your dress and your skin."

"I may never wear the dress, but there is my skin."

"It's really pale. You must have to smother yourself in sunblock to be out all day."

"Didn't you ever want to be a counselor?"

"I was an assistant two years ago." Sheryl is a year older than I am. "They nearly arrested me for assault. Listen," she says, propping my leg on her knees, "I don't know what kind of guys you go out with, but I never thought someone like Hank Einhorn would show up here. Forget how he looks. He has money, he has a car, he likes books, like you. Seth told me Hank's crazy about you."

At first he was jealous, but now Seth desperately wants me to elope with Hank. I think psychologists call it "transference." Having buffed my toes and inserted cotton between each of them, Sheryl is applying the pink polish, which is lovely.

She persists, "If Hank's a little forward—"

"Compared with Hank, Warren Beatty is a little forward."

"So you're going out with Warren Beatty. The problem is...?"

"He can be mean."

"To you?"

"Not so much to me, but take his roommate, Leon."

"*Leon*?" Sheryl makes a face.

"Why, what's wrong with him?"

"Hank went to see him in the hospital. He takes Leon along to movies and bowling. He's like a pet."

"Then he insults him. Hank insults a lot of people."

Sheryl moves her nose within an inch of my big toe, as much as to say, that's where my brains must be hiding. Silently she continues applying polish while I look out from the porch, down to the pond, the playground, and the flagpole. They're all so romantic as dusk starts to descend. I display my elegant toes, kiss Sheryl on the cheek and tell her, "Sorry. But I don't think I like Hank Einhorn."

"Kiss someone else. I still like men."

10

Leon

There's one guest who defies all the rules, and he isn't really a guest. If Cully is the Wizard of Oz, Seth Perlman's father apparently is the guy who lets Cully duck behind his curtain. Whose loans, as Seth says, keep Salzman's afloat.

Sonny prepared me for my first glimpse of Si Perlman, but it doesn't register because of two distractions. First, Mr. Perlman's car. I know nothing about cars except that Uncle Max's needs new shocks after hauling my family and all our earthly belongings. Sonny instructs me that this is not a car, it's a limousine. A Cadillac Fleetwood 75 with a window inside to screen out the chauffeur who's not anyone's idea of a chauffeur. The bruiser has more hair in his eyebrows than on his mop-top head. Instead of a uniform he wears a suede jacket and bell-bottom checked pants. He doesn't open the driver's side back door for Mr. Perlman. He saunters over to the other side of the limo and opens the door for a woman lounging there. Running up to help, I can see why. This luscious redhead is wearing a miniskirt so short, it barely qualifies as a belt.

While I reprise my open-mouthed goldfish stare, Si Perlman struggles out of the limo and climbs up the front steps to the lobby. Distracted and discombobulated as I am by his companion, I still notice two things about Si. His head bends over his sunken chest like a horse in a photo finish. And he has the heaviest black glasses I've ever seen. The kind of frames I wanted as a kid to look like Zorro.

As Si's shaky legs propel him up the stairs, he nearly gets bowled over when Seth bursts through the glass doors. Seth gives his dad a hug that touches me. Si musses his son's hair. Seth kisses Si. That's nice, but I swivel my head at warp speed to catch another glimpse of Si's mistress. The chauffeur is helping her out of the back seat and ordering me to pull the luggage out of the trunk. She smiles at me. It's not spectacular, just a sweet smile, almost shy. It becomes mischievous when Seth rushes up to her.

"Geez, Louise."

"*Sethie*." They hug. Seth is a hugger.

"Hi, Anthony," he says to the chauffeur.

Anthony curtly nods his bowling ball head. "An-tony," he growls in a strange accent. Cockney? Australian? "It's pronounced An-tony."

"Part of his new English thing," Louise whispers to Seth.

Louise's luggage is all pea soup green spangled with golden LVs. She's brought more luggage than my mother or Liz Taylor could dream of. For Louise, I carry it cheerfully.

Seth's filled me in about his father and Louise. Also about his late mother.

Mrs. Perlman died in 1964 when Seth was ten. She'd been a chain smoker. Seth said the cigarettes dropped her voice down an octave and made her sound like a foghorn when she hollered, which was often. Not at Seth. She was devoted to him—and to his dad, in Pearl's rather belligerent way. That was her actual married name, Pearl Perlman. She and Si didn't have Seth 'til Pearl was well into her thirties and Si was forty-six. Pearl had been a dancer in the chorus of Broadway shows. Seth said she'd hoofed in a bunch of shows including her last one, *Wish You Were Here*, which coincidentally is about a Catskills summer resort like Salzman's. Si was an aging stage door Johnny, slouching around night after night hoping to coax a smile out of Pearl. If she wasn't a beauty—though Si thought so—Pearl was a cutie, a personality dancer with hair like dandelion fluff. Seth's is like that, but he straightens it.

Si was a CPA working for the IRS. He was clean until a boyhood friend from Brooklyn hooked him up with the Mancini Family. The confirmed bachelor wasn't ambitious. Pearl was. They started going out every night to the Carnegie Deli. Pearl persuaded Si to do the Mancini family a few favors.

When they got married, "the Family" made Pearl a present of a dirt-cheap dance studio in Canarsie. Pearl was getting too old for the chorus, so she'd become what Broadway calls a "character," complete with rhinestone glasses and tap shoes with ankle socks. She yelled out dance steps at little girls in her booming contralto and bossed Si around more than the Mancinis did. Si loved Pearl, and Seth did too.

Pearl taught Seth not only to dance but to be an entertainer. Little Seth imitated Donald O'Connor at talent shows. "Make 'Em Laugh" was Seth's theme song. By the time Pearl died from lung cancer, Seth says she knew he was different. Her last words to him, in front of Si, were a prayer that he'd find a nice Jewish boy, and that maybe they could adopt.

Enter Louise. While Anthony parks the limo, Louise is slowly shimmying to the front desk. Si's attraction doesn't require much explanation.

Marion is on duty. Oh, Marion. She's an old timer, one of Izzy's first guests after the war. Marion's son Bobby graduated from day camp and became Salzman's head waiter. Now Marion tells me he's a big shot, the president of the Diner's Club. That's not unusual. A lot of guys and girls have worked their way through college on Salzman's tips and have gone on to do big things. When Marion's husband died, Cully asked her to run the front desk. Bobby lets his mom do it because she loves kibitzing with all the guests, old and new.

Thanks to Si Perlman, Marion has to do something she dreads, what she calls "fibbing." Usually her fibs are about little things, like telling guests that fresh towels are on the way, even though Marion knows Al Salzman is up to his neck in soap bubbles thanks to a broken washing machine. Now Marion sheepishly tells me that when Louise finally makes it to the desk I should take her and her mountain of bags to room 115.

"But Marion," I whisper. "Don't you remember? I checked that family from Staten Island in to one-fifteen yesterday. The Waldmans."

"Sonny's moved them upstairs."

"Why?"

Marion looks down at the room key and blushes. "I told the Waldmans that the air conditioning in one-fifteen isn't working."

"It is working. I was there an hour ago bringing them toilet paper."

Marion is near tears. "That's what they said, and I told them you spotted a mouse."

"What?"

"That's what they said." Poor Marion rattles on in one breath, "They wanted to check out and go to Pine Hill Lodge, but Sonny calmed them down and gave them a voucher for drinks and moved them upstairs, so one-fifteen is free for..." She takes a breath. Marion isn't judgmental, only embarrassed. "It's free for Mr. Perlman's friend. Oh, here she is." Marion beams, "Hello. Welcome to Salzman's."

I get it. Now that I've seen the limo and the lady. All the rooms are pretty much the same in the main building except for 115, which is maybe a third larger and has the only air conditioner that never breaks down.

"Mr. Perlman is talking with Cully," Marion gushes to Louise. "Would you like to join them, or can Leon take you straight to your room?" Marion is so warm and welcoming that Louise flashes her a megawatt smile.

Seth had followed his dad to Cully's office but now returns and says accusingly to Louise, "Did you just come from Sassoon?"

Louise bobs her geometrically cut hair. "It's what Vidal calls his 'five-point cut.'"

"Please." Seth shakes his own head with mock disdain. "Tell me something I don't know."

"Do you love it?"

"Love it? I want it. I want any makeup you brought from Charles of the Ritz. I'm going to be in a show here, and I can't go on without Ritz lips."

Which gets me thinking about the performance I have coming up, in a hall a lot bigger than Salzman's playhouse.

11

Leon

Bellhopping begins each morning at nine, but that's not when my day begins. On cat's paws before dawn I steal out of our barracks at Sadie Hall—if I'm not quiet Hank hurls a book at me—and make my way to the casino.

This isn't a gambling casino. Gambling is supposed to be illegal, although Tilly's nightly poker game would break the bank at Monte Carlo. No, this casino is where the hotel puts on shows. Its playhouse has knotty pine walls and fake crystal chandeliers. Long tables fan out from the stage, taking aim at performers like guns on a battleship. Which is fitting since the audience, suffering after-dinner heartburn, lies in wait like the enemy. At the back of the playhouse there's a dimly lit, smoky bar with a plate-glass window that offers a view of the stage. Across from the bar is a bustling junior bar—a coffee shop with an ice cream fountain. Campers stay up as late as they're allowed, playing pinball and slurping egg creams. That's a New York drink made with soda water, milk, and chocolate syrup, but no eggs.

By early morning the playhouse is a wreck, yet I'm glad to be given access at 5 a.m.—the same time as *Modern Farmer*—so I can get in four hours of practice before work. Although Alyssa doesn't know it, she was unfair. I practice, only not softball.

We haven't discussed it until now, but I am a pretty serious pianist. Not a prodigy. At sixteen I have little hope of becoming a virtuoso. Still, playing the piano is all I can do.

My first teachers in Queens were routine. Had I been a major talent they would have ruined me. "Stop with the show tunes. Stick to your scales." That was the drillmaster, Mr. Orzehowski. His apartment reeked of cabbage. He made me take off my shoes, which I hated because my socks often had holes in them.

My next teacher was anything but tough, to play for or to look at. Miss Federoff was dismayed that I knew so little great music beyond "The Great American Songbook." Like most every kid in America, unless you were Toscanini's grandson, I had no idea the *Lone Ranger* theme came from an opera. Dad may have hailed from Vienna, but the only hometown music he liked was operetta. So gorgeous Miss Federoff made sure I became acquainted with Mozart, Schubert, and Chopin. "And don't let anyone tell you Rachmaninoff is second-rate, Leon. There's no one more beautiful." Miss Federoff was more beautiful, especially when she played for me. Which was more often than I played for her. This wasn't her fault. I begged Miss Federoff to play so I could sit back and look at her.

Nevertheless, I got good enough to win a few minor competitions and give a few recitals, and even concerto performances at small halls with pick-up orchestras. Next month I'm set to compete in another lower-tier competition, this time in Newark. The lure of the grandiosely titled World Piano Competition is college scholarship money and the chance that someone influential might hear me.

Even without that lure I'd be at the keyboard before dawn because by now it's deeply ingrained habit. At home while my parents sleep I silence our upright piano with towels and blankets. Or I depress the keys so slowly that there's no sound. After school Dad is always away, and my mother doesn't object to hours of practice, especially now that I've won prizes, however piddling. She has the idea that I might get a full ride to college. I hope she's right. Otherwise, I have to rely on tips from bellhopping.

The early morning crew at Salzman's cleaning up the playhouse sometimes stops their sweepers to hear a nice passage. I return the compliment by taking requests. We all love jazz. But one of the guys, a bandy-legged old sailor called Smitty, keeps asking for a classical piece by Debussy that he calls "The Girl with the Flossed Hair." Smitty leered when he told me, "A gal with hair like cotton candy played that for me at a bar in Samoa during The Big One. She said they wrote it about her, but I don't know." Probably not. Still, I'm glad to oblige a veteran.

One morning last week a gnome appeared. He was suddenly sitting on a chair beneath the stage. A bald man, even older than Smitty, he couldn't have hit five feet in elevator shoes. I thought my glasses were thick, but his lenses were telescopic thick.

"How do you play a piano so out of tune, boychik?" His Viennese accent was more pronounced than my father's.

"I don't know how to tune it, so I don't listen."

"A pianist needs to learn how to tune, at least somewhat. That's the hardest part of our job. A pianist can't carry his instrument in a case like a fiddler, and you never know what you'll run into."

"Like this piece of garbage."

"Hold on." The gnome, a lot more agile than I would have guessed, hopped onto his chair and then onto the stage. I jumped up from the piano bench and took a step back. He looked mad. Meaning both angry and crazy. "Would you insult a woman who's old and run-down but filled with beautiful music? Have you played your Bach this morning?"

"Which Bach?"

"Any Bach. Every morning Pablo Casals plays something from *Das Wohltemperierte Klavier*. *The Well-Tempered Clavier*. On the piano, and he's a cellist. You understand German?"

"It's my parents' first language."

"Ah, but do you listen to your parents? My children never listen to me. Come, play me some Bach."

I did. The Toccata from the sixth Partita. He didn't interrupt, but at the end, silence.

"You like that?" the gnome asked.

"Yes."

"And you like Rachmaninoff? Because you swooned like it was movie music."

That forced me to stand up again, this time for Miss Federoff. "I'd like to hear you play it."

The gnome paused and then said, "Can you wait?"

"I need to be at work by nine." It was only seven-thirty.

"Be right back." He scampered off.

Twenty minutes later he returned with a folded soft leather case filled with tools and set to work on the piano, striking keys and turning his lever to adjust strings one at a time.

"There's nothing I can do about that," the gnome muttered. "Or that. *Was zum Tuefel?*" And he did look bedeviled for nearly half an hour. At last the old man shook his head and said resignedly, "Well, Bach never heard a real piano, so he won't know they should sound better than this." He sat down and played the Toccata. Not flawlessly but perfectly. One thing distracted me. The numbers tattooed on his arm. The only people I knew who had tattoos were in the navy or the circus. Or concentration camps.

"It's a quarter to nine," he said. "You have to go."

"My name is Leon."

"My name is Herman."

"I'll be here tomorrow."

"You better be."

12

Alyssa

Even when I couldn't wait to be with Hank Einhorn, the heart of my evenings has been lowering the flag. Every night after the dinner hour the entire camp gathers to watch the sun dip below hills, its last red and purple rays lighting the clouds so spectacularly you expect Turner to come back and paint them.

But tonight, as Neil is putting the trumpet to his lips, one of the campers has cried out, "*Look at that.*" We see the Stars and Stripes flying upside down under an effigy of Richard Nixon.

The commotion draws my father out of our bungalow, which is a stone's throw from the flagpole, up the hill near the lodge. Dad looks up, then puts his head down like a bull and charges straight toward Hank, knocking him over. Then he grabs the rope and quickly lowers the flag. Campers shriek. Neil almost swallows his horn.

But is this really a surprise?

The counselors and older campers all immediately suspect who's hoisted the flag upside down, the sign of a nation in distress. We all know who wants to hang Nixon, and not just in effigy. In the name of political discourse,

Hank has been staging daytime debates in the playhouse among his teens. The subjects range from Vietnam to the Stonewall gay rights riots. At first a few, and then a growing number of parents and other adults have been attending these debates. They applaud Hank. "The kids are learning more here than in school."

But Vin Lawrence did not applaud. Certainly not after word started reaching him that the handsome teen counselor was acting fresh with his daughter. I've assured Mom and Dad that I can handle myself.

Yet the problem with the debates goes deeper than that.

Vin Lawrence's given name was Vincenzo Lavingna. He grew up in the Bronx, learned to love history, and played baseball and saxophone at Stuyvesant High School. As a teenager, to make money, Dad joined a band that worked weddings and bar mitzvahs. The bandleader discovered he had a voice that made girls wilt. In 1944, when he came of age, Dad tried enlisting in the Army. Ironically for a musician, they found he had a punctured eardrum. He wound up singing with the USO. After the war, Vincenzo Lavingna anglicized his name. He knew he'd never challenge Perry Como and Dick Haymes, much less Sinatra, so Vin wisely used the G.I. Bill to earn a degree. Teaching and coaching at Long Beach High, he met a demure English teacher named Beth Donnelly.

Dad kept singing on weekends in clubs. During summer breaks he crooned for more than a decade in the Catskills, and for the past two years at Salzman's.

This Italian breaks a lot of Jewish hearts singing "Quando, Quando, Quando" and offering to "Volare" with any matron who will "Come Back to Sorrento." Even Tilly Mintz is dazzled by my dad, who has gleaming teeth, his velvet bowtie, and pointy patent leather shoes.

The flirting is all an act. I'm happy to tell you that Dad is completely in love with Mom. By extension, he's fiercely protective of their son and daughters. It's the memory of their son—who died in Vietnam—that got Hank shoved on his ass.

Pumped up by Dad's defense of the Vietnam War, Johnny Lawrence chose the Army over college. Mom, usually so quiet, vehemently objected. For all his talk, Dad's heart ached too. Johnny wasn't singing for the USO. When he was on patrol last year in Da Nang, the Vietcong killed my brother. He was nineteen. The kindest and funniest brother in the world. I still remember the way he took Brian Cooper aside and nicely taught him how to treat girls, especially Johnny Lawrence's sister. Brian idolized Johnny, and I did too.

His loss has kept me from ever wanting to discuss politics. Maybe that's wrong, but I can't. A lot of grieving parents might have become anti-war activists. Dad sees things differently. He honors his son as a patriot who gave his life to contain communism.

Hank's debates make Dad sick. One time a girl in a blouse knotted above her midriff argued, "You know we wouldn't even have had to be in Vietnam in the first place if, you know, that other president—"

"Eisenhower," Hank prompted. He's the moderator.

"If Ike Eisenhower hadn't blocked democratic elections there."

"Ho Chi Minh would have won those elections," Hank told the audience.

Put up to it by Dad, my sister half-heartedly stood up to defend the domino theory of communist expansion. "If the Vietcong take over, they could be in Japan next."

"But Vanessa," Hank asked, "isn't that simply an excuse for American imperialism?"

Vanessa nodded and rolled her eyes.

Sitting that afternoon beneath the stage that he owns at night, Vin Lawrence could hardly contain himself. The history teacher wanted to stand up and argue that communism condemns tens of millions of Europeans to cower behind the Iron Curtain, and countless more people around the world. Dad tried persuading Vanessa that Hank was brainwashing her. It's been a losing battle. The fourteen-year-old misses her brother and blames warmongers for his death. And like all the girls—and Seth Perlman, who attends every debate and can barely keep his eyes open—Vanessa is smitten with Hank.

So Dad's shove by the flagpole tonight has been a long time coming. Hank didn't anticipate it or he might've defended himself. Vanessa is the first to run over and offer comfort.

"Are you okay, Hank? Daddy, are you *insane*?"

After making sure Sandi has our campers in hand, I'm close behind my sister. Not to side with Hank, but to make sure he's okay. You can imagine how that infuriates Dad. He orders Vanessa to our bungalow and—however wrong it is for a co-worker, and an adult and a father, to behave this way—Dad looms over Hank, ready to take on all comers.

***

Leon

My part in all this is to do nothing. Nothing that anyone can see.

I never speak up at Hank's debates. Now, I don't run over to help Hank to his feet, even though I'm his roommate, the only member of our motley crew who saw Vin Lawrence push him down. I do nothing even though Hank helped me when I collapsed in short center field. I do nothing except in my own head. My own damned head, which is where I live most of my life, such as it is.

In my head I do all kinds of things that people never suspect. Like Zorro, who pretends to be a fop, a putz, while he secretly champions truth, justice, and the Mexican way.

While Hank springs back onto to his feet, tells Vin Lawrence to go to hell, and gets cheered by his teens, I fantasize about being the true hero of their battle. I imagine being the one who confronts Hank. Not knocking him to the ground. Better than that. Grabbing the rope that raises and lowers the flag, and climbing the pole to pull down that mocking image of Richard Nixon. I'm no fan of Tricky Dick, but this is my way, my fantasy way, of defending the office that Washington created and Lincoln preserved. In my fantasy, Hank's teenagers cheer my derring-do.

Wait. It gets better. More pathetic, but let me take you inside this fantasy, because it's so typical.

I'm now sliding down the flagpole and telling Hank, in front of Alyssa, "Don't pretend that by protesting the war in Vietnam you're some kind of a hero. I know you. I know your whole stinking anti-war movement, and you're a bunch of cowards."

"Cowards?" Hank laughs derisively and addresses the crowd with a flourish. "Leon Kraus stays holed up in a two-bit playhouse practicing Beethoven—and you call me a coward?"

"Most assuredly," I sneer, nose to nose. My voice rings out like glinting steel. "Because the dirty little secret is that you wouldn't have been willing to fight—any—war. Not against Hitler. Not against slaveholders. Not against the British when Washington crossed the Delaware that icy night before Christmas with real revolutionaries—not pampered campus radicals—and turned the tide of the war that gave us... INDEPENDENCE"

"War? You talk about war? I stood up to tyrants at CORNELL."

Now we're fencing. I'm wearing my bellhop uniform with the short red jacket and gleaming brass button that looks dashing as hell. Hank Einhorn is wearing some kind of canary yellow outfit that also seems to be out of the nineteenth century. We're dueling with épées because they're deadlier than foils, but not as clunky as sabres. The campers are now peasants of old Spanish California. Alyssa looks drop-dead gorgeous in a white satin gown and black lace mantilla. I hear the pounding, swashbuckling "Polacca" from Tchaikovsky's Sleeping Beauty, *because I always thought it sounds Spanish even though it's a polonaise, and would make the perfect theme song for Zorro.*

Dismissing Hank's sally, I taunt, "Tyrants at Cornell?" Cut. Thrust. "You mean the nursemaids your rich parents pay to look after all you spoiled Ivy League brats? Maybe your father was a hero." I have no idea, but Hank bridles at the idea, so I press on. "Your father and your mother." This incenses him. He swings his weapon wildly. "Your father and your mother and their whole generation survived the Great Depression." I lunge. He parries, feebly. "They won World War Two." I riposte. Hank staggers back. "They made the world safe…" I leap forward, "for subversive sex-crazed villains…like YOU."

Sudden low inside lunge. Hank Einhorn drops his sword and falls to his knees. Vanessa Lawrence shrieks. Vin Lawrence leads the peasants tossing their sombreros in the air. Alyssa Lawrence looks at me with all the longing in the world.

Until I blink. Aannd I'm back.

In reality, Hank Einhorn is marching toward Sadie Hall flanked by his teens. Vin Lawrence is walking sheepishly back to his bungalow with Vanessa in tow. Alyssa and Sandi are herding campers to the side door of the kitchen to hand out half-pint cartons of milk before their parents take them off to bed.

I stand alone next to the flagpole. It's nearly dark.

I'm a schmuck.

13

Leon

I don't deserve it. I didn't earn it. Yet a magician has granted my fondest wish.

There was nothing romantic about how the day began. At the habitual hour of 5 a.m. I tripped over Phillip's stack of *Playboy*s. He'd joined Hugh poring over them overnight, frustrated that Sandi Lerner once again shot him down. Seth slept through my pratfall, but Hank sprang to his feet and hissed, "Why can't I ever sleep 'til seven, six? Any normal time? Who the hell's ever going to listen to that crap you practice?"

Knowing that for all Hank's bluster, last night Vin had taken him down a peg, I didn't protest. Honestly, Hank doesn't intimidate me. He's not a violent guy, and maybe he's right. Practicing at this point is mostly a compulsion. Also an evasion. Starting with my parents, it annoys more people than it will ever entertain.

Nevertheless, I trudge off to the casino, say hi to Smitty, promise to play his favorite Debussy, and sail into a Prelude from Bach's *Well-Tempered Clavier*, a piece welling up with impatience, but also hope. Two hours later, Herman arrives. His Bermuda shorts this morning are particularly vivid. For dinner, Herman's married granddaughter dresses him in quieter clothes, but he begins each day in a riot of color that jolts anyone who doesn't drink coffee.

We get down to work on Beethoven's "Tempest" Sonata. Herman and I argue over a tricky fingering. Beethoven didn't always write pianistically, meaning in a way that's natural for the hand. Maybe he was being malicious. Ludwig could be that way and laugh about it. When I complain, Herman nudges me aside and plays 'til his fingers hurt too much to go on. Watching him is not like looking at Miss Federoff. Still, I learn more in an hour from him than she and Mr. Orzehowski taught in ten years.

Not only about technique. We talk about why people call this sonata the "Tempest." Beethoven supposedly told his assistant, a guy named Schindler, that it was inspired by Shakespeare's play. Maybe, maybe not. Schindler made a load of money stealing mementos from his boss and concocting myths about him. But Herman takes the nickname seriously. He says this sonata contains Prospero's magic.

"I don't mean hocus pocus. This is the magic of discovering love." He has me play a stormy passage that suddenly, unexpectedly, breaks into stillness and wonder. Is this the magician's lovely daughter? I look at Herman. He repeats the quiet in the midst of the storm and then quotes Miranda's line,

How beauteous mankind is. O brave new world, that has such people in't.

***

Alyssa

That's when I walk in. Leon doesn't notice. He tries to play as beautifully as Ardis's great-grandfather, Mr. Pressler, does. Instead, Leon is stumbling and cursing under his breath. Peering owlishly into the darkness with his thick glasses, Mr. Pressler sees me but says nothing. He motions for me to take a seat a few rows back.

***

Leon

Herman says we ought to take a break, and that this might be a good time to play Smitty his Debussy, "The Girl with the Flaxen Hair." That's the real title.

I play it well. You won't often hear me say that, but this morning I'm playing it well. Smitty usually breaks into applause. Now he stands silently by his vacuum. I look to see if he's still there, and I see...Alyssa.

She rises from a metal folding chair and comes toward us. I jump up from the piano bench. Herman remains seated. As always, which is to say on this second or third time I've ever actually addressed her, I begin by stuttering.

"G-good morning."

"Lovely morning. You played that beautifully. Who wrote it?"

Alyssa's lynx eyes glitter like lapis lazuli from the *Arabian Nights*. Now they spread even wider with her smile.

Seeing I had trouble managing "good morning," Herman answers, "Debussy. '*La fille aux cheveux de lin.*' Like yours."

"My hair is more like straw."

She speaks French. I feel like Gomez Addams. I want to kiss Alyssa up and down her arm. Instead, I stammer.

"This—Herman, this is Alyssa Lawrence."

***

Alyssa

Mr. Pressler stands up, though tiny as he is you can hardly tell the difference. "Your great-granddaughter is in my group."

I walk toward the apron of the stage. Mr. Pressler makes a courtly bow and grasps my hand. He has a delightful accent.

"I hope Ardis isn't giving you too hard a time. She's, how shall I say, rambunctious."

"She's a little fiend," I say with a smile, and he smiles back.

"That too. You're the singer's daughter, aren't you? He's quite good. As good as Tony Martin."

Tony Martin sang in movies and at clubs like the Copacabana.

"Thank you. I'll tell him."

"The other night your father sang my favorite song, 'Night and Day.'"

"That's your favorite song?" Leon seems to have found his tongue. He's talking to Herman without stuttering and clearly isn't shy with his friend. "You never told me. That's *my* favorite song."

"My favorite too," I say.

They stare at me. It's a big coincidence, but I can prove it.

"You know who called 'Night and Day' the best song of all? Irving Berlin. My father told me that. It's my parents' song, the one they danced to at their wedding."

Herman Pressler smiles slowly and then prods Leon. "Go ahead. Play it for her."

***

Leon

How to play it? Lately I've been trying to imitate a dizzying recording by Art Tatum. I've also heard a ponderous late version by Sinatra. I don't know how Vin Lawrence sings it, so I close my eyes and picture Fred and Ginger.

After a beat at the end of silence, Alyssa asks, "Do you dance too?"

I laugh and say, "No."

"What were you practicing before? Was that Beethoven?"

"That's not ready. It'll never be ready."

"It better be ready next month," Herman says. "Leon is entered in a competition."

"Only a minor one."

"In Newark. I'm going." Herman takes Alyssa's hand again. It's so easy for some people. "You could also come. It would be nice to bring friends from the hotel. In Europe we call it a claque. It doesn't hurt. You could heckle the other contestants."

I ask him to stop, but Alyssa laughs. Then, emboldened by the Debussy and the thought of Fred and Ginger, I blurt out a proposal that's totally out of character.

"You know, there is a nice way to meet Beethoven. Do you like old movies?"

"Sure."

"Did you ever see *Born Yesterday*?"

"Oh, I love that. Judy Holliday."

I step down from the stage. "Remember how William Holden takes her to a concert outdoors and the orchestra plays—"

"Beethoven's Second Symphony," Herman says. "The *Larghetto*. I like that movie too. The gin game." He laughs.

"You can't come," I growl.

"Where?" Alyssa asks. "Is there a concert with that coming up?"

"No," I say. I'm trying to gather courage, and continue in a rush, "Would you be willing to meet me tonight at the pool? Late tonight when nobody's there?"

"What?"

"Trust me." I reach to take her hand but stop. "I mean, you're not afraid of me."

"No, of course not," she says.

"Of course not," I repeat. I don't want her to be afraid of me, but it wouldn't be bad if I was a little intimidating. "I think you might like this."

"How late?"

"I don't have to service a card game 'til after the show," I tell her. "Any time before midnight."

"I would hope so," she laughs. "Mr. Pressler's great-granddaughter and my other campers eat breakfast at eight."

"Herman," he prompts.

"Herman." She smiles. "I have to run now."

"How about eleven tonight?" I ask. Implore. "We only have to hear the slow movement of the Beethoven."

"We have to?" she asks.

"Yes."

"How?"

"You'll see."

She seems to be considering it. Herman looks at her even more anxiously than I do.

"Okay." She smiles. "Eleven, at the pool. But don't they lock it?"

"I'll get a key," I say. "Remember, I'm a bellhop."

"How can I forget? It's the uniform that got me," she says. "Am I supposed to wear a bathing suit?"

Deathly silence. I'm picturing Alyssa in her polka dot bikini.

"No, of course not," I say aloud. "See you at eleven. Tonight."

"Now you're trying to get rid of me."

"Yes," Herman says. "He has a competition to win."

14

Leon

The rest of this endless day hasn't been any more romantic than the way it began, with me tripping over Phillip's *Playboy*s. Everyone at the hotel, everyone in the world, is talking about how last night Teddy Kennedy drove a young woman off a bridge on Chappaquiddick Island, Massachusetts. Then he left her to drown. As the day's worn on it seems Kennedy tried to cover up the crime. He went to police only after two fishermen discovered the car that contained the body of Mary Jo Kopechne.

At Salzman's, most of the guests and almost all the staff are loyal Democrats. Teddy is the heir of their martyred first family. We now know Jack Kennedy was no saint. Reluctantly, some people have linked women, including Marilyn Monroe, to Bobby Kennedy, gunned down only a year ago, the same terrible year that saw the assassination of Dr. Martin Luther King, Jr. Kennedy defenders note that Eisenhower, FDR, Warren G. Harding, and God knows who else kept mistresses. *Boys will be boys.* Especially when they're under a lot of stress.

There's at least one person here who does not accept that excuse. Sonny Jones. My boss and I haven't gotten around to discussing politics. Grabbing a bite in the kitchen after lunch when Big Sol's taken his gun and his dog home for a nap, I overhear Sonny arguing with a dishwasher feeding plates onto a conveyer belt. Like the dishes, Sonny is steamed.

"Lemme get this straight," he shouts over all the clattering. "Teddy Kennedy. You know his real name is Edward Kennedy. As in Edward Kennedy *Ellington*."

"Jesus," Tyrone the dishwasher wails, his voice as high as Sonny's is low. "Can you cut that Duke Ellington crap?"

Sonny puts down his pound cake. "You're calling Duke Ellington crap?"

"What the hell does he have to do with Ted Kennedy?"

"Because Ted Kennedy is crap. The man's got a beautiful wife. She plays the piano."

"Who cares?"

"He's got beautiful children."

"Would it make a difference if he had ugly children?" Tyrone lifts a tray of dishes from the other end of the conveyor and shakes them at Sonny.

"The point I'm trying to make, you moron, is that if he's screwing around and letting some young girl drown, Edward Kennedy might as well have walked out on his children. Abandoned those children. The way my old man walked out on me."

"Oh, so that's it," Tyrone says, spreading his arms and then pointing at Sonny. "This is about you. If it's not freaking Duke Ellington, it's all about you."

"It's about being a responsible father. Teddy Kennedy calls himself some high and mighty defender of colored folks."

"Black people." Tyrone shoves a rack of goblets into his machine. I'm amazed they don't all shatter.

"What's the biggest problem Black families are facing these days?" Sonny asks. "The biggest problem."

"Being a dishwasher and getting paid crap."

"Being a father and not being there for your kids. Voting rights, welfare rights, the right to check into this freaking hotel—"

"You can keep that right." Tyrone spits.

"None of that matters if you abandon your kids. None of it. When Senator Edward Kennedy was doing what he was doing to that girl before she drowned, he abandoned his kids. You agree with me, Lee-on?"

Great. Now I'm getting roped into this.

"I think we have to wait for all the facts," I trail off, hoping to slink out while taking a bite of an apple.

"Hold on. Your father works five days, sometimes six days a week so you and your fine mother can stay here and enjoy a summer vacation."

"Yeah, this is some vacation. Maybe we can take a side trip to a coal mine."

"Am I overworking you, Lee-on?"

"Lemme get back to work. There's no one in the lobby."

"Because," Tyrone sneers, "you can't have the head bellhop hanging around the lobby. Not when he can be here busting my chops about Ted Kennedy and Duke Ellington."

"I'm educating you," Sonny says loftily. "The point is that Leon's father is responsible. When I have children, I'm going to be responsible."

"I bet you already have a busload of kids."

That really riles Sonny. He steps into Tyrone's face and says softly, "You're ignorant. You're a smart mouth. There's a reason we picked you up off the street in the Bowery and you were glad. Glad to come here to wash dishes for cigarettes and hooch. I hope you don't have any children. 'Cause those children wouldn't have a chance."

Sonny pokes Tyrone in the chest and beats me back to the lobby.

***

Alyssa

Something romantic is already happening today.

Herman Pressler's great-granddaughter and the rest of my girls are playing prisoner's base down in that dell by the flagpole. I see Ardis as a future convict, so we make sure that she's closely guarded.

Albert Fallick is not part of the game. The assumption—not mine, but that of the camp directors, Mr. and Mrs. Goldman—is that girls are not fast enough to play with boys. Parents also fear roughhousing. They don't worry about inappropriate touching. After all, these kids are only six and seven.

They don't know Albert.

He's supposed to be swimming with Neil Esposito's junior boys, but Albert slipped away to watch our game from behind a tree. Now Albert sees his chance.

The girls guarding Ardis are facing forward, like the Turks at Aqaba in *Lawrence of Arabia*. That's one of my favorite movies—

and not because my last name is Lawrence. Peter O'Toole reminds me of Richard Chamberlain with a British accent. *Sigh.* Anyway, like Lawrence of Arabia, Albert sneaks up from behind, taps Ardis on the shoulder and, when she turns, he plants a kiss.

It may detract from the romance, but I must note that Albert has been nicknamed The Kissing Bandit. He accosts junior girls, intermediate girls, he's indiscriminate. He kissed me one night when I handed him his milk carton. I boxed Albert's ears. It's against camp regulations, but I'm not Vin Lawrence's daughter for nothing.

However, it seems Albert's love for Ardis is the real thing. To prove it, he's dug into the inner pocket of his bathing trunks and pulled out a Cracker Jack toy ring. Ardis is flabbergasted. Her gasp grabs the attention of the jailers, who send up a war whoop. Both teams pursue Albert. He puts the lie to the idea that boys are faster than girls, largely because Albert eats whole crates of Cracker Jack, and looks it.

Before our Amazons can pummel Albert, Sandi and I call them off. Ardis is crying.

"Did he hurt you?" I ask, worried, especially about Mr. Pressler.

"N-no."

"So why are you crying, sweetie?"

"Well," Ardis whimpers. "Do I have to give back the ring?"

I tell her no, but there will be no honeymoon.

Sandi keeps watch over all our prisoners while I frog-march Albert back to the pool.

The rest of the girls giggle, shout curses, and admire Ardis's jewelry.

15

Leon

By 10:30 I've almost completed my preparations. Blanket, battery powered record player, Beethoven, bowtie.

Earlier, when I asked Sonny about the pool key, he waited a long moment and finally said okay, but told me not to try anything. He'd be keeping an eye on me. Then he gruffly offered, unasked, to cover the late card game, "so you won't have to ditch your date." Thank you, Sonny.

At 11:05 the only Lawrence voice I hear is Vin's. The casino is close enough that some of the show is drifting over. Vin is singing "Fly Me to the Moon" in honor of tomorrow's big day.

Five minutes more and still no Alyssa.

But a minute later at 11:11, my traditional lucky time, oh my God. A vision has unlatched the gate. Wearing a swishing summer dress as sparkling blue as her eyes, she steps warily through the darkness. I rush to meet her only to hear, would you believe, an apology.

"I'm late."

"You're here."

"You didn't say what to wear... I'm glad I changed."

She sees I'm in my tuxedo, the one I wear for concerts and competitions. I also have on a bowtie Seth lent me. It's nicer than mine, subtler. "My Cary Grant tie," Seth said. He saw me dressing and was as excited as I am. Seth calls Alyssa a showstopper and has almost forgiven her for dating Hank.

Seeing me now, I'm afraid she'll laugh. The whole night is a gamble.

***

Alyssa

Wow. No kidding. Wow.

"You look elegant," I tell Leon. Which I now realize is a wonderful name. Distinguished. Urbane. "Like Peter O'Toole in *What's New Pussycat?*"

Leon seems confused. Maybe he's not a fan. Or maybe he thinks I mean he looks like the other star of that film, Woody Allen.

"Not Woody Allen," I assure him. "You look like Peter O'Toole. He wore glasses in the movie too."

Leon seems relieved. Actually—and I can't believe I'm thinking this, because I never thought it about my old boyfriend Brian Cooper, much less Hank Einhorn—Leon looks like Dr. Kildare. He's not wearing hospital scrubs, and he's a little scrawnier than Richard Chamberlain, but Leon Kraus is slender and elegant and…dreamy.

He closes his mouth—I have to get Leon to stop gaping like a fish when something impresses him. He says, "You look… Well. You've seen how I've looked at you for the last three weeks, so you know how you look. Tonight it's by moonlight."

"With Beethoven. How are you managing that?"

Chaise lounges ring Salzman's huge rectangular pool, yet Leon leads me to a blanket spread next to the deep end, on freshly mown grass that smells heavenly. Fireflies bring the stars within reach. I've never seen so many stars outside the Hayden Planetarium.

***

Leon

I considered sneaking wine, but thought better of it since I don't drink, and I don't know if Alyssa does. Also, we're underage. Maybe Sonny really is watching.

"This record player doesn't sound like much," I apologize. "Still, it's not bad if you rest your head right next to the speaker. I got the idea from James Agee. Have you read *Let Us Now Praise Famous Men*?"

"We did last year in school. Those photographs."

The book is about rural people struggling through the Great Depression. Walker Evans took photographs that are like x-rays of those poor people's souls.

"You remember how Agee tells you to lie down on the floor, beside the speakers, to get inside the music. To let the music embrace you."

Alyssa's eyes widen. "I remember he said that was painful."

"Well," I laugh, thrilled that she remembers. "Agee was listening to Beethoven's Seventh Symphony. Or maybe the Ninth." My memory isn't as good as hers. "They're both loud. This will be different. Trust me."

"I do."

"What?"

"I do."

I think about that.

"Why?"

"You seem quirky, but kind."

"What did I ever do that's kind?"

Alyssa considers. "You haven't killed Tilly Mintz. I've watched that woman for two summers and can't believe she still lives."

"The night is young."

"No, it's not, Leon. I've got to be up early."

This is the first time Alyssa ever said my name. Without another word I escort her to the blanket and help her down as tenderly as Fred helped Ginger. Then I put on the record. Bruno Walter conducting Beethoven. The Second Symphony. Its celestial second movement.

***

Alyssa

For maybe a dozen minutes neither of us breathes. This magical music rises and falls as softly as the water in the pool illuminated by lights below the surface that glows with the same fathomless blue as Leon's eyes. I never really noticed he has beautiful eyes. The stars are shining all the brighter because tonight there's only the sliver of a moon. When the music ends, we remain side by side lying on the blanket. I don't recall at what point during the music we began holding hands.

"Tomorrow at this time," I whisper, "someone will be walking up there."

Leon and I are way ahead of the astronauts.

***

Leon

Turning my head, I see that Alyssa's hair has fanned out on the blanket, silver in the moonglow instead of gold. The scent of her hair is more fragrant than roses.

"It's an age of miracles," I reply.

"Sometimes." Alyssa turns to me and smiles. "On a lovely night like this, yes. Other times I think it's all… I don't know." She looks away. "Vanishing."

Vanishing? I pray this moment will last forever. What is it that Alyssa is trying to hold onto? Certainly not me.

Then I remember what Hank had said about her being stuck in the past, and stupidly can't help asking—maybe because it's so hard to believe that Alyssa is actually here with me, "Is that why Hank razzed you? Called you a fascist?"

She releases my hand. I see a flash of temper. She's not Vin Lawrence's daughter for nothing.

"Why are you bringing up Hank?"

"Sorry."

"You're…"

"What?"

***

Alyssa

I refuse to say what Ardis would've said: Leon Kraus is an idiot. Instead, waking from what had been an enchanted moment, I'm now forced to take a breath and explain, "Hank calls me a fascist and a reactionary—I can't believe he actually talks that way, like we live in the U.S.S.R.—because of something I was reading."

Leon looks worried, like I've been reading *Mein Kampf.*

"It was *The Fountainhead.*"

He raises himself on one elbow.

"You know," I clarify. "By Ayn Rand."

"Hank censors what you read?"

"He tried. But that's the whole point of *The Fountainhead.* Not going along with the crowd. Having the courage of your own convictions. Not being afraid to try to be something different. Really different. Not what everybody calls different when they all share the same opinions and listen to the same stupid music and wear the same awful clothes."

"Peer pressure."

"The pressure to conform. *That's* fascist. But if you told him—"

"Hank." Leon wants to make sure we're actually criticizing Hank.

I stand up to emphasize the point, and because I'm aggravated. "When you call Hank a conformist, he doesn't believe it. He and every radical out there believe they're all thinking for themselves. They want us to be members of a collective, but don't understand they're not thinking for themselves."

Leon furrows his brow, which is endearing, and says, "That architect in *The Fountainhead*—"

"Howard Roark," I prompt, kneeling next to him.

"And the woman. Domino."

"Dominique."

"They're like supermen. To be honest with you, I'm not crazy about Ayn Rand's style of writing. She hates communism, but she sounds like clunky socialist realism." Is this Hank all over again? Leon blunders on. "I'm talking style. Ayn Rand's characters—they're made of granite. They're bigger than life. They never have any doubts."

"Because they have courage."

That gives him something to think about. After toying with a blade of grass, he admits, "I don't have much courage. It took all the courage I've ever mustered in my life to ask you to come out here tonight and listen to a record."

"It was beautiful," I say. "Thank you."

We're quiet until he adds, "My favorite character in all of literature is Russian, and he has plenty of doubts. He's always worried that he's not doing the right thing. He hates conventionality. He's not sure about religion. He's not sure that anyone could love him, that the woman he loves could ever love him back. Even after they come together in this incredible scene where they read each other's minds."

"Are you talking about Levin?" I sense he is like I have telepathy. "In *Anna Karenina*?"

***

Leon

I love that she knows and, impulsively, I grasp her hand again. "When Levin and Kitty complete each other's thoughts, writing on the table, is there anything—"

"More romantic?"

"Of course, when Levin joins the peasants mowing his fields. That's about the greatest thing ever written. It's almost music."

"It's Zen," Alyssa says.

That cools me off a little. "Are you into Zen?" I don't know much about it. I assume the Lawrences are Christian. Of course, Zen Buddhists and Christians are all gentile. Not that I'm religious, but who knows how she sees me.

"No," Alyssa says, smiling. "We're Friday fish Catholics."

"Oh." A Buddhist would have been less intimidating. I rattle on, "César Franck is a great Catholic composer I can play for you. Francis Poulenc too. He wrote a wonderful *Gloria*. Also music for *Babar*."

"The elephant?"

"Yes." I laugh along with her.

"But I don't want to listen only to Catholic composers," Alyssa says. She sits down again, next to me. She must sense I'm not comfortable talking about religion. Our religions. You don't need to read minds to sense that. Still, I guess because we're on the subject, she asks, hesitantly, "Was Beethoven Catholic?"

"Not really. He wasn't much of anything. Like me. I mean, I'm not Beethoven."

Alyssa laughs again. "Not yet. That's why Mr. Pressler wants you to keep practicing." Then she's silent for a moment until she muses, "Tolstoy got religious later in life. But you're right about Levin. He certainly doesn't have all the answers."

"He doesn't. But you know what's also romantic?"

"What?"

"When Levin screws up." I sit up straighter and move closer so we're almost touching. My face is inches away from hers as I murmur in the dark, "When he forgets how much he loves Kitty. When Levin almost takes the miracle of their family for granted. Because that's life. People screw up. God knows I screw up. I just screwed up, bringing up that bozo—"

"Mr. Bozo to you," she says it like Groucho in *Monkey Business*.

"All right, *Mister* Bozo."

Alyssa squeezes my hand.

"But real love," I say, "is not listening to music in the moonlight. It's having the chance, over a lifetime, to show someone, every day, you can be kind and caring. In all the little ways and the big ones."

"You can't rush that," she says softly.

"No," I respond even more softly.

Then, as I'm about to release her hand, she squeezes it again. "We can still enjoy the moonlight." She laughs such a wonderful, affectionate laugh. "I know someone who'd love to be out here right now with the girl he's going to marry. I saw him give her a ring today. Maybe it wasn't real love, but it was as romantic as you can be…when you're six years old."

"What?"

"They're six years old. Albert Fallick had the courage to give Ardis Greenberg a kiss."

I think about that. Then I stop thinking and kiss this special girl gently, and then ardently, and then tenderly, and then with all my heart.

She kisses me back.

16

Leon

What happened to taking things slow? I don't mean physically. We don't get beyond kissing, and hugging. That's enough. More than I ever dreamed possible. After walking Alyssa home, I meet her mother, which is more intimidating than meeting the Pope.

She's waiting at the door. Did someone see us at the pool and send out an alert? I guess not, because Mrs. Lawrence greets us with a warm smile. "Isn't this a lovely night? Come on in, please. Calm down, Blinky." Blinky is their cocker spaniel.

That's how Mrs. Lawrence greets us. Not "where have you been," or "look how you've been keeping me up." Her sentences end on an up note, like a soap bubble popping. She's so pretty, petite, and bright-eyed. The kind of mother who seems to be holding a plate of cookies. Beth Lawrence has the gift, she gives the gift, of making you feel instantly like an old friend of the family. She's transformed their creaky bungalow into the cover of *Good Housekeeping*.

I'm not saying Mrs. Lawrence is a chirpy housewife out of a '50s sitcom, but there's nothing wrong with having a nice disposition. With smiling. I don't try that often enough. Neither does my mother. My father smiles, but not really. Not his eyes. I want to change, if only to be a better musician. Something a critic wrote about the young pianist Martha Argerich made a big impression on me. Martha—I call her Martha because I like her so much, and she's beautiful—Martha is stupendously talented. She's won major competitions. She's also had nervous breakdowns, and at one point, Martha stopped playing altogether to become a secretary. This critic, who meant it kindly, said Martha would never become a great musician until she discovered "a talent for happiness."

As we sit down in the living room, Mrs. Lawrence asks, "Did you get to hear your music?" Alyssa had confided in her mother. My mother couldn't have pried that out of me with matches under my nails—assuming she'd been interested.

"It was gorgeous," Alyssa gushes. "Leon played Beethoven at the pool on this. This is a record player with batteries." I'm still clutching the case. "And," Alyssa adds, "here's the album."

"This will sound silly," her mother says, "but is this the symphony from *Fantasia*?"

"I love *Fantasia*." Not wanting to be a snob, I cheer like *Fantasia* was the shot heard 'round the world—*"The Giants win the pennant. The Giants win the pennant."* Anyway, I actually love *Fantasia*. Especially the flying horses. I keep to myself that Walt used Beethoven's "Pastoral" Symphony, the Sixth, not the Second.

Mrs. Lawrence smiles and tries restoring our conversation to normal tones so as not to wake Vanessa. "Leon," she says quietly, "you look so dashing."

But it's too late. The cranky kid pads into the room wearing a rumpled yellow nightgown. "What's going on? What time is it?"

"Leon is bringing your sister home."

"Who's Leon?" Vanessa demands. "Are you a waiter?"

"Young lady," her mother admonishes.

"The *maître d'*?"

I do look like a juvenile *maître d'*. I want to serve Vanessa a knuckle sandwich, but at that moment, the man of the house—the vanquisher of handsy young men who dare to go out with his daughter—Vin Lawrence strides in from work.

"What's going on? Everything all right?"

Vin is handsome, but in a peculiar way. His head is enormous, the way Napoleon's was enormous. It doesn't make him look top-heavy, since Vin is fairly tall. His big head gives him more authority than he has, being Alyssa's father and the guy who toppled Hank Einhorn.

"Vin, do you know Leon?" Mrs. Lawrence soothes. "I'm sorry, Leon, I don't know your last name."

"Kraus," I croak.

"Looks like you've been to a prom," Vin observes.

"Leon was playing Beethoven by the pool for Alyssa." Mrs. Lawrence hands her husband the album. He examines my tuxedo.

"You must really like Beethoven."

"I hate Beethoven," Vanessa contributes. "'Roll Over, Beethoven.' Words to live by."

"Thank you for that critique, Vanessa," her mother says with what, by her standard, must be a withering look. I now know who she reminds me of. The movie star from the *Thin Man* series, Myrna Loy.

***

Alyssa

"Leon is not only a classical disc jockey," I joke, giving my father a peck on the cheek—as much for Leon's sake as for Dad's, to let Leon know not to be afraid of him. "He plays the piano incredibly well. He's going to be in a competition next month. What do you think is his favorite song?"

"Enlighten me."

"'Night and Day.'"

"That's our song," Mom says. "It's sort of our family song. We all love when Vin sings it."

"Do you play popular stuff?" Dad asks. "I mean for this Salzman's crowd. Old songs, standards?" Dad is suddenly businesslike.

"All the time," Leon says eagerly. He wants Dad to know he doesn't think his music is sentimental sludge. "When I'm not practicing, you know, the other stuff."

"I'm going to bed," Vanessa announces, telegraphing that we're all hopelessly square.

Dad continues. "Can you play from a fake book?"

"What's a fake book?"

"Melody and chords, not written out."

"Like guitarists play?"

"Yeah."

"I could try."

Dad turns to Mom. "Danny collapsed tonight."

"What?"

"Nothing serious. Sounds like he has appendicitis. But we had to make do for half the show, and there's no piano for tomorrow."

***

Leon

Mr. Lawrence turns to me. He's still not smiling. "I'm sorry, what's your name again?"

"Leon," Alyssa and her mother say at the same time.

"Leon," I mumble.

"Can you meet me tomorrow morning, Leon? I know you have to work."

"It's Sunday, so we'll be busy with check-ins," I say, reluctant as always to commit myself. Dammit.

"How about early? I wake up early."

"I wake up at five. That's when I practice in the playhouse."

Mr. Lawrence raises his eyebrows. "Well, it doesn't have to be five. How about, say, eight o'clock there. Or even seven?"

"Better make it seven."

"You don't have to dress." He smiles sarcastically.

"Vin," his wife scolds gently.

"Actually, I do have to dress. I'll be the guy in the bellhop jacket."

"I'll be the guy in pajamas. Let's get to bed."

17

Leon

Turns out a fake book is as thick as the Manhattan phone book. It contains every song ever written, going back to King Solomon's *Song of Songs*. The band has to be ready for any and all requests.

Mr. Lawrence is prompt, and once again, businesslike. No "good morning," but he has brought a Styrofoam cup of coffee I pretend to sip. I don't like coffee. Egg creams are another story.

He sits in a folding chair next to the piano bench. "I don't know how our piano guy, Danny Lapidus, is doing," Mr. Lawrence says. "He's still in the hospital. But even if Danny's fine, it's good to know someone else here can play. Let's see. Why don't you find, 'Those Were the Days, My Friend.' It's recent and everyone likes it."

Each page of this fake book can fit three or four songs because of the short-hand chords. There's an index.

"Yes, I know this," I say. Not cocky, I just do. I play it for him by ear.

"I like that one too," Smitty calls out. "Reminds me of a bar I know. A lot of bars." He stopped his sweeper when we went onstage. Now he's arranging chairs in the back.

"You've got great taste, Smitty," Mr. Lawrence says. He doesn't comment on my playing but turns back to me. "How about something old? 'Polka Dots and Moonbeams' in F sharp. Can you transpose?"

"Yes."

I know the recording Sinatra made with Tommy Dorsey before the war but look the song up in the fake book so as not to seem like a smart aleck. At the phrase, "The music started, and was I the perplexed one," Mr. Lawrence joins in. When we finish, Herman—

who always pops out of thin air—calls from the back, "You really sound like Tony Martin. I hope you don't mind my saying that."

Mr. Lawrence grins. "It's a compliment. I gave up a long time ago hoping people would say I sound like Vin Lawrence."

"No, you're good. You have your own feel for a song. Is Leon going to play with you?"

I jump in. "We're kidding around. You remember, we met Mr. Lawrence's daughter."

"That beautiful girl who—"

I don't think her father would mind that Alyssa showed up yesterday, but it seems a good time to change the subject.

"Mr. Lawrence, this is Herman Pressler."

"You were here last summer, weren't you Mr. Pressler?"

"My granddaughter brings me. They like to get me out of the City, and it's a nice chance to spend time with my great-grandkids, and to enjoy your shows. It's no bad thing to sound like Tony Martin."

"He's got the best pipes in the business," Mr. Lawrence says appreciatively.

"And he's got Cyd Charisse. Hey, I wish I sounded like Artur Rubinstein."

"Are you a pianist?"

"Used to be." Herman waves the question away. "But let's talk about Leon. He's promising."

"You don't find many kids who like the old songs," Mr. Lawrence says. It's the only nice thing he's said to me so far. That is, if he means it nicely, and not to say I'm an oddball.

"Oh, Leon is an old soul," Herman says. "But I'm interrupting you. Mind if I listen?"

"Have a seat." We get back to business. Alyssa's father is unbending a little. "Leon, play something you like."

I try the love theme from *Spartacus*. Yes, *Spartacus* has a love theme, along with other themes for all the killing. Bill Evans owns this beautiful piece, but I give it a whack in what I hope is my own style.

Mr. Lawrence sits with his eyes closed. Then, "Have you ever played with a band?"

"A little. A couple times at school, Mr. Lawrence."

"Vin."

Vin?

"All right," he continues briskly. "Let's check on Danny. I bet he won't be up for tonight. Luckily, it's not a real show. Most everyone's going to be watching the astronauts. We're talking about moving a TV set into the playhouse. Anyhow, on Sunday nights we play Stump the Band. You know, the guests call out song titles."

"They can be sneaky." Herman whistles. "You know these people."

"And love them."

"There's no real pressure on you," Vin assures me.

"Don't underestimate this kid," Herman says.

"If you start singing," I assure Vin, "I'll try to follow along."

Vin eyes me. "I already know you have a tuxedo."

"That was kidding around."

"It was nice to see my daughter get dressed up." For the first time, her father smiles.

"I bet," says Herman. He's so old that Vin lets it go.

"Clear this with your boss," Vin tells me. "Who is your boss? Can Sonny give the okay, or do you have to go through Cully?"

"I don't know Cully," I admit.

"Do you?" Herman asks Vin. "He makes Howard Hughes look like the welcome wagon."

"I'll ask Sonny," I say.

"Tell him we'll play Duke Ellington. I'll ask my wife to request 'Sophisticated Lady.'"

"Or maybe," I suggest, 'I Got It Bad and That Ain't Good.'"

Vin, Herman, and I laugh.

18

Alyssa

I hit a duck. No, I didn't mean to. I'm sorry. *I'm sorry*. She's scooting away faster than I thought ducks could swim. Now I bet all her friends are going to attack me, like in *The Birds*. Why can't I get any good ideas like Hitchcock's? How about a variation?

Campers' parents one day suddenly attack their counselors because…

Because?

Because unbeknownst to the counselors, Salzman's Hotel—

I can't say Salzman's.

Salter's Hotel… no, Altman's Hotel… Maltings Hotel—*the hotel has supplied counselors with containers of… curdled milk. Maddened by his great-granddaughter's blood-curdling cries, old Herman Pressler—make that Henry Preston—lures little Alice's counselor out to the fire escape on the second floor of the main building and—*

I'm losing my mind. You think that story line is bad? Let me retrieve the crumpled-up page I threw at the duck.

Reading books is great. *Fun with Dick and Jane* got me started, and about the only time since first grade that I've been without a book is when I take campers like Herman Pressler's great-granddaughter into the water. After all the grief Ardis gives me, Mr. Pressler would still owe me even if she did sip a little curdled milk. I don't mean that. Ardis is not bad. And that was probably a nice duck.

The point is that ever since I learned to read, I've been trying to write a book. It's not easy, at least for me. Jane Austen as a teenager wrote a hilarious parody of English history, with illustrations by her sister, Cassandra. Fat chance asking Vanessa to collaborate with me.

We'd wind up killing each other. Hmm. That might be an idea for a book.

I try. I do. After discovering this rusty seat next to the pond—the pretty much abandoned pond that was Salzman's original swimming hole—I've been coming here with my lined composition book. The pond is overgrown and mosquito-infested, but I enjoy a little solitude. For all the good it does me.

Hank and I never discussed my literary ambition. With nothing to show for it, I was afraid he'd laugh. Hank can have an unpleasant laugh. What St. Matthew calls "laughter to scorn." That's all Leon needs is for me to quote Christian scripture. But it's hard to fault Hank. He's writing what will probably be a bestseller about his tumultuous first year at Cornell.

The only life experience I have to write about is not hilarious. Sorry, I don't mean to be cryptic or coy, but I don't want to go into it. Except to say that every time I try writing about something else, it's all I keep thinking about. That summer at the literature camp. How's that for irony? Or a copout. A literature camp keeps me from writing anything that resembles literature or even parodies—anything but trash.

What I have been telling you is stuff that's fun to remember, assuming I'm even remembering it correctly. Like how I was obsessed with Dr. Kildare. Why do we become obsessed with anything? Is there something not so delightful that we're trying to forget?

I look at this pond, this abandoned pool halfway filled with filmy water teeming with mosquitoes. I'm sitting on a rusty metal chair hoping my shorts are protecting me so I don't get tetanus. I see cracked concrete and a metal railing. Before World War II, before it was owned by the Salzmans, kids swam here who are now parents or grandparents. They may now be as old and abandoned as this rusty chair. Who knows what stories are floating in what's left of this pool? I'm not going to try to imagine them because I'm not that imaginative. That's why I may never be a writer.

I'm also not brave enough to tell you some of the stories I know about myself and others. Do I have the right to tell you about other people? It would hurt them to see their stories. That would cause anger and fights. Maybe even abandonment.

As for my own stories, isn't it easier to laugh about Dr. Kildare and forget the rest? To remember the fun stuff and let the rest become overgrown with weeds and rust?

Writers who don't want to write "the truth," or the most painful part of what they believe is the truth, wind up scribbling a crummy variation on someone else's story—my version of Hitchcock's *The Birds*—when what you're actually writing is a variation on Hitchcock's *Marnie*. That's the one about Tippi Hedren becoming a sneak thief, until Sean Connery helps her confront her terrible past and escape from it.

I'm not about to dive into anything like that, so here I am scribbling awful versions of other stories, other people's stories, that I wind up tearing out of this composition book and crumpling up and tossing.

Who pays the price? The duck.

I'll bring bread tomorrow and maybe we can make up.

19

Leon

Check-ins turn out to be light this Sunday, July 20th. I suppose because we're in the middle of the season. There aren't many errands to run since everyone's glued to the TVs in the lobby and the lower lobby, and the portable sets some guests have in their rooms— all to watch the moon landing. I'm excited too. This is the most momentous thing since Columbus sailed across the Atlantic and didn't fall off the Earth. Today, for the first time, all of humankind will set foot beyond our small planet.

"How can they send pictures back like that? Television pictures?" My mother is watching the set in the lobby. Nothing world-weary about her now. This is earthshaking for most of us.

"I hear the whole thing is a fake," Tilly Mintz assures everyone.

"Why would they want to fool people?" Mrs. Lawrence asks.

Tilly looks at Mrs. Lawrence like she's a fool. Tilly has a crush on Vin. "To put one over on the Russians," she explains, as if she's speaking to a two-year-old. "God, I can't believe how gullible you all are." Tilly lights a cigarette and stalks off to play gin.

The shuttle lands in the afternoon. Neil Armstrong is supposed to walk on the moon tonight, sometime after our show gets underway. We rehearse after dinner. Vin, Ben Bauer on trumpet, the drummer Buddy Kelly, and Harvey Shapiro alternating clarinet and sax.

Turns out Harvey is a classical music nut, a single guy who makes money off-season tootling his clarinet and wearing *lederhosen* at German beer halls in New York. His hobby is collecting albums, 78s, and even the original Edison cylinders. I can tell we're going to be friends.

Then there's Connie Sims. You can't call Connie a girl singer. For one thing she isn't a girl. Before she arrived late to the playhouse, Buddy told me Connie is a grandmother. She doesn't look old enough, but it's hard to say. Connie wears more makeup than a geisha. Even without makeup it would be hard to see her face behind the curtain of smoke, some of which Connie blows in my face. If this is meant to be seductive, I ruin the moment by coughing up a lung.

Besides not being a girl, Connie isn't really a singer. She's a *tummler*. It's not really translatable. It's Yiddish for a combination emcee, social director, and all-around live wire. Buddy says at most summer resorts men do this, like Mel Brooks when he was young. It seems last summer, Vin Lawrence tried taking over for the previous *tummler* at Salzman's, but Vin doesn't have the kind of personality to run around the pool and push people in. Instead, women and men warm to Vin's singing and his Dean Martin brand of cool. To light a fire under their guest's tushes, Salzman's relies on Connie.

"Who are you?" she asks in a voice as furry as her chinchilla wrap. It's eighty outside, seventy-five in the playhouse, yet, like a lot of guests, Connie is wearing a summer fur.

The men at Salzman's—and not only the band—wear a tux or white dinner jacket on Wednesday, Friday, and Saturday nights. Except for the ones who are hip, like Ronny Mintz with his Sergeant Pepper getup.

I've already talked a little with Harvey and Buddy. Now Vin arrives and formally introduces me to the band. Nobody seems thrilled, although it's become clear they're going to need someone long-term. Danny's appendix burst on the way to the hospital. That could have been fatal. Recovery will take two or three weeks, and Danny's parents want him to come home. They blame Salzman's food.

Danny Lapidus is the youngest member of the band, a twenty-year-old working his way through Fordham. I listened to him, and we chatted once. Danny isn't into classical piano or jazz. Still, he has a nice cocktail touch. A ladies' man, he gave Sandi Lerner a loony excuse for not being able to drive. It seems a week before arriving at Salzman's, Danny lost his license for speeding. But he told Sandi he wasn't allowed to drive because he had taken a speed-reading class that revved up his brain so much, he wasn't able to focus on highway signs. Sandi—the only person in the world who would have bought this—sympathized with Danny. Then she set her sights on Hank and his red Peugeot.

Anyway, Danny's classes at Fordham resume at the end of August, so he couldn't have stayed through Labor Day even if he'd kept his appendix. It's not lost on Vin that my high school, like his, doesn't restart 'til September.

***

Alyssa

Leon's first night in the band is historic because of the moon walk, and he's genuinely impressive. He looks wonderful again in his tux and sits quietly when he plays, not like pianists who toss themselves around. We have a kid at Long Beach High who plays well, but almost winds up on the floor.

With Neil Armstrong's walk about to start, only a few cynics show up at first. Then word filters out that Dad has arranged for a color TV, a twenty-five-inch Zenith, to be set up on the playhouse stage in front of the band. They play until the astronauts are ready to emerge. Then, a few minutes before eleven, it happens. The audience and I, and Leon onstage, can't be confined to our seats. We crowd around the set and stand transfixed as Neil Armstrong climbs out of the lunar module and says,

"That's one small step for man, one giant leap for mankind."

We all cheer and hug, even strangers. Armstrong and Aldrin are bouncing around. We are too. Not long before midnight they plant the American flag and Buzz Aldrin salutes. That chokes me up, and I can see Dad's close to losing it.

Leon walks down the stairs they have on the side of the stage, comes over and gives me a kiss. Not a peck. A lip-smacking smooch. Mom is next to me, and he kisses her too. We're all laughing, and the audience applauds us. How Dad is reacting I don't know, because I try not to catch his eye.

As Dad said, this isn't a show night. On Sundays they play Stump the Band. In honor of the landing, tonight there's a twist. We can only call out moon songs. Besides "Fly Me to the Moon," we've already heard "Moonlight Serenade." Dad's sung "It's Only a Paper Moon," which Mom requested. Connie Sims did "Moonglow." The game resumes after the astronauts have been walking around for a while. A lot of the songs stump me, but not Leon and the band.

Seth's dad, Mr. Perlman, asks for "Blue Moon" by Rodgers and Hart. Louise is *très chic* in a high-waisted cocktail dress, white—like the moon? Seth says it's by Halston, Jackie O's designer. I couldn't wear the same blue dress from the pool two nights in a row, and besides it has grass stains. Thankfully Mom did not ask why. So this is my second-best outfit, a pink and white cotton check—yes, pink, Sheryl—with a thin white belt. Not by Halston, but not bad. I do love my low-heeled pink shoes.

Louise is now asking, wistfully, for "Moon River." You remember who first sang that? Audrey Hepburn in *Breakfast at Tiffany's*. I could be wrong, but maybe Louise sees herself not as the men see her, as Marilyn Monroe. Maybe she sees herself more as Audrey. Or Audrey's character, Holly Golightly. Holly is a New York party girl. A call girl, but fragile. We find out she's really a country girl.

Louise intrigues me. I hope we become friends.

***

Leon

I'm scoring points tonight with Sonny. He's helping Seth serve tables. They both volunteered since they love the shows. Sonny's impressed that I know a song by Duke's son, Mercer Ellington, called "Moon Mist." Herman requested the first movement of the "Moonlight" Sonata. Vin asked Connie and the guys to back off so I could have the stage to myself. Beethoven got a nice round of applause.

The long night's winding down in the bar. By law, I'm not old enough to be here, but everyone's attitude is, "Shut up and give the kid a break." The hotel has an alcohol-stained upright crammed next to the taps with room for two raised stools. Vin's loosened his tie and he's sitting on one of them. Connie's crossing her legs on the other. I assume. The cigarette and cigar smoke in this bar is so impenetrable, I keep expecting Smokey the Bear to warn everyone, "Only you can prevent forest fires."

I manage to follow the singers, who really are quite good, through half the fake book, with patrons in varying degrees of inebriation caterwauling along. They even ask me to warble "Night and Day" after Vin tells everyone that's my favorite song.

I haven't mentioned the most important thing, infinitely more important than puffing myself up because I know how to play "Moon Mist."

Alyssa has stayed up with me all night.

***

Alyssa

The bar reeks from a combination of beer, various kinds of liquor, and not having been hosed down properly since it was built. Smitty may have refined taste in music, but even if this is the way things smelled back in Samoa, he's got to start mopping up with more bleach. I'm not used to bar aromas because neither of my parents drink. Mom never has. As for my father, when a student of his, three years older than me, was killed driving drunk, Dad took me out in our car and confessed that he became a heavy drinker during the war. They didn't serve booze at USO canteens, but Dad would drink on the side out of embarrassment and frustration that he was singing, not fighting. He went cold turkey when he met Mom and she told him she couldn't date a drinker. It was because of my grandfather. But this is a happy night, so let's not get into that. Suffice it to say, I don't drink.

Mom, of course, insisted on taking me back to the bungalow when everyone tumbled from the playhouse into the bar, but Dad—what did you do with my Dad? A man bearing an uncanny resemblance to Vin Lawrence said it was okay for me to sneak into the bar as long as I ordered a Shirley Temple—soda water, or what they call seltzer here, with a splash of grenadine, topped off with a maraschino cherry. Ridiculous, but it's my passport to a stool next to where Leon is playing a piano that can barely be heard above the roar of the crowd. Which is just as well, since he says it's dreadfully out of tune.

Dad knows this is a special night. There's the moon walk. There's Leon, who I think Dad's beginning to like a little. Mom already does. Vanessa hates anyone nice, so I'm relieved she hates Leon. Ardis calls him an idiot. All is right with the world.

Until... Oh no. Look who's swaggering in. Hank Einhorn. At nineteen he's still too young to be served at the bar, but Hank clearly got sloshed elsewhere. Now he's pounding his fist so hard that glasses jump, and roars at Leon, "*Kraus.* You lousy Beethoven Kraut-lover. Play me a minuet."

Sonny the head bellhop takes Hank by the elbow. Hank resists until Sonny twists his arm. Hank yelps. Sandi, who's wearing a green dress with a neckline that plunges to her navel, slaps Sonny on his arm and leads Hank out of the bar. Leon smiles and plays what sounds like a minuet.

***

Leon

I walk Alyssa home. We talk about the moon walk, which was so staggering that perhaps Tilly is right: it was a hoax. I agree with my mother too. How did they send back that video?

As for my playing tonight, Alyssa says I did well. At the bar before we left, Vin said nothing beyond, "See you tomorrow afternoon at two. Sonny's cool with it."

See you... Cool... *Really*?

When Vin said that, I found Sonny still in the playhouse and, believe it or not. I gave him a hug. He told me to go to hell. That he'd still be keeping an eye on me—and congratulations.

I have to be up to practice with Herman. Alyssa has to be up for the flagpole and breakfast, so we don't dawdle. Except outside her door for a goodnight kiss.

Talk about moonglow.

20

Leon

I am now a professional musician. The playhouse isn't Carnegie Hall but hey, Brahms got his start playing in a bordello.

The rhythm of my life has changed. Roosters now crow alone. Staying up so late every night, I don't wake up 'til seven. That leaves plenty of time to practice before Connie needs the playhouse for group dance lessons, which include my mother. Dad is never here for them, but she finds plenty of eager partners.

Herman still shows up to coach me. He doesn't worry that I'm spending too much time with popular music. He worries that I'm spending too little time on my competition program, that I'm slacking off. But then he's a worrier.

***

Alyssa

Leon's playing is in great demand. Sandi and I brought our group to the playhouse to hear Mozart's variations on the French song, "*Ah vous dirai-je, Maman,*" better known as "Twinkle, Twinkle Little, Star." Then our maestro accompanied each camper in "Chopsticks."

For tonight's talent show, Leon's helped us work up a performance of *Peter and the Wolf.* Ardis makes a terrifying wolf, or as she says, "woof." Mr. Pressler is applauding wildly.

Donna Salzman opened the talent show to both guests and staff, hoping the staff might be more entertaining. They are, starting with Mrs. Salzman. She sings, "How are Things in Glocca Morra?"

Cully's beautiful wife explains to the audience that she sang that song as a teenager at Camp Lokanda in upstate New York. The audience is glad to hear her without the booming outdoor loudspeakers.

Guests have come up with stuff like Sandi Lerner's dad doing card tricks. No one can see them beyond the first row, and he's screwing them up at that. Sorry. I don't mean to be mean, but like father like daughter. I don't say that because Sandi is now going out with Hank, who claimed only to like girls who love *Great Books*.

The show also features Tilly Mintz accompanying herself at the piano while yodeling "Hey Jude." By the time Mrs. Mintz gets to the third verse, we all realize this must be Tilly's torch song. But for whom? She's wailing by verse four, and Tilly's gyrating on the piano bench for verse five, the part about letting it in and out.

At this point parents are scooting their children out of the playhouse. Still, Tilly tries enlisting us all for the chorus—

Na na na nana na naaaa

—but the audience drops away as the *na nas* go on and on. Tilly seems unaware that the song has an ending. In fairness, "Hey Jude" never does end on the record, it only fades out. Dad finally puts an end to the woman's misery, and ours, by sitting down next to Tilly on the piano bench and applauding her.

There are rumors that the Beatles may break up. Tilly's performance could be the final straw.

***

Leon

The surprise hit of the talent show is Seth Perlman. We ran through the entire fake book looking for songs until Seth decided he wanted to be the emcee from *Cabaret*. I wasn't sure how this would go over. The emcee is a Nazi. Sure, all the guests have probably seen the show, and in the funniest movie of all time, *The Producers*, Mel Brooks gets a laugh out of making fun of Hitler. I checked with Herman to make sure he wouldn't be offended, and my friend said it was okay with him. Seth even persuaded some counselors to join the

Kit Kat Club chorus. Alyssa begged off, but Sandi Lerner loves writhing around in underwear and a garter belt. Hank must love it too, since he showed up for the dress rehearsal with his teenagers. Maybe this was their class on the Weimar Republic.

Wearing tails, and made up in white pancake, false eyelashes, and bright red lipstick, Seth is strutting, leering, and preening like a pro through "Willkommen." He moves well and has a strong voice. By acclamation, and to Tilly's chagrin, the audience chooses Seth as the winner. His prize is a season pass to the miniature golf course down the road from the hotel.

None of the other contestants begrudge Seth his success. Sandi's father is showing anyone who cares the secrets of his card tricks. Parents are making much of Alyssa's little girls who did *Peter and the Woof*. I mean *Wolf*. And all the male staff except me—because Alyssa's right here and I know what's good for me—are congratulating the Kit Kat chorus girls, trying to keep them from changing clothes.

Hugh is too shy to look at the girls anywhere but straight in the eye. Andrew is sizing them up like an all-you-can-eat buffet. I'm curious to see how Seth's dad reacts to all this.

My dad is still in the City. So is Ronny Mintz. He was spared Tilly's humiliation. Si Perlman watched the show front and center, and he seems as delighted as his girlfriend. Louise, who lent Seth her lipstick, is getting it back by kissing it off Seth's lips.

Mr. Perlman gives his son as big a bear hug as a shrimpy guy like him can, and doesn't hesitate to talk about his late wife in front of his mistress, and how proud Mrs. Perlman must be up in Heaven. I'm beginning to see that Louise isn't some cheap squeeze Si Perlman stows away for a quickie. Mismatched as they appear at first, Si and Louise are almost as cute and devoted a couple as Vin and Beth Lawrence. It makes me envy Seth. He gets a lot of support, for all his lunacy, from Si, Louise—even Anthony. Although Anthony tells me the best part of the show was the card tricks.

Si thanks me warmly for helping his son. I tell him I enjoyed it, and it's true. Not least because Seth loves talking about Alyssa. Guys are usually more like Phillip. If they talk about girls, it's only about sex. Seth goes on about Alyssa's clothes, her hair—it's like she's his Barbie doll. More important, Seth talks about what a kind, funny person Alyssa is, besides being "smart as a whip."

Seth wishes Hank could be more like Alyssa.

21

Alyssa

Hank wishes he'd never met Seth. Not because he's homophobic, but because Hank has no desire to become a "made man" with the Mob.

Here's the account Seth gave Leon and me about how Hank met his father the day after the talent show. I told Seth about my trouble finding something to write about and Seth suggested the subject, mostly because he wants to be "immortalized." Fat chance of that, but I'll try to write a little like Dashiell Hammett, who's terrific.

Leon says Mom sounds like Myrna Loy playing Nora Charles in *The Thin Man*, minus all the drinking. I love that. I also love Dashiell Hammett's lover, Lillian Hellman, the great playwright. Long Beach High did *Watch on the Rhine* two years ago. It's about a family that flees Nazi Germany until the father goes back to join the resistance.

My dad says Lillian Hellman is a communist. But that play—and I'm sure the movie they made of it with Bette Davis—was very moving.

In this scene with Hank and Si Perlman I'm making up the dialogue because Seth only remembers things he says himself, and even that's not accurate. But he insists this is essentially what Mr. Perlman told him, and I'm still angry enough with Hank to hope it's true. By the way, I'm including some things they said about me that are flattering. I hope they're true as well. So here goes:

That afternoon, after the talent show, when Hank Einhorn dismissed his teens so they could change for dinner, he saw Si Perlman waiting for him outside the pool gate. Perlman was not dressed for swimming. Neither was his chauffeur, Anthony.

Einhorn had been laughing off Seth's boasts that his dad was a member of the Mob. After all, Si Perlman doesn't look like tough guy Lucky Luciano, or even Meyer Lansky. Mr. Perlman's sports jackets seem two sizes too big for him. He has at most three strands of gray hair on top of his head, and his big nose, glasses and fuzzy mustache look like a novelty Groucho disguise. Hank Einhorn figured this was not someone who pals around with the Rat Pack. Maybe Si Perlman did lend Salzman's money. So what? Hank had him pegged for a shylock. But a Mafia don? No. Still, the man had a limo, and he had this weird driver, who was wearing a flowered shirt, red pants with white stripes, and a corduroy newsboy cap. A Carnaby Street gorilla.

"I'm Seymour Perlman. Seth's father." Although Si's vowels were echt-*Brooklyn, he had a soft, refined voice. His girlfriend, Louise, thought he sounded courtly. Hank did not.*

"Okay," Hank said warily.

"How are you?"

"I'm getting ready for dinner. Sorry, gotta go."

"To the place where you sleep with my son?"

"Excuse me?"

"I mean where you and the other fellas bunk. I'll walk you over there." Si walked slowly. Anthony took Hank's arm.

"Hey," Hank said as he tried freeing himself from Anthony's grip. First it was the bellhop strong-arming Hank last night. Now a chauffeur. Hank Einhorn was used to more deference. He was in for a rude awakening. Well, not really rude.

"Sorry," Si Perlman said. "I didn't introduce you. This is Anthony."

"An-tony," the driver corrected.

"Forgive me. A friend of the family."

They marched through the lobby and out the side door that led to Sadie Hall. To get to Sadie Hall you have to go through some woods. Hank was beginning to wish he had called for help in the lobby. Sonny was on duty, but Sonny couldn't stand him.

"Kissing up to Black Panther, Nation of Islam-type radicals," Sonny thought when he saw Hank. He'd heard about Hank closing down Cornell. "Don't ask me about how he treated that sweet Alyssa. She might be too good for Leon. She's way too good for this a-hole."

Leon tells me, "Thank you for getting me into the story. You are too good for me, and now it's official."

"I'm only writing what Sonny must've been thinking." I nudge Leon with my elbow. "Can I continue?"

He nods.

Now Hank Einhorn found himself in the woods with a Mafia boss and his hit man. Oh yes, Einhorn believed it now.

"Hank, may I call you Hank?" Si tried to smile, but the only time he smiles is when he's hugging his son. Occasionally also Louise. "I'm sorry," Si apologized again. "But I want to talk with you about something rather delicate. Something that requires privacy. And discretion."

Hank still said nothing.

***

Leon

Have you ever noticed that the best way to seem smart and powerful is to shut up? I got to know the principal of my elementary school. Remember Mr. Smith? The guy who liked to take conferences with my beautiful mother? I had conferences with him too, because I was having so much trouble reading until Mrs. Stonehill got me on the Helen Keller blocks. One day Mr. Smith asked why I was always so quiet. I said nothing. He waited and then smiled and said it was okay to be quiet. "Don't tell anyone, but I like to keep quiet too. When you're quiet, people don't know what you don't know." Then he winked.

Alyssa's annoyed. "Are you going to keep interrupting? You sound like Seth. I'm trying to write about people other than myself."

"Sorry. Go ahead. Please."

***

Alyssa

Why was Hank silent? After all, he went to a top school, so he didn't have to fool anyone. Si Perlman actually brought that up.

"I know you're a smart fellow, Hank. You go to an Ivy League college. I went to City College. Not that I'm ashamed. More Nobel prize winners went to City College than anywhere else. Did you know that? Jewish fellows mostly. I'm also proud of being Jewish, as I hope you are. I work with a lot of Anthony's people, Italian people, and some of them think I'm—how shall I say—out of my element. But we're all simply people. I'm proud of what we do. I'm proud of being able to help businesses, like this hotel." Si took a deep breath. "Thanks to this hotel a lot of hard-working people are able to spend a few weeks every summer in the fresh air. Are there any chairs around here, Anthony?"

"We're in the woods," Anthony said with his bizarre accent.

"Maybe a bench?"

"What am I, bloke, a forest ranger?" Hank recognized it now. It was a Beatles accent. A fake Liverpudlian accent to go with his mod clothes. Anthony continued, cheeky, "This is the first time I been here. Ask the kid." Meaning Einhorn.

Einhorn was surprised Anthony could get away with such insolence, but Si was broad-minded. Anthony wouldn't've talked this way to Fat Tony Brindisi. Fat Tony was not a glorified accountant.

"Hank," Mr. Perlman asked, "do you know if there's a bench around here? I have a heart condition."

"There's no bench. Can I go now?"

"Hank. Hank. I'm trying to get acquainted. I'm introducing myself. Telling you I'm proud to be a Jew, a City College graduate, with honors." Si chuckled. Hank and Anthony didn't. "I'm proud to be a businessman. To be able to help this business, and another business you may know. A club in Greenwich Village. It's been in the papers lately. The Stonewall Inn?"

"I know it," said Einhorn, sneering. "I mean I've read about it. Like everyone."

"Sure," said Mr. Perlman. "I'm proud of the people who made a stand there. For their rights. I'm proud of them. I'm proud of my son."

Si Perlman waited a moment to let this sink in.

"But I also have to protect him. I promised my darling wife, may she rest in peace, on her death bed, that I would protect our son *because he's special. So, when I hear that he's made a friend, I want to make sure that friend is special too. I've gotten to know a lot of people like Seth. My Pearl had many special friends from her show-business days. Good people. Some of them a little—how shall I say— out there. But not everyone. Anthony won't mind my telling you, as long as we're keeping this among friends, that he's special. He enjoys meeting friends at the Stonewall Inn. People come in all sizes and shapes and it's not for me or anyone,* anyone, *to judge. Since we're talking about my son, I want to be sure. Frankly, Hank." Si Perlman paused. He was short of breath. Also, he thought he'd made a joke, which was unusual for him.*

"Frankly, Hank. That's funny." Hank and Anthony didn't think so. "Can I be honest with you, Hank? This is for us. I wish sometimes, not always, but sometimes, that Seth could be more like you. Or Anthony. Strong. Because it would be easier for him to fit in. He has a good heart. I don't want to see anyone break his heart."

Hank Einhorn looked down. Looked up at Anthony. Looked down a little at Si, and then said, "Are you crazy?"

Anthony gripped Einhorn's arm again. Hank spun around 'til he was nose to nose with Anthony, and then swung back even faster. Then he took a step toward Si and got snapped back by Anthony. It was almost a dance routine.

"Easy, Anthony," Mr. Perlman said gently.

"Do I look like a faggot?" Einhorn almost spat. Anthony tightened his grip. "A homosexual?"

"You look great," Si said. "You're handsome."

"What the hell does that mean? That I'm homosexual?"

"There's no need to raise your voice."

"People don't raise their voice to us," Anthony said. Now he sounded more cockney. Like Bill Sykes, the tough guy in Oliver Twist.

Hank Einhorn wasn't laughing. He took a deep breath. "Listen, Mr. Perlman."

"Si. Call me Si."

"Listen. I didn't choose to sleep with your son. To bunk *with your son. For God's sake, there are six of us in that room."*

"Seth likes everyone. But not like he likes you, Hank."

"I can't help who he likes. If you're fine with it, that's good, but I like girls."

"You can like girls and everyone. You can be honest with me."

"What did Seth tell you?"

"We're close, my son and me. But to be honest, it's what he told my friend. Have you met Miss Maxwell? Louise?"

"Oh my God," Einhorn said. "What did he tell her?"

"Why do you keep bringing in God? If you're an atheist, Hank— yes, I've read up on you—you can still respect other people's religion. Louise is not Jewish, but I respect her Catholic religion. Seth and my friend Louise, I'm delighted to tell you, are particularly close, and Seth confides in her. The way I confide in Seth. Louise knows there is nothing more important to me than my son. He's all I have left."

Anthony at this point was rolling his eyes. In his family, if his father wanted to show affection, he smacked you.

"So, I'm trying," Si continued, *"to become acquainted with Seth's friends. I'm telling you, Hank, as a friend, that I'm not a bad friend to have. You need a summer job? Seth wanted a summer job. He needed to get out of the City, into the country, away from people I was not happy to see him becoming acquainted with. I figured, I know, let's send him to Salzman's. It's a nice wholesome place, on the whole. Seth can wait tables. They were going to make him a busboy, but I told Cully Salzman that my son is not a busboy. He's a waiter. He's earning tips and learning the value of a dollar. I figured Louise can stay here, get a little fresh air, keep an eye on Seth. Everyone's a winner. And then..."* Si paused, more to catch his breath than to be dramatic. *"Then, Seth meets you. Bunks with you. Goes to the movies with you."*

"When?" Einhorn demanded. *"You mean—when a whole bunch of us went. I went with my girlfriend for crissake."*

"You mean the singer's daughter?"

"That Neanderthal's daughter, yes."

"The pretty blonde girl?"

"Yes."

"I thought she's going out with the piano player."

"She is," Anthony volunteered.

"Explain that to me," Si suggests, but really orders.

"She was my girlfriend at the time," Einhorn said slowly, losing patience. *"Now I'm with the girl she's a counselor with. The other counselor for the little kids. Sandi Lerner."*

"You go out with a lot of girls, Hank?" Si asked gently. "That's good. I wish Seth would go out with some girls. All I'm saying, Hank—"

"Oh, for crissake."

"Why do you keep bringing Christ into this?" Si asked not so gently. "He's not my God, but he's Anthony's God."

"Oi, mate," Anthony said to Si. "You don't have to stick up for me. Or the Church."

Si shrugged and went on. "Look, Hank. Look at me, Hank. Then we can go, because I'm getting tired and Anthony must be getting tired. You too, for that matter. You don't have to work as a counselor. I can get you a great job. Back in the City. Or wherever you like. Not only for this summer. I'm talking about for life. What do I want? I want you to look out for my son."

"Because we're looking too," Anthony said.

"Please, Anthony, did you hear me make any threat? Hank, did you hear me make any threats?"

"That's why you have me," Anthony muttered.

"Well," Si said, and he reached for a low-hanging branch to hold onto. "How do they not have any chairs out here? A single bench? Where can you sit to get some fresh air if you want to get away from the pool and the lobby and the dining room?"

Si chuckled again, to himself. "Can you believe how people stuff themselves in that dining room? Eat that way at the Carnegie Deli and you have to rob a bank to pay the bill. I don't know how Cully Salzman does it. Actually, I do know. He has me. But that's another story.

"Hank, I'm glad, I'm truly glad we had a chance to talk. When you see me around, or Louise, say hello. I'd love to hear about Cornell. It's a great college. Who knows? Maybe you'll win a Nobel prize."

"You know something?" Leon tells me.

"What?"

"That's funny," he says sincerely.

"You want to make out?"

"No, really. Tell what happens next."

I smile. He's really winning my heart now.

A few minutes after this meeting, back in Sadie Hall, right next to Hank Einhorn's poster of Che Guevara, there was something new hanging on the wall.

Seth.

Einhorn caught Seth on his way out to the dining room. Seth should've left an hour earlier, and he wished he had. But that was Seth. Who had the nerve to fire him? Not even Big Sol.

Einhorn was holding Seth up against the wall with one hand while threatening to smack him with the other. Si Perlman might not have made threats, but Hank Einhorn did.

"I'm going to kill you," Hank growled.

"Why? What's the matter?"

"What did you tell her?"

"Tell who?" Seth was perplexed.

"Your father's bimbo."

Seth wriggled so furiously that Einhorn had to let go. "Louise is the loveliest person I've ever met."

"Oh, she's hot."

"I mean altogether lovely. Yes, I told her how I feel about you."

"Who cares how you feel?" Einhorn thundered. "What did you tell Louise I felt for you?"

"I was vague."

Einhorn lunged at him. Seth held his ground. Einhorn picked up a red feather boa on Seth's bed.

"What the hell is this?"

"What does it look like?"

"I don't know. I don't know many... what? What are you? A female impersonator?"

"It's only for fun. But, yes, I was going to work it into the Cabaret *number at the talent show."*

Silence. Einhorn slowly shook the boa and shook his head. Seth waited a moment more and then said, "What did you think?"

"About what?"

"About my number. Me. I don't mean Sandi Lerner in her bra and panties."

Hank Einhorn looked at him. "I liked Sandi. I don't like you."

Seth took this in. "My performance?"

"No, you."

Seth looked down. He was wearing shiny black shoes. Big Sol wanted all the waiters, and even the busboys, to have shined shoes, creased pants with no spots, and clean white shirts to go with their bowties and short gold jackets. Seth satisfied on all counts. He did nothing else right. His guests wanted to switch tables, except for the grandmothers who thought he was adorable. Seth did not waste his good Cary Grant bowtie on his guests, so it truly was an honor that he lent it to Leon for his magical first date with Alyssa at the pool.

He explained to Hank, in a rush, "Leon talked me out of wearing the boa for the talent show. It's not that it was out of place. What could have been out of place in Germany back then? Before Hitler. After Hitler, but not before." Seth rattled on. He felt awful about Einhorn saying he didn't like him.

"Will you shut up?" Hank demanded. He meant generally, but especially about Leon. Hank didn't want to hear anything about who was now with Alyssa. Seth had forgotten about Alyssa, although he was quite fond of her. He started to cry.

"Quit whining," Einhorn ordered. "Oh, for crissake. I get hauled into the woods by your father and that goon—and what is it with him and that accent—and you're crying."

Seth made a sincere effort to stop, snorted up tears, and asked with dignity, "You didn't like my performance at all?"

Einhorn could only laugh mirthlessly. "Don't you have to be in the dining room?"

Seth took the boa from Einhorn, laid it lovingly on the bed, and prepared to make a grand exit. Seth wasn't into old movies, but instinctively he imitated Joan Crawford.

"Hold on," Einhorn said. "Are you going to tell your father?"

"What?" Seth bit off the 't' nicely. He had style.

"That I like girls. Only girls."

"If the subject comes up. I'm sure my father and I have other things to discuss. By the way, even if she wasn't devoted to my dad, a woman like Louise would not give you the time of day."

With that Seth swept out. Though it was still on the bed, you would have sworn he was tossing the boa around his neck.

The End.

"Is this what you're going to be writing about now?" Leon asks.

"Maybe," I tell him.

Leon takes my hands and peers into my eyes. "Us?"

I grin. "We'll see. Wanna make out?"
He shakes his head. "Not if it's going to be in a book."

22

Leon

As big a surprise as how much time I spend with Alyssa is how, even away from the band, I'm also spending time with her dad.

It started with paddleball. Salzman's has a tall cube of a building with no windows. The kitchen help sleeps there, including Tyrone.

Two sets of paddleball players smack Spaldings against opposite sides of that cube. You hit the rubber ball against the wall—this is one-wall paddleball, not the fancy kind with four—the next player has to return it on one bounce, and Tyrone and his colleagues inside the cube suffer shellshock. If you think living inside without windows is torture in the summer heat, consider hearing that from dawn 'til dusk

Vin is rabid about paddleball. After seeing me do not too badly playing Phillip, he invited me to be his partner in four-man games. Vin's a burly guy with a barrel chest to go along with that pumpkin head and curiously skinny legs. He anchors himself in a muscle shirt only a couple of feet away from the wall and makes quick killer shots. I scamper around the back of the court in long sleeves to avoid sunburn and mosquitoes. By the end of each game Vin's right arm has gotten a good workout, while I'm prostrate and panting.

We lose more often than we win, thanks to me. I've got to think that's why Ronny Mintz challenged us. Ronny the rock star wannabe is no great athlete, but he seems serious this Saturday morning. No Beatles wig or other borrowed hair. Instead, a white polo shirt and his signature pink shorts that are short enough for Sandi, though, thankfully, they're not see-through.

What's giving Ronny courage this morning is not his wardrobe but his partner. Hank Einhorn, so far as I know, has never played paddleball before. Basketball, softball, and tennis are his games.

Probably also polo, if Salzman's had any horses. But here's Hank twirling his paddle, bouncing a Spalding, and looking murderously at me.

Hank has not talked to me since he broke up with Alyssa in our room. Not a word, except to warn me about waking him up. The silence grew more ominous when Alyssa and I began going out. Hank doesn't talk to me now.

He glares.

***

Alyssa

Dad acts like he never shoved Hank to the ground, perhaps because Vanessa is still in Hank's group. Maybe Dad feels guilty, being a teacher and all. Anyway, my father speaks only to Ronny while Ronny stretches and preens. Leon is trying to blend into the wall.

Usually, there isn't a crowd to watch paddleball. Even if you don't play gin or mahjong, as Mom does—mahjong, not gin—it's more fun working on a tan by the pool than watching guys keep the kitchen help awake by smacking a ball against a wall.

Today, however, since Tilly's come to watch Ronny, Mom has come to cheer on Dad, and Leon. As the game's about to begin, a pretty big crowd is pulling over patio chairs. There are so many spectators that Sonny figures he can earn tips bringing beer and sodas from the coffee shop.

I hope Sonny wishes Leon luck. They've remained friendly despite Leon having quit bellhopping in favor of the band. Among the four players, Sonny is catering only to Ronny Mintz, who is, after all, a big tipper. From what I hear, Sonny also caters to Tilly Mintz, but I'll tell you about that later.

Seeing all the people milling around the court, Sandi and I steer our campers over. Instead of playing dodgeball on the softball field, our iron-lunged little girls form the loudest cheering section, drowning out Dad's aging bobbysoxers. Ronny Mintz is flirting with nobody in particular, and everybody. Anthony is taking bets on the match.

The crowd favorite is Hank.

Dad moves to his usual place a few inches from the wall. Ronny hunches over to Dad's left. He can't make Dad's kill shots, but Ronny doesn't have to. They begin, and Hank is playing like the Rod Laver of paddleball. He actually hangs back and swings with a wide tennis stroke, and that's throwing Dad off. He has to stretch high for Hank's returns, or move back, or let Leon get them. And when Leon tries…Hank trips him.

At first it seems accidental. Then Hank does it again. The third time most of the crowd cries foul and starts to cheer for Leon. Hank grins. Leon bends over, ties his shoe so that his butt is almost in Hank's face, and glances at me.

"*You've got this one*," I yell encouragingly.

"*You've got to be kidding*," yell my disloyal girls.

***

Leon

Vin has kept the game within reach. Ronny helped. Compared to him, I'm Arthur Ashe. We're playing to 21 and you have to win by two. Ronny and Einhorn have pulled ahead 17-15. But now, Vin is putting on a clinic, furiously smacking ball after ball into the crack between the wall and the floor. Even Hank's half-pint fans are impressed. Vin's fans shriek like he, not Ronny, is the fifth Beatle.

At 20-19 for us, with only this next point needed to win, Vin sends the pink Spalding rocketing into the left back court, an inch from where I'm standing. Hank lunges for the ball and scores a two for one. He hits the ball and also gores me with his paddle, like a bull at Pamplona.

Between softball and paddleball, I'm getting good at taking punishment. Another Alan Ladd. In his old movies, you always knew Alan Ladd would come out on top—but not until someone knocked the crap out of him.

What I'm trying to say is that Hank's paddle-blow to my solar plexus hurts like hell. If Alyssa weren't standing there cheering, I'd ask her father to call for an ambulance. But Vin's daughter—my girlfriend—is here, and before she can run onto the court, I seize my chance. Hank Einhorn's high shot has bounced off the wall, sailed over Vin's head, and landed in the back right court, five feet from where Hank floored me.

The greatest moment of my life was Alyssa kissing me at the pool in the moonlight. It still is. But this comes close. In slow motion—you'll never convince me it's not slow motion, because I can read the word Spalding on the ball—I hurtle the whole five feet without touching the ground and stick my paddle out far enough to make contact with the ball. I can't swing. All I can do is extend, but Hank sent the ball flying so fast, it ricochets off my racket and bounces, like a wounded bird, gently against the wall. Ronny could easily smash it, but Ronny, bless him, stands paralyzed—exactly like I stood that day in short center field—and the point, and the game, belongs to the good guys.

The crowd, the entire crowd—including Hank's new girlfriend Sandi—erupts in amazed jubilation. Alyssa runs onto the court, not to nurse me but to kiss me. When Alyssa's little girls try hoisting me in the air, it must look like a miniature flag raising at Iwo Jima.

Ronny shakes Vin's hand and slips me five dollars. He *is* a big tipper.

As for Hank, if he was looking daggers at me before, now he's wielding a battle axe.

23

Leon

Win or lose after our games, no matter how exhausted I am, Vin insists on having long talks. Not about how we played. Not about music. Apart from Harvey the sax player, most musicians I've known, classical or pop, don't talk much about their music. They prefer to play, or like Herman, teach. To unwind from our games, Vin talks about his day job. Teaching history.

It's more than a job. Vin has a vision of history he pushes as much as Hank hawks Marxism. Vanessa gives all her attention to Hank, which drives her father crazy. Alyssa's six-year-old mischief makers leave her too wrung out to listen to her old man's ranting. Mrs. Lawrence is too kind to say so, but she's heard it all before. Even Vin's old pal Benny Bauer, our trumpeter, only wants to talk in his machine gun monotone about horses or his beloved Mets. Benny's bet heavily that 1969 is finally going to be the year they win the pennant.

Therefore, until his high school classes resume in the fall, Vin is stuck with me.

"You know it all comes down to two revolutions." That's Vin's opening salvo after today's epic victory. Nothing about my miraculous shot. Instead, two revolutions.

"What comes down to that?" I gasp between gulps of water.

"America. Politics. Hank Einhorn."

Like a good teacher, he's grabbed my attention. The Hank Einhorn part though is perplexing. "We pulverized him," I say. "Why is Hank still eating at you?"

"Well, first he goes out with my older daughter."

"Before she met me."

"Yeah. After seeing you, she wouldn't give him a second look."

"After all, I'm in the band."

"You're calling Alyssa a groupie?"

"No, no."

Vin runs his hand through his thick black hair. "My younger daughter thinks this guy Einhorn is the Second Coming. Anyway, you want to hear about the two revolutions or not?"

"Sure." I shrug.

We're sitting—I'm sprawled—on the elevated patio in front of the casino, at a small metal table with a big green umbrella. There are only two chairs, or some of the male guests, and certainly some of the women, would have joined us by now. Many have stopped by to offer congratulations. Vin's brought a bottle of Ballantine beer from the coffee shop. Instead of more water, he kindly bought me an egg cream.

"What makes America different from France?"

Odd question, but I ponder. "We have Pat Nixon, they have Brigitte Bardot."

"Cut it out. The answer is our revolutions."

When Vin talks like this, he isn't pompous or professorial. He's trying to reach me. Must be intense in his classroom, but hard to resist, especially after Vin takes off his reflective sunglasses and stares at me with those dark eyes.

"The American Revolution was about liberty, individual rights, limited government. It all went back to the Mayflower."

"My family doesn't go back to the Mayflower."

"Neither does mine, but the idea, the whole idea of America does. What did those Pilgrims want?"

"Religious liberty."

"Right. Plus something else."

"A turkey dinner."

"Self-government, you clown. The Pilgrims signed the Mayflower Compact before they even got off the boat. From there, you had New England town meetings and then colonial legislatures, and you know—don't make that noise with the straw, it's annoying—you know, the French didn't have any of that. When they finally launched their revolution, thirteen years after ours, they had no tradition of self-government. The king and the aristocrats never allowed that."

"So, what's your point?" I badly want to slurp up the last of the foam.

"My point is that the French Revolution, instead of leading to limited government, led to the Reign of Terror and dictatorship. Napoleon. Don't tell me Napoleon was some great liberal."

"I won't." They both had big heads, but clearly Vin doesn't like Napoleon.

"He was a dictator and he killed. He was responsible for the deaths of more than a million of his own people in all his wars. You know, France never recovered from that."

"Hitler killed six million Jews," I tell him.

"I know." Vin sighs. "That's what dictators do. They kill people."

I consider this. "You're saying Hank Einhorn is anti-American because he supports big government. That he wants socialism."

"Socialism is anti-American," Vin claims. "It's not merely another choice, another viewpoint." He's really worked up now. "You know what Jefferson wanted to put in the Declaration of Independence when he first drafted it? Life, liberty, and *property*. John Adams changed it to the pursuit of happiness, but Jefferson wanted property. Because even though Einhorn and all those kids would hate me for to say it, the United States is about private property. Not only real estate, or a bank account, but intellectual property. Everything. Property makes you free."

Vin looks like he's about to get up and fly from the intensity of his fervor.

"Religious freedom drew people here from tyrannies all over the world. What also drew them was the chance to own property. Like Izzy Salzman. You know why Izzy and other Jews, and a lot of other immigrants, were successful when they got here? Because they'd already suffered so much back home. Getting the hell away from Europe and Asia was liberating. Think of it, Leon. They were no longer peasants, serfs. Having the gumption to get on a boat made them entrepreneurs. Remember, and this is really important, Izzy and my parents didn't come here to get welfare, because there wasn't any. You had to find a job or create one. My father sold cigars on street corners."

"Boxes of cigars?"

"If you wanted a whole box and could afford one. Otherwise, he'd sell you one cigar at a time on the Grand Concourse and cut it for you with a guillotine. Then he'd light it."

"A guillotine?" I laugh. "Was it really, what, a little guillotine?"

"No. You've seen them. A lot of guys here use them. A single-blade cutter. But don't start smoking cigars. You'll stink up the playhouse even worse."

"Alyssa wouldn't like it."

"Oh then, by all means puff away."

"Come on," I say, a little hurt. "You don't really mind that we go out. I'm not a bad guy."

"Let's get back to the revolutions."

"Guillotines. But hold on. How did your father support a family selling cigars on the street?"

"That was only at first," Vin explains impatiently. "He wound up selling used cars. He sent five kids through school. I always hate when people put down Nixon by saying he looks like a used car salesman. My father looked great. He sang the way he looked, like Lou Monte, always with a smile in his voice. Around the house, not professionally. He was proud to sell you a beautiful Buick Riviera. That was his favorite car. I've still got one.

"I'm proud of my father," Vin says, smiling. "And the Salzmans ought to be proud of their family. Izzy and his sons had even bigger dreams. They worked hard, took risks, and thanks to them, *we have jobs*. All of us, including Hank Einhorn."

I mull this over. "Okay. I'm grateful," I say, sincerely. "I'm grateful to them and I'm grateful to you. Still, Hank would say not everyone in America has property. Not to mention that some people with property," I lower my voice, "got it by belonging to pretty shady organizations."

Vin grasps my wrist and whispers, "The less said about that the better. Do you talk with that kid about his father? Alyssa's friend. Seth."

"Not really."

"Don't. I might have had a bigger singing career, but I steered clear of their clubs. Actually, Beth made me."

Vin looks at his beer.

Then I say, "It's not only *those* people. 'Legitimate' big businesses push people around too. All over the world. Paying them almost nothing, if they pay them at all. Speaking of property, Sonny would tell you that when Jefferson was drafting the Declaration of Independence, his property included Sonny's ancestors."

"And that stinks," Vin agrees, slapping the table. "It's America's original sin, along with the mistreatment of Indians and women and Chinese railroad workers and a whole lot of other people. Including Jews and Italians. Your people and mine. Never forget, eventually, everyone who comes here has a chance. Even if your neighbor spits in your face, at least the government leaves you alone. Unlike Hitler and Brezhnev and Castro. And Ho Chi Minh. Who killed my son. The greatest kid in the world, and I'm not just saying that." With balled fists, Vin pounds his knees. "My kid's dead and Hank Einhorn has the gall to fly the flag upside down."

Vin is more emotional than I've ever seen him, including at the flagpole. I don't know what to say.

"Look." He seems to be making an effort to calm down and swallows more beer. "You're a good kid. You used to be more respectful, but you're a pretty good kid. What I'm trying to say is, don't think life is all music. Don't leave the real world to guys like Einhorn with their endless grievances and their Great Society handouts that buy votes for politicians. Believe me, I include Republicans who repay their cronies. If you don't do something we'll wind up losing this country, and my son will have died for nothing."

24

Alyssa

My boyfriend is getting a swelled head.

It's intense, a kid at sixteen joining union musicians, making good money onstage and at the bar, and having the power to entertain people by playing any song they like.

We haven't talked about the women left alone five days a week while their husbands stay in the City, but now's the time. A lot of those ladies are ravenous. They satisfy themselves with the staff.

I found this out from Sheryl the switchboard operator. "Look," she said smiling wickedly. "I plug in a cord to connect a call. Then all I have to do is flip this switch." Now Sheryl can eavesdrop on the whole course of an affair, from seduction to assignation and, if the wives aren't careful, retaliation by husbands threatening them long-distance from New York. Of course, what the husbands are up to in New York is anyone's guess.

The better-looking waiters are in high demand. As well as Lou Sherman. He's the lifeguard in a Speedo who leaves nothing to the imagination when he "rescues" ladies behind closed doors. Sheryl claims Hank Einhorn is also cheating on Sandi, as he might well have been cheating on me, with at least one camper's mother. I choose not to believe this, and we certainly don't tell Sandi.

***

Leon

Has Alyssa heard that the biggest stud is supposed to be Sonny Jones? Hope not, because my former boss and I still spend a lot of time together.

Sonny is Tilly Mintz's Jude. He told me, and I *do* choose to believe it. This was their second summer together, until Sonny couldn't stand her kvetching anymore. Kvetching is Yiddish for being a pain in the tush. Tilly wanted Sonny to visit her every weeknight that Ronny was in the City. They met at precisely 1:00 a.m. Not a minute sooner, since Johnny Carson doesn't sign off till 1:00 a.m. And not a minute later, because Tilly is impatient.

The trouble is, Sonny had other women demanding a visit. Sometimes he wanted to watch Johnny Carson too, especially when Richard Pryor was on. One night, Sonny raced away from the playhouse as soon as he could, arriving at the Mintzes' room in the main building right after midnight. He looked up and down the hallway and then scratched at Tilly's door.

"Who is it?" Tilly called.

"*Shhh*. It's me."

"Come back in an hour. Fifty-five minutes."

"I've got to come in now. Let me in."

"I can't hear you," Tilly lied. "Come back after the show."

"The show's over."

"I mean *The Tonight Show*."

"That's what I need to see. Has Richard Pryor been on yet?"

"Oh, he's impossible. I don't know why Johnny books him."

"What did he say?"

"Go away. I can't hear Joan Rivers."

"Did he call Johnny a honky?"

Tilly laughed.

"Did he?" Sonny demanded.

Tilly didn't answer. She was in hysterics over Joan Rivers. Sonny stormed off, for good. Hence Tilly's meltdown at the talent show.

Sonny never talks much about Tilly Mintz or any of his women. We talk about other things. When I can't be with Alyssa, I spend a lot of off-time in Sonny's room in the basement of Izzy's original lodge listening to records, his and mine. Unless it's Billie Holiday, whose meowing voice I can't appreciate. Not because it isn't "pretty." I like a lot of singers who don't have beautiful voices. Fred

Astaire. Maria Callas. Unlike them, Billie's voice seemed to limit what she wanted to do, like Sinatra these days. Sonny kicks me out when I draw that comparison.

We do both like—love—Miles Davis. Once Sonny saw that I "got" Miles, he helped me picture this genius at New York's Birdland—center stage in his designer suits—with his huge, slanted eyes and space alien face, turning his back on the audience. Not insolent, not insulting. Miles faced away so he and the audience could have a private moment. Later, I shared with Alyssa Sonny's account of how cops beat up Miles simply for standing outside the jazz club with a white woman.

Sonny's now leading me beyond Miles. After the show tonight, when I brought Alyssa back to her family's bungalow, I didn't feel like listening to the guys at Sadie Hall pump Hank about college and girls. I've stopped by the lodge to see if Sonny is still up. He is, in his undershirt, listening—not so loud as to tick off Connie next door—to a female singer I don't recognize.

I take off my tuxedo jacket and sit on the floor. Sonny visits women in their rooms and doesn't care what his looks like. It's small. A narrow iron bed, the gray paint chipping. A tiny bathroom. A closet full of off-duty clothes—elegant enough to impress Ronny Mintz. An old photo of his mother, who was beautiful. Sonny tells me that in the '40s she was an usher at the Howard Theater in Washington, D.C.

"You ever heard of the Howard?"

"No," I say, guessing this made me a dummy in Sonny's eyes.

"You've heard of the Apollo."

"Of course."

"Of course," he mimics. Do I really sound like that? Smug white bread? Challah, anyway. That's Jewish egg bread. "Well, the Apollo was nothing. I mean it didn't exist when the Howard was introducing D.C. and the whole freaking nation to jazz. Not only for colored people. I remember." His baritone goes down to a whisper.

He savors a slow drag on his cigarette. "I remember the most splendid nights." He makes it three syllables. *Sp-len-did.* "The Howard was spellbinding. Young Ella. Pops. You know, that's Louis Armstrong." He pronounces it not Louie but Lou-is. "We didn't call him Satchmo, like you. He was Pops. Ethel Waters. Oh, Miss Ethel Waters. That's who you're hearing now, boy. With bird of paradise feathers in her hair and that million-dollar smile. Miss Ethel could have stayed on The Great White Way, but she told Mama the audiences there didn't have any spunk."

Sonny looks at his fingernails. They're polished, or maybe only buffed, and tapered. Not like mine, that I have to stop biting. Sonny almost whistles. "Ellington was from D.C., like me. That man isn't a duke, he's a king. Back then you had to see his sky-blue dinner jacket with satin lapels. The Duke called my mother—my mother—his satin doll. I was there. He winked at me. Colored people and white people, at the Howard anyway, they sat and cheered together. It was the future, and it showed me there could be a future. Not the numbers-running and the dope my uncles and cousins went down, down, down with. Mama kept my brother and me away from all that. She took us to the Howard, and we saw a future."

We listen next to Johnny Hodges in Duke's "Prelude to a Kiss." Johnny's alto sax sounds like an ibis taking flight. When it ends, Sonny blows out a wisp of smoke. We sit in silence.

Then I ask, quietly, "Why didn't you stick with music? Something to do with music. That's what you love. I think you love it more than I love Beethoven. Or as much."

Sonny stubs out his Camel. "I was lazy. Don't tell Tyrone I said that. He'd say I'm 'playing up to the white stereotype.' But it's true. My mother pushed me to take lessons. Horn lessons. I didn't stick with it. I didn't work at it. It didn't come easy enough. Listening came easy. Looking good, and I did look good, that came easy. The ladies came easy. Too easy."

<u>25</u>

Leon

The only women who ever make a pass at me are drunk. Late nights at the bar I sometimes feel a hand under the keyboard on my thigh. It's probably playful. After all, my mother is perched a few stools down, getting plenty of attention while keeping an eye on me. The women who stroke my thigh also pinch my cheeks and tell my mother she must be proud of me.

Alyssa doesn't take this seriously. After that first night, her parents, quite rightly, don't allow her to go to the bar. She goes to most of our shows in the playhouse. Besides the band, they feature everything from comics who end every joke with a Yiddish punchline even I don't understand, to impressionists, magicians— you name it. Cully would probably book plate twirlers, like Ed Sullivan does, but the busboys break enough plates.

One night we had a hypnotist. I may be giving you the impression that all the talk at the hotel is pretty serious. No. The hottest discussion at Sadie Hall that night was whether a girl can be hypnotized to take off her clothes. Phillip tried it on Phyllis Salzman. She threatened to tell her father, Big Sol. Nevertheless, they're now known as Phil and Phyl.

***

Alyssa

The shows are not really dates for Leon and me. Actually, some of our best times are hanging out with my girls. I know he enjoys them because Thursdays are Movie Night at Salzman's, and Leon is off. That's when Mickey Katz, a wonderful man, comes to the hotel with his teenage son, Howie, who struggles with a mental disability. I'm happy to tell you that everyone, including Tilly Mintz, treats him with respect and affection. Mr. Katz is a teacher, like my parents. I suppose we have so many teachers on staff because of their summer breaks. Mickey brings his own 35-millimeter projector and big reels of film. He's a movie buff. Leon and I talk with him in the playhouse while he's setting up—Mickey puffing away on his pipe while Howie painstakingly threads the projector.

Howie's favorite film is *Yankee Doodle Dandy* with James Cagney playing the Broadway legend George M. Cohan. Mr. Katz shows it every year. Afterward, everyone thanks Howie, who usually wears a determined expression but now grins and seems to want to say, along with George, "My mother thanks you, my father thanks you, my sister thanks you, and I thank you." I'm so touched by Howie and his dad that I'm writing a story about them and, if it's not too treacly, I'll share it with Mr. Katz, and with Leon.

You figure Mr. *Million Dollar Movie* would be front and center for the films, but after shooting the breeze with Mickey Katz during the set-up, Leon instead joins me at Spooky Hollow. That's what we call the woods behind the pool that lead to Sadie Hall, the woods where Mr. Perlman had his chat with Hank. One thicket there is cleared for campfires. The first time Leon tried gathering firewood, my wood nymphs laughed their heads off. That's because Leon brought back green wood, as we all learned after it belched enough smoke to fumigate Mount Freedom.

Tonight, Neil Esposito's boys are joining us, and campers like Albert—more interested in eating than savoring the great outdoors—are wolfing down gooey marshmallows right off the twig. Sandi and I make the braves and squaws work off some of those calories by dancing around the campfire, wearing arts and crafts headdresses and chanting, we imagine, like Apaches. Neil and his co-counselor, Harry, join in. Leon gets out of dancing by volunteering to beat the tom-tom. Our dance starts off as a spoof. Soon though, in the darkness—with the flames turning the kids' faces red, and casting long, eerie shadows—I can tell that Ardis and even Albert are connecting, really connecting, with ancient rituals and myths. Leon and I are feeling it too.

When the dance winds down and everyone's dead tired, I drape a sheet over my head. The children huddle to hear me. I drop my voice down an octave to lure them into this week's episode of—spooky pause—*The Twilight Zone*. Well, my version of it.

Like Leon, I was too young to stay up and watch the show when it first aired years ago. Instead of singing lullabies to Vanessa and me, my father would sit under a sheet with us on the floor between our beds, training a flashlight under his chin, and he'd tell us Rod Serling's scary tales. How my sister and I don't have continuing nightmares is beyond me. At first Mom ordered Dad to cut it out, and she refused to join us under the sheet. but she couldn't help listening by the door. Dad is a great storyteller. From him is where I got the idea.

Trying to sound like Boris Karloff, I begin, "The night before she died, Sally's grandmother promised that she and Sally could always stay in touch on a special toy telephone."

"Was it like a walkie talkie?" Albert asks.

"No."

"Then how can you talk on a toy telephone? It's a toy."

"Grandma was a witch, and she put a *spell* on the phone." I raise my arms under the sheet. The kids cower. Sandi does too. You know how gullible she is.

"After her funeral," I resume in the sepulchral voice, "the toy phone—with the spell on it—rings. Grandma tells Sally they can still see each other if Sally puts down the phone right that minute and runs into the street. *Into traffic.*"

"You should never run into traffic," Lisa, the littlest camper says, starting to shudder.

"That's right," I state with emphasis.

"Then," Ardis demands, her voice shaking, "why would her grandma say that?"

Vanessa and I used to love this tale, but maybe we were twisted kids. I assure the campers, "It's only a story."

"How does it end?" Albert looks scared but stalwart.

"Well," I conclude reluctantly, "a truck comes speeding right at Sally, and—"

"*Oh no,*" the kids shriek. Albert once again leads the other six-year-olds. This time they're not chasing him. They're trying to get the hell away from *me*. Sandi stares at me in horror. Even Leon's eyes are bugging out. But my biggest worry—besides having to find where the kids are hiding—is how to explain to Herman Pressler why Ardis turned against her grandma.

***

Leon

Since the band is free during the day, I accompany Alyssa on field trips. Last week we visited Washington's Headquarters in nearby Morristown. The general stayed in this stately Georgian mansion from late 1779 to early 1780, during the cruelest winter of the Revolutionary War. His seven thousand troops weren't so comfortable. They froze their toes off in unheated log huts.

The person whose fortitude impressed Alyssa most was Mrs. Washington. When George married Martha, she was one of the richest young widows in the colonies. He could have retired from the army to their plantation at Mount Vernon and lived like a king. By fighting for independence, George risked Martha's fortune and his own neck. You'd figure she'd want no part of the Yankee Doodle revolution. Instead of staying home, Martha made the dangerous trek from Virginia to New Jersey so she could spend the winter at her husband's side and comfort the sick and wounded soldiers.

"How patriotic, and romantic, is that?" Alyssa asked. I bought her a small portrait of Martha and George from the souvenir shop, the first gift to my girl.

Ardis, on the other hand, was most taken with George's teeth, made out of hippopotamus ivory. Perhaps still thinking of *The Twilight Zone*, Ardis said they reminded her of teeth she wore for Halloween. "I like mine better," she sniffed. "They had fangs."

This week's field trip is also taking us back in time. For fifteen miles, we're all bellowing "A Hundred Bottles of Beer on the Wall" until the bus driver, who must wear earplugs, drops us off in Tombstone, Arizona Territory, 1880—also known as Wild West City.

This is the place I saw on the highway sign when my father drove us to Mt. Freedom. The sign was more appealing. What we find are dirt roads, ramshackle buildings, a saloon, a sheriff's office, and a jail. We all wear cowboy hats. The kids take pony rides. When Alyssa isn't looking, I join the male counselors ogling hussies in flounces and garters.

Zorro wasn't really a cowboy. He fought with a sword and a whip and, as I mentioned, I always preferred swashbuckling to shoot 'em ups. Zorro lived in a hacienda. Cowboys roughed it almost as miserably as we do in Sadie Hall.

Someone else who doesn't like westerns is my pudgy pal, Albert. We have to rustle up a posse to find him. While our other desperadoes pose for fake wanted posters, Sandi, Alyssa, and I have to go on a real manhunt. Sandi searches the saloon, hoping to find Albert downing a sarsaparilla. Alyssa comes up empty at the blacksmith. Finally, I find him in the parking lot. Seems his fellow campers had laughed at The Kissing Bandit because holsters handed out for the Gunfight at the O.K. Corral didn't fit across Albert's middle. I try kidding him as we trudge back toward town. He keeps crying and refuses to rejoin the group.

A voice calls out in a resonant yet gentle tone. Even a dork like me knows that voice from *The Lone Ranger*. It's Tonto. Jay Silverheels in a leather headband and buckskin vest. He's waiting to make a guest appearance, stretching out behind the stable.

Mr. Silverheels calls us over. "What's the trouble?" he asks. Albert stops crying. We both freeze and stare. "You don't have to tell me if you don't want to. But," Tonto says gravely to Albert, "if you like, you could be my *kemo sabe*."

"What's that?" Albert asks. *The Lone Ranger* first aired before Albert's time but, come on, don't they still have reruns? Mr. Silverheels isn't the least put out. He kneels in front of The Kissing Bandit.

"In my language," Tonto says, placing his hands on Albert's shoulders and looking deep into his eyes, "*kemo sabe* means faithful friend. Someone you can trust with a secret."

The six-year-old seems tongue-tied, so I say, "It's no secret," and explain the other kids' cruelty. Tonto inhaled deeply, and then slowly let out his breath.

"My friend," he says "I know what it is to be an outsider. You know what I am speaking of."

"You're an Indian," Albert says.

"I'm Comanche. I'm proud to be Comanche."

"But you're… you're," Albert hesitated.

"Yes?" Tonto prompts.

"Nobody calls you fat."

"If I was fat, I wouldn't be able to ride my horse, Scout. I wouldn't be able to help my other *kemo sabe*, the one they call The Lone Ranger. Are there things you would like to do if you were thinner?"

Albert kicks a pebble and says, "I don't care about playing ball, but it could be good to play better."

"So no one would laugh," Tonto guesses.

"What about girls?" I ask. For the first time Tonto looks like he might smile, but he doesn't.

"That too," Albert says.

"The Comanche way to honor your body is to ride a horse every day. Do you have a horse?"

"No." Albert frowns and mutters, "But my dad has a lot of cars. He's a Cadillac dealer."

"A car does not give you exercise," Tonto says. "You have legs. Instead of riding too much in a car, walk. Or even better, run. Run every day. Climb stairs. Fast. Eat food the ancestors and healers tell us to eat. Earth food. Good food. Not so much food that it would be hard for a horse to carry you, because you never know if you need to ride to help your *kemo sabe*. Will you do that?"

Tonto crooks his right arm and holds up his palm and fingers. Albert does too. So do I.

I explain that we have to go because people are looking for Albert. I thank Tonto and tell him, "Truly, it's been an honor."

Albert waits a moment and then gives the Comanche brave a hug.

When I tell Alyssa about Albert, she says she admires Tonto even more than Martha Washington, then she says, "Tonto must also be your *kemo sabe*, since the Lone Ranger's friend seems to like people who wear masks."

<u>26</u>

Alyssa

Now that I've finished *The Fountainhead* and heard a little bit of Beethoven, my mission this summer is to teach Leon how to swim. Not everyone knows how, especially city kids. Of course, not every landlubber is afraid of the water. Leon is, so our lessons take a while. His favorite part is rubbing Coppertone all over my back and legs.

Not everyone at the pool goes there to swim. Take Louise. She doesn't like to soak her Sassoon cut in chlorine. Louise visits the pool for a tan and to play mahjong. That's where she met Leon's mother, and mine—and Tilly Mintz.

Twice a week Mom plays canasta in the card room. Mostly though, it's mahjong by the pool. Do you know this game? Four women sit around a collapsible card table. Each of them has a rack holding green jade tiles with Chinese characters and pictures of dragons and flowers. I don't know how to play, but they push around these tiles calling out "one bam," "two bams," "three cracks," "five cracks" while the tiles crack against the racks and people nearby—trust me—get a wracking headache. Which is why I never let Mom teach me. Leon says it's no more annoying than the all-night poker games he used to service. One good point for mahjong: unlike the men at Tilly's poker games, the ladies she plays with take a little time between games to get to know each other.

Mom is afraid to learn too much about Louise for one reason: she doesn't want Dad near any nightclubs owned by the Mob. One night at the bar, Si Perlman kindly told Dad he had an associate in Reno who would be impressed. When Dad thanked Si but didn't follow up, Mr. Perlman accepted the rebuff with good grace.

Tilly doesn't ask Louise about herself for three reasons: she assumes Louise is a hooker; she's jealous, and, being utterly self-absorbed, Tilly doesn't give a damn.

It's now left to Leon's mother to play Barbara Walters.

"Dahlink, vhere ver you br-haut up?"

Mrs. Kraus is asking where Louise was brought up. Louise is barely getting the hang of Anthony's mangled English. Now she's being subjected to German-accented English. Hoping she is not "Darling," Louise silently stares at her tiles.

"Vhere are you frr-ahm?" Mrs. Kraus follows up.

Nothing.

"For God's sake. Louise." Tilly heaves a sigh and slams down her gin martini. "Magda's asking where you come from. When are you going to stop being so—exotic—Magda?"

Mrs. Kraus smiles sweetly, and as best I can tell, mentions Leon's father. "Fredi tells me I talk just fine."

"I'm sure Hitler would have loved the way you talk too," Tilly says. "But no one between here and Deutschland can figure out what the hell you're saying."

"Oh," Louise responds. "I'm sorry. I'm from Ohio."

"Is this the way people dress in Ohio?" Tilly asks. When Louise plays mahjong, she places her chair so that it's in the sun, and she wears an itsy-bitsy bikini.

Louise answers, for the first time seeming self-conscious. "When it's hot. By the pool. Sure, we wear bathing suits."

"Where in Ohio?" Mom asks, to change the subject.

"Cincinnati. The West Side."

"Not the Upper East Side?" Tilly drawls.

"I know Cincinnati," Mom says enthusiastically. "Well, Vin does. He appeared once in a club across the Ohio River. It's called the Beverly Hills Supper Club."

Tilly puts down her drink again. This time it nearly shatters. "The Beverly Hills Supper Club?"

"Yes," Mom smiles. "He said it's beautiful."

"Across the river. In Kentucky." Tilly wants clarification. "Beverly Hills, Kentucky."

"Well," Magda says, "we have a casino here, and I hate to tell you, but Salzman's is not Monte Carlo."

"It's beautiful," Louise says defensively. "The Beverly Hills Supper Club is beautiful."

"So why did you leave?" Tilly pokes.

Once again, Mom tries to smooth things over. "I'm not surprised you moved to New York. Vin says a lot of the most talented people in New York come from the Midwest."

Louise blushes. "I'm not talented."

Tilly coughs. It's all she can do with a drink at her lips, and a cigarette too. By now Louise must wish she'd passed up playing mahjong and gone shopping with Seth. With flushed cheeks she explains to Mom, "My cousin Billy is a bartender at the Copa. The Copacabana."

"This is the Copa on Sixtieth Street?" Tilly asks. "Not the one in Kentucky?"

Ignoring this, Louise asks Mom, "Did your husband ever sing there?"

"No, not yet."

"I think he's good enough," Louise says, making Mom's smile blossom. "He's better than a lot of the singers there."

"You would know this how?" Tilly asks. "No, don't tell me. The costumes suit you. You're in the chorus."

"No," Louise says. She doesn't seem insulted. "I was a hat-check girl. But," Louise adds cheerily, "we wore skimpy outfits too, so you can still look down on me."

Tilly takes a long sip and says nothing.

"You must see a lot of great entertainers there," Mrs. Kraus says supportively.

"Oh yeah. When I was working I did."

"You're not still working?" Tilly asks with a sneer. "Oh, you mean, you're not checking hats."

Ignoring this jibe—because you have to ignore a hell of a lot with Tilly Mintz—Mom circles back to Magda's question. "Who was your favorite entertainer?"

"I loved The Supremes. *Stop. In the Naaame of Luuuv.*" Louise does a little straight arm action, bobs her head, and blushes again. "Also Marvin Gaye. *He* was nice to everyone." She says that looking at Tilly, which is the closest Louise comes to returning the insults.

Refilling Tilly's cocktail, Sonny can't help breaking in.

"You know Diana Ross?"

"I wouldn't say I know her." Louise smiles while Tilly burns. "Only to say hello. Mary Wilson, now she's a sweetheart. She was always joking with us to get a job where we could wear full-length gowns like hers because it gets cold in New York, and besides, you get old. Customers won't want to see your legs forever." Louise laughs. This is the most she's said since being invited by Mom to join the mahjong set.

Mom noticed, when Si Perlman was away, Louise had no one to talk with except Anthony and Seth. Now Mom and Magda Kraus are laughing with Louise, not at her, so of course, Tilly has to put a damper on things.

"Is it true," she asks sweetly, "that the Mob runs the Copa? Frank Costello?"

Louise looks down. Si must've asked her never to discuss business.

Tilly doubles down. "Is that where you met your…friend? Mr. Perlman?"

"I checked his coat, yes. He couldn't've been more of a gentleman."

"Uh-huh." Tilly nods.

Louise says defiantly. "That, that was six months ago. The first time I saw Mr. Perlman. Si. Then he introduced me to Seth. His son. The waiter."

"The waiter in a manner of speaking," Tilly drawls. She sits at one of Seth's tables waiting to be served.

"Now," Louise says, all aflutter because she had not yet told anyone at the hotel except Seth and Anthony, and she wants Tilly to know, "we're getting *married*."

"What? When?" Mom exclaims. My mother is genuinely happy for Louise.

"October eleventh. Eleanor Roosevelt's birthday."

"That's the day you chose?" Tilly chokes. "Eleanor Roosevelt's birthday?"

"Not because of that. Si looked up who was born that day. For good luck. He's a big fan of Franklin Roosevelt. We chose the date because it was the first Saturday we could book a famous temple in Cincinnati. The Plum Street Temple."

"Are you Jewish?" Mrs. Kraus asks, politely.

"Not yet. I'm converting. My real name is not Maxwell. My family's name is Boeckmann. Which almost sounds Jewish. Si is religious. Reformed but religious."

"He's not reformed from what I hear," Tilly rasps. She's drunk by now, or even she wouldn't be so mean—or foolish. Louise ignores her. It's clear Mrs. Kraus and Mom share Louise's happiness. They don't ask, but Louise displays her bare left hand. "I don't have a ring right now because a friend of Si's is making it up specially."

"Specially," Tilly echoes, like the drowsy dormouse in *Alice*.

"I'm going into Morristown tomorrow to look at gowns. There's supposed to be a wonderful little shop all the society brides in Peapack and Gladstone use. They go fox hunting. Can you believe it?"

"I believe you will. With a machine gun." Tilly is running out of steam and now everyone ignores her, including Sonny when Tilly demands another drink.

"Do you have anyone to go with you?" Mom asks.

"Now that you mention it," Louise says hesitantly, "I was going to ask. Seth is coming. He wondered if Alyssa could come too. You know they've gotten friendly. It's Alyssa's day off, and—"

Mom interrupts because Louise looks embarrassed. My lovely mother lights up. "That will be so much fun for both of you. For all of you. I can't wait to hear about it."

"Would you like to come too?" Louise asks shyly.

"I would," Mom says. "I don't want to hone in."

Louise seems unsure. I know Mom doesn't want to crowd us. She's glad to let me have a girls' day with Louise, and Seth. I'm going to ask Leon to come.

***

Leon

Any chance to be with Alyssa, I'm there.

Anthony drives the four of us into Morristown. We sit in the back on seats that face each other. Blasé as the town is about society brides on fox hunts, Si Perlman's limo causes a stir. When we park, it hogs three spaces on the village green.

The mansion that had been Washington's headquarters still fits right in. Take away the modern storefronts and Morristown remains smugly stuck in the eighteenth century. Our New Jersey native, Hugh McMahon, is proud of this town. As Hugh says, "If you took the nice parts of New Jersey and put them in Connecticut, they would be Connecticut." Hugh meant Morristown, which is charming.

The girls, plus Seth, Anthony, and I look at shops bordering all four sides of the green. Then we ask around for the bridal shop. We elect Alyssa to accost strangers, since she seems the least likely to scare them. I am, as usual, non-descript.

Louise's mini is short enough for the Ice Capades. Seth has on tight black pants and a turtleneck with horizontal stripes that make him look like a scrawny escaped convict. Anthony looks like a *Mod Squad* reject, and how he mixes with other wise guys I can't imagine. Alyssa is wearing a yellow sundress and a straw hat. If anyone looks at her twice it's because she's adorable.

An old lady who might be a Daughter of the American Revolution points us to a quaint narrow street a block behind the green. The cartoonist Thomas Nast lived here a hundred years ago. You can still visit his home, replete with caricatures of Tammany Hall bosses and the first modern Santa Claus. Our gang passes that up and walks nervously into a colonial shop called Sarah's Closet. Louise is disappointed not to find the racks and racks of gowns she had seen at Loehmann's in the Bronx, but one swift glance around assures Seth everything here is in vogue. As in *Vogue* magazine.

A matron named Linden—that's her first name—doesn't so much wait on Louise as grant her an audience. The biggest problem with Louise's skirt is that it gives Linden a full view of her shaking knees.

Selecting one dress is tough for Louise because money is no object and everything is swell. Alyssa and even Seth are overwhelmed. We leave the choice pretty much up to Linden. She suggests an ivory satin gown with a scoop neck, a plunging back, and a train that encircles Louise. It's swanky and sultry yet restrained. The kind of dress the '30s siren Jean Harlow could not sit down in because it was too tight. Louise looks radiant and predicts

Si will love it. He never says anything about her clothes that isn't complimentary. Although, Seth tells me, having first been smitten with Louise's legs, Si is no longer crazy about showing them off publicly. He'll love any full-length gown.

On the twenty-minute drive back to Salzman's we all shout our joy loud enough for Anthony to hear up front. Louise asks if Alyssa dreams about wedding gowns, the way Louise and Seth have since they were kids. It disappoints me, unreasonably, when Alyssa says she's a long way from getting married.

"Have you ever met anyone you might like to marry?" Wait. Is Louise asking about me? Is she asking about *Hank*? Louise adds, "I don't mean marry now. I don't think it's only in Ohio that people marry their high school sweethearts."

"Everyone?" I ask. Do I qualify as a high school sweetheart? Alyssa and I are both in high school, but we met at Salzman's.

"No, not everyone." Louise laughs.

Seth notes, "My dad didn't meet Louise in—where did you go to school, sweetie?"

"Cincinnati's Western Hills High." Louise cheers. "Graduating class of sixty-one."

"Dad went to Erasmus High in Brooklyn. Class of—"

"A little before nineteen sixty-one," Louise says protectively.

"Dad may've mentioned that he's a proud graduate of City College. In fact, Seymour Perlman could be their only graduate who has *not* won—"

Louise and Anthony sing in unison, "a Nobel prize."

"At least not yet," Seth adds. They all laugh affectionately.

"Did you spend any time in college, Anthony?" Alyssa asks.

"Did I do any time?"

"I mean," Alyssa rephrases, "did you go to college at all?"

"Luv, I went to the college of hard knocks."

I ask, "Was that tougher than the school of hard knocks?"

"Believe it, you little nob."

"At the college, I bet you give as good as you get."

"Better."

"Do you know where you want to go to college?" Louise asks Alyssa. "My family didn't have money for that. When my dad died, I was twelve. My brothers—I have three older brothers—they offered to chip in, but I wanted to get to New York after Billy, my cousin Billy, told me how exciting it was. I'm sorry. I was asking about you, Alyssa. With all the books you read, you must want to go to a great college."

"We'll see where I get in, and where I get a scholarship. Seth is a year behind me."

He shakes his fists. "Two more whole years until graduation, God help me."

"That means you have more time to think about it, and to study," Alyssa says, leaning forward and tickling Seth in the ribs.

"What I think about," Seth giggles, "is Louise introducing me to some of her Copa pals, so I can go to the University of," he belts it, "*B-road-way.*"

Louise, sitting next to him, pinches Seth and he howls. "Buster," Louise says, "you'd better hit some of Alyssa's books this summer." Then Louise turns to my girlfriend and says mischievously, "Before you started going out with Leon, I hear you dated a college man."

Now I know Louise is talking about Hank.

Seth knows it too. "They broke up and he's all mine." Conveniently ignoring that Sandi's still with Hank.

"You can have Hank Einhorn," Alyssa says. "Leon's not older, but he's better."

I want to kiss her. Hell, I want to marry her.

Alyssa must be reading my mind because she asks Louise, "Do you think you'll like being Jewish?"

"Not if she has to wear black all the time, and those corkscrew sideburns," Seth laughs. Louise pinches him again.

Anthony calls out to Alyssa from the front, "Are you asking because you're going out with a Jewish kid?"

Alyssa blushes. "Leon and I have known each other for…only a few weeks."

"Seems longer?" Anthony chides.

"It does. In a good way."

"That's sweet," Louise says. Maybe she realizes how uncomfortable I feel. How unworthy I feel to have Alyssa, for however long I have her. "That's how I felt when Si took me for the first time to the Carnegie Deli. I didn't feel like a sandwich, so we shared blintzes, and we talked and talked. He listened. After a couple hours, the waiters wanted the table but, well, they didn't say anything."

"They were either romantic or petrified," Anthony says. "Guess."

"Leon," Louise says to me, "is an old-fashioned name. I suppose you're old-fashioned like Si. Look at your music. I like you, Leon." She leans forward and gives me a peck on the cheek.

"I like you too," Seth says. He leans forward 'til I push him back.

"Me too," Alyssa says. She rests her head on my shoulder.

Anthony leans back and says to Alyssa, "You could do better."

27

Leon

"How do you feel about Jews?" I'm surprised to hear myself asking. Alyssa is taken aback too.

"What?"

"You never talk about it."

"What am I supposed to say?" We've come out of the casino after the show. Tonight there was a comic. I'm thinking about what Louise and Seth said. Especially what Anthony said.

Alyssa considers and then admits, "Okay. I wish Jewish comics would stick to English."

"You must have picked up a lot of Yiddish by now. Two years here, and didn't you spend every summer before this up in the Catskills? You've spent more time with Jews than I have."

"That's ridiculous."

"No, it's not."

It's a gorgeous night. We walk the long way back to the Lawrences' place, past the pond, where the pitch dark lets a million stars dot the water.

"It's not ridiculous. Before you, I spent most of my time with Fred Astaire, Zorro and Beethoven. Not a Jew in the bunch. Although I always wondered about Zorro. The cape is so theatrical."

"Superman wears a cape," Alyssa notes. "Is he Jewish too?"

"Yes. And it's his mother who thinks he's super."

"Like your mother?"

I say nothing.

She presses. "Don't you spend time with her and your father?"

I say nothing.

We walk up to the edge of the pond and kiss. Of course, being me, I can't let it go. "So, do you like Jews?"

"I'm starting to tolerate you."

"Do I seem very Jewish?"

Alyssa draws away, looks at me, seems about to make a joke, but doesn't.

To me, Jewishness doesn't seem that big a part of Salzman's, but that's like saying water doesn't seem wet to fish. The hotel's menus feature treats like latkes—a kind of potato pancake—and matzoh balls as big as beach balls. Still, people don't talk that much about being Jewish. Well, apart from the time Izzy Salzman flushed Philip Roth's new book, *Portnoy's Complaint*, page by page down a toilet, calling it "*a schande vor de goyim*." A disgrace for gentiles to see. Izzy's son Al never read another novel. Not after he had to fix the plumbing.

I read *Portnoy's Complaint* and other Roth books and marveled at how brilliant boys from Newark—presumably all Philip Roth—managed to attract nymphomaniacal *shiksas*. That's a gentile girl. The girl I'm clutching is romantic, not sex-crazed. Does she like me—tolerate me—despite what I am? Does she truly like me at all?

"I don't know what you want me to say, Leon. Who's Jewish? Is Herman Pressler Jewish? Because he's nothing like Tilly Mintz."

It is, of course, Hank who I'm thinking doesn't seem Jewish. But I bite my tongue. Alyssa adds, "Everyone's different. Can't we be ourselves?"

Maybe. Maybe. At least when we kiss or simply talk in another enchanted spot.

Behind the casino there are more woods, bigger than the grove leading to Sadie Hall. About a hundred yards in there's a small circular clearing. Maybe these woods are nothing special. I don't have much basis for comparison. Opposite our apartment on Queens Boulevard, between a Chevy dealer and the synagogue my family never attends, we have a green patch with a few trees. People go there to sit on benches or walk their dogs. Since we've never had a dog or even a cat, I pretended when I was little that the squirrels were pets. My mother called them rodents and wanted them shot. Magda Kraus made random but implacable enemies.

This wood behind the Casino is sinister. For one thing, it's dark, no matter how bright the sun is shining. When you walk, the ground crunches, which I like, since I figure it scares away animals and snakes. Also, the rocks are always damp, with moss crawling all over them.

Sinister though it is, I resent any sign that other people have been here. Sometimes, we see crumpled cigarette packs or a crushed beer can on the way to our circle, but not many. This one spot is pretty much ours.

Now, waiting to change into evening clothes before the next show, Alyssa and I lie on our blanket from the first night at the pool. We listen to my record player. Gazing up through the wreath of trees we watch clouds like the ones that a Brahms song calls "silent dreams," until at sunset they turn volcanic in their intensity. Alyssa says, "If you could see clouds only once, people would travel half-way around the world."

A leaf falls. We watch it flutter. Did a breeze or a bird dislodge it? This must be a sign that next month is autumn. Labor Day and the end of this summer idyll are only three weeks away. I don't ask Alyssa what she feels because I'm afraid she isn't as fearful as I am.

We caress listening to a limpid piece by Handel, an oboe floating over strings. Then we hear kids hooting in the distance. The rest of the wood is not our exclusive preserve. Hank and his teens erected a treehouse, "Chez Swiss Family Robinson." It's impressive. Luckily, the guests I checked into old bungalows didn't see Hank's treehouse first. They might have preferred it.

Alyssa says how nice it would be to have a treehouse of our own. "I bet you could build one, if you put your mind to it." Putting my mind to things has become a lighthearted but persistent talking point for Alyssa, despite seeing me tackle the piano while most people sleep. It bugs me.

"You build one," I yawn. "You're the feminist."

Feminism is another bugaboo for us. Alyssa finally agreed that Dominique from *The Fountainhead* is a bitch, daring the architect to sleep with her, and then marrying some other guy because the world isn't ready for the union of Superman with Superwoman.

Alyssa's better feminist icon is Jane Austen. We're reading *Pride and Prejudice* aloud to each other. Alyssa knows it almost by heart and slips into a delicious British accent. I know the old MGM film and try to sound less effete than Laurence Olivier did. Effete or not, in the movie and in the book, Darcy is a different kind of superman. A rich man, like Hank Einhorn. Once again I feel inadequate.

"Of course," I say. "Like Elizabeth, you could marry a guy with a castle."

"Or I can earn enough money to buy my own castle."

"Is that important to you? Having a lot of money some day?"

Alyssa is silent. Suddenly she sits up. I assume she's angry, until I follow her stare and see a deer. A full-sized deer the size of a horse. With antlers. It's maybe five feet away.

Dogs frighten me. Big Sol's beast, and the little dogs on leashes in Forest Hills. Even the incessantly yapping Blinky with Mrs. Lawrence. I hate to admit it, but this deer is terrifying with shiny black eyes as big as fists staring right back at us. In a flash, I try remembering if deer are aggressive, like moose. I know moose are, and this thing looks like a moose. Time is suspended. The only sound is the Handel which, dammit, the deer seems to like. Thankfully the needle drifts to the end of the record. The deer bends its head and lopes away.

***

Alyssa

"That was scary," I say, sensing how Leon feels.

"That was scary," he fervently agrees.

"What would you have done if he'd charged us?"

"Thrown myself on you," Leon says. "Not that I need an excuse. I would've thrown myself on you and screamed for dear life."

"Well," I laugh, hugging him, "I would've thrown myself on you, so Bambi would have gotten quite a show."

We cuddle quietly. I think about Leon's anxiety, not about the deer, but about Hank.

"You know," I whisper, "Lizzy doesn't really want to be rich."

Leon, of course, cites the least romantic part of the book. "Elizabeth says she first realized she was falling for Darcy when she saw his huge house."

"Lizzy was joking," I insist, although I've never been entirely sure, and maybe Jane wasn't either. "She was joking with her sister.

You should hear how I talk to my sister. Anyway, my parents aren't rich and they're happy."

We're silent some more. Hank's teens trail off. They're probably heading to the coffee shop.

I add another argument, because that's what I do. I must get it from Dad. "When Lizzy first sees Darcy at Pemberley, it's not like he's suddenly struck it rich. Lizzy already knew he was wealthy. But by then he's kind. He asks about her family. He's sweet and shy, not proud. She only really falls in love when Darcy rescues Lydia, even if it means humbling himself. With Wickham, no less. Think how much love that took. How much goodness. That's what Lizzy wants. A good man."

"Who happens to be rich."

"She would have been happy with Darcy's poor cousin," I contend, and it's probably true. "Colonel Fitzwilliam's the one who wouldn't marry without money."

I fall silent again. Then I tell Leon, quietly, because he has this crazy idea that his family's not as good as my family, "My father has to work two jobs, teaching and this. We don't live like kings, but my father is a better man than Lizzy's father, who doesn't care what happens to his kids. That's why my mother loves him." I hesitate, and then tell Leon, "My mom had a terrible father."

He stops arguing and listens.

"Have you heard about this?" I ask, feeling tense.

"What?"

"Not that I care," I say defiantly, but unconvincingly. "It was big news when it happened, but that was thirty-five years ago and my mother… She likes you, Leon. She wouldn't mind if I told you."

"What?" He takes both my hands.

"Her father, my grandfather, killed my grandmother."

"*What?*"

"He shot her. When she was drinking tea with my great aunt. He shot them both."

"Why?"

I stifle a sob. I never knew my grandmother, so I guess I'm crying for my mother. "Because he was drunk. My grandfather was a violent drunk. He was awful. He didn't drink because he was poor and miserable. He came from money. You think I'm attractive? My grandmother was breathtaking. I'll show you her picture. She was poor. She had come over with her sister from Ireland. Enniscorthy. I'd love to see it someday, and Montesilvano, in Abruzzo. That's where my dad's family is from. He says the beaches there shimmer, and they look out onto Greece. He loves ancient Greece. I'm rambling. I'm sorry."

"It's all right. I want to know everything."

Now I'm really blubbering, but I can't help it.

"It's awful. After my grandmother and her sister died—were murdered—they sent my grandfather to prison. Their daughter—my mother—didn't have any other family in America that would take her in. The Church found an orphanage for her. St. Vincent's in Baltimore. I've seen it. Mom took me there about ten years ago because she didn't want me to think she was ashamed. I remember it was a big Roman stone building that went back to the Civil War. I thought how strange it must have been for children to live in a place that looked so grand when they had nothing, not even parents. Then we visited the newer building where they moved Mom. We saw the kind of junior bed she slept in. Some of my mother's nuns were still there. They were wonderful to us."

"Is that why your mother is so neat?" Leon asks, "because she never owned anything as a child?"

"It makes me ashamed that I don't always take care of the things she gives me. Vanessa is impossible. But it's hard to live with someone who had such a terrible childhood. Even if she never brings it up. Especially because she never brings it up. My father doesn't either. Anyway, it's not like she's possessive about things. I mean materialistic. Mom wanted to become a nun, but the sisters arranged for her to go to college. Then she became a teacher, and that's when she met Dad. She didn't know he sang. He wanted her to love him because he was a history teacher. He thought that was more respectable, more important. My mother says none of that mattered. She loved my father because he was kind. She knew he'd be a great father because he's so great at school with kids. I'll be in his class this year. You'd love him as a teacher."

"I already do."

I think about that. Then I give Leon a tender kiss.

He doesn't kiss me back, but says, "I wish I was half the guy your father is."

"You're as good as anyone, Leon. You're as good as you want to be. I'm not going to tell you right now how extraordinary you are. I don't like to see you whining and begging for compliments."

"You've never had to beg for compliments," he whines.

"I'm not interested in compliments. I want a companion I respect. I don't trust compliments. I trust good character. That's why Lizzy marries Darcy. Not because he's rich. Because he's good."

28

Leon

I love Alyssa more each day, but don't always show it. You'll find this impossible to believe. I can't believe it. Leon Kraus taking Alyssa Lawrence for granted?

I hate to think it's because she shared her mother's story. Whoever would have guessed it, when Mrs. Lawrence seems as perfectly turned out as Myrna Loy? Even I'm not a big enough creep to despise her for being damaged. For overcoming so much. Let me believe instead that it's my well-earned insecurity. I'm not as good as Alyssa's father, much less Mr. Darcy. Hell, I'm nothing compared to Hank Einhorn.

Like a moron, I keep testing Alyssa. Little things, like expecting her to sit through the most idiotic shows because I'm onstage. How many times can you watch some clown impersonating Al Jolson? He's the entertainer who starred in the first talkie movie, *The Jazz Singer*, singing "My Mammy." In blackface. No excuse for that today, and you might say no excuse any day. I'm not going to argue. Though other groups got treated abominably too in the movies. Chinese people. Watch a Charlie Chan movie sometime. Indians. Not so much Tonto, but most every other Indian. And yes, Jews. Fagin in *Oliver Twist*. Shylock in *The Merchant of Venice*. Although Shakespeare at least gave Shylock the speech,

Hath not a Jew eyes? ...
If you prick us, do we not bleed? ...
If you poison us, do we not die?

That last line hits home to me. Not in a self-pitying way. It makes me ashamed because Herman, for the first and only time, got really angry with me yesterday when I said I listen to records by musicians who stayed in Germany under the Nazis, while Hitler was gassing millions of Jews. Some of those musicians joined the Party. Others, like the conductor Furtwängler, I don't think were Nazis. I think Furtwängler hated the Nazis but stayed in Germany during the war because he wanted to keep making music for his people—the decent Germans—so they'd remember that they used to be human beings. In a way, I guess Al Jolson is less defensible, because the only reason he wore blackface was to make money. It's tough to judge people in the past by our current standards instead of theirs. To which Herman said, if no one stands up for higher standards, how are we ever going to change?

I keep testing Alyssa. I pout if, instead of listening to me play with the band, she once in a while wants to go out with girlfriends. I also assume she'll listen to anything I like on my record player in the woods, instead of asking what she'd like, or wants to try. To top it all off, I pontificate about composers and performers 'til Alyssa almost starts to hate classical music.

In fairness to me, Phillip manages to be even more pretentious. He isn't a musician, merely a "conductor." Phillip never wants to hear me play. But when we listen to records sometimes with Alyssa and Phyllis, Phillip will begin tapping one finger. Then he makes tiny arcs in the air. Then, when the music reaches a crescendo, he throws back his head and his eagle beak and raises his arms to embrace heaven. Alyssa takes all this in stride, but Phyllis smacks Phillip's afro and demands to hear the Stones or Led Zeppelin.

Phillip puts up with a good deal of abuse from Phyllis because he lives in fear of Big Sol. Also, he can't believe a girl's finally giving him a glimpse of her body. Phillip can be quite eloquent about this. I don't know as much as he does about art—paintings and sculpture—and he rubs it in. One night he said to me, "Think about it, Leon. You go back to Minoan goddesses with their bare breasts. Their beautiful bare breasts."

"Thousands of years old," I reminded him.

"They still don't sag. Then you have Greek goddesses. I've never been that turned on by them, because their waists are kind of thick."

"If they had wasp waists, you would be turned on by a statue?"

"Yeah," Phillip sighed. "That's what the Minoan girls had. Wasp waists."

"You know," I said, "we're not talking WASPs, as in Protestants."

"Like Alyssa."

I swung out from my bunk and glared at him. "Don't talk about Alyssa."

"Okay."

"Who happens to be Catholic."

"Okay. I'm saying small waists, not Alyssa," Phillip bleated. "I'm saying you go from ancient times to Titian, then Ingres—that odalisque by Ingres, and Bouguereau. Do you know Bouguereau?"

"No."

"Oh," Phillip panted. "Bouguereau is better than Playboy centerfolds." Hugh, our bashful Playmate fan, was taking all this in, wondering how to spell Bouguereau. "What I'm saying," Phillip went on, "is when a girl takes off her clothes, when she lets you take off her clothes and you're looking at her, she's like all the girls there have ever been. She's... *woman*. You want to thank her. It's amazing."

Which was a lot more sincere than Phillip is about music.

You know, I kind of agree with him. The real problem with Alyssa and me is not my being Jewish, or not being Mr. Darcy. It's that I'm becoming more and more sexually demanding.

I'm not going to go into what we *have* been doing, but Alyssa made it clear early on that she takes Catholicism seriously and does not believe in full premarital sex. I've been wondering if this is really about religion because Alyssa doesn't simply turn me down. She didn't simply turn Hank Einhorn down. She flinches, she dumps popcorn, she's almost about to cry.

What is really going on?

It's late afternoon, and the children have been dismissed. They're with their parents until dinner. We're in Sonny's room in the basement of the lodge. He's on duty in the main building. I'd told him I wanted Alyssa to hear Miles Davis and, of course, I wouldn't dream of borrowing his *Kind of Blue* album and taking it off to the woods. A deer might eat it. Sonny said Alyssa and I could listen in his room, unaccompanied. His neighbor, Connie, smirked when she saw us go in.

We're listening to Miles, Bill Evans, and the guys in the most haunting jazz track I've ever heard, I bet that anyone's ever heard, "Blue in Green." Every member of the quintet wails his own sad story, including Jimmy Cobb on drums.

We're on the floor. There's no window and we haven't put on the light, so it's dark. The basement can get cold. Fresh out of the pool, Alyssa is shivering. I take off my t-shirt, which is dry because I didn't swim—although I can swim now, fairly well—and wrap it around Alyssa's shoulders.

You know what happens next. I don't have to draw a diagram. When things go too far, Alyssa shoves me away, hard.

"Why did you have to ruin that?" She's angry. "It was so beautiful."

"A lot of people think…"

"What?"

"That sex can be beautiful too. Everyone we know."

"You took a poll?"

"What do you think we talk about in Sadie Hall? Ayn Rand? Even she writes plenty about—"

"All right."

"Sex. Sex. I have a condom. You're not going to get pregnant."

The truth is, I know what to do with a rubber only theoretically. I'm a virgin. Don't tell me you're shocked.

Alyssa is crying. "Turn it off. Turn off the record player." She starts to get up. I try to stop her. *"Get your hands off me."*

Can Connie hear us? I let Alyssa go. She doesn't get up, but she's still crying.

"What is it?" I ask as gently as I can, and not because I want her to change her mind. She's not going to change her mind.

At last, Alyssa tells me what happened.

At twelve, she was invited to a literature summer camp. I like books, but a literature summer camp sounds to me like a contradiction in terms. Remember though, Alyssa is the daughter of English and history high school teachers. When I was still learning the alphabet with Helen Keller blocks, Alyssa was already reading Nancy Drew and *Charlotte's Web*.

This camp was on the campus of a Chicago university. I don't want to say which one because this isn't going to reflect well on them and maybe they've cleaned up their act. I'm sure they had to.

The invitation had come in response to Alyssa's staggering scores on standardized tests. The principal at her middle school recommended the camp, suggesting Alyssa would get more out of this program than from another summer in the Catskills. Beth and Vin checked it all out carefully.

"Sending me was going to be a sacrifice," she says, not looking at me. She hasn't looked at me since she started telling the story. "We'd built an addition to our house in Long Beach, so it was a difficult time. Still, after they looked into it, they wanted me to go."

Besides playing ball on campus and visiting museums and street fairs, the young scholars swam in Lake Michigan, which Alyssa says had high waves and was surprisingly cold, even on hot days. Mostly, though, these brainiacs read. Heavy stuff like Homer's *Odyssey* in translation. Each camper also got to pick a book for their group to read. One pimply show-off made everyone wade into *Finnegan's Wake* by James Joyce, until they battered him with their books and he admitted the thing is incomprehensible.

Alyssa went the other way. Instead of trying to impress her group, she asked them all to read one of her favorite novels, *I Capture the Castle* by Dodie Smith. When the Ph.D. wannabes discovered that Dodie Smith also wrote *The Hundred and One Dalmatians*, the little snobs scowled and wanted to banish Alyssa back to Long Beach. Once they actually read *I Capture the Castle* they found it's a droll, delightful book about two poor English girls who live in a crumbling castle with their dad, a burned-out genius who got that way—I'm guessing—because he wrote crap like *Finnegan's Wake*. Anyway, I love that Alyssa is smart but not pretentious.

Here's the thing, though. Someone else loved Alyssa that summer. In a way that's made her flesh crawl for years. One of the counselors, or maybe they called them instructors, who was a graduate student. We're talking twenty-two years old or more, and Alyssa was twelve. Not a jaded, experienced twelve despite spin the bottle. This smart but hang-dog creep kept staring at her. Especially when she wore a bathing suit. She stopped wearing bathing suits, except with long t-shirts, claiming she was afraid of sunburn, but really, she was afraid of him.

Then one night, when they were camping at Starved Rock Park after a day filled with horseback riding and canoeing, the pervert found Alyssa by herself, gingerly stepping down rocks next to a waterfall. He clamped his hand over her mouth and pulled her behind the curtain of water. Then, stifling her cries—it's hard for me to write this, but it's important, especially for parents, to know what's out there—this instructor, who Alyssa says, "went to a good school and had been vetted by the camp and even knew the camp director," this monster started pawing Alyssa. She still had her shirt and bathing suit on, or I don't know what he would have done next. Probably he thought he could get away with anything because he saw that Alyssa was naïve and reserved. Thank God one of the other campers—actually, the *Finnegan's Wake* kid—dimly witnessed what was happening and yelled out to the director.

The director fired the instructor. Alyssa begged the director not to tell anyone. Especially her father. She knew he would tear the molester to pieces. The horrible, awful, insert expletives here, thing of a human being was gone, and Alyssa finished camp.

She tells me, "What's sad on top of the horrible is I never had a better time in my life until that degenerate started stalking me."

The damage was done. The Lawrences didn't know why, but for years after that all of Alyssa's romance was reserved for books and movies—and stories she wrote for herself.

She says, "Vanessa couldn't understand why I turned down dates. There weren't so many boys asking—"

"I bet there were a ton," I tell her.

"Anyway, my sister warned that I was going to be an old maid. At sixteen. Then… You heard everything else, so I'm sorry, but you have to hear this, Leon. The first guy I finally wanted to go out with turned out to be Hank. Apart from everything else, I was flattered that from all the girls at Salzman's, he chose me. At first, Mom and even Dad were glad I wanted to be with anyone, and they overlooked the age difference."

As with the other daughters of guests who work at Salzman's, Alyssa stays with her parents. Sadie Hall is for the male staff. The Lawrences must've thought they were keeping an eye on their daughter.

Alyssa assures me they were.

She drew a red line about physical intimacy. I hate to think that's why Hank dumped her.

Reading my mind, she says, "He didn't dump me, he lost me. I dumped him."

29

Leon

We sit quietly, saying nothing more. Then, I walk Alyssa back to her family's bungalow, planning to see her briefly after dinner at the flagpole. It's Wednesday and we have a show, but I haven't asked Alyssa to come because there's another comic who she won't understand. Also, after all she's relived—all that I've forced her to relive—she needs a break from me. Mrs. Lawrence is driving her to see a movie in town with Sheryl. *True Grit* starring John Wayne. Shades of Wild West City.

Weeks ago, I'd been delighted with Alyssa's red line, for Hank and for me. I didn't know the whole story and thought, hallelujah she's Catholic. Hell, I wanted to convert and patiently wait until we could marry, enjoy marital relations, and have nine kids.

Then I kept hearing what other guys were doing, not only with Salzman's weekday widows like Tilly Mintz, but also with nice teenage girls—girls like Alyssa. Insecurity fed my lust. I became more demanding. That led to fights. Two or three days sometimes went by before I apologized. Then it would start again.

Now I know Alyssa's heartbreaking story. Though I wasn't her first choice this summer, I should still be honored and grateful that she's chosen to go out with me at all. I am.

However.

You'll hate me for saying this. I hate me.

It's not enough.

You know who must sense this? Even though she sees me with Alyssa all the time, including going into Sonny's room this afternoon? Connie Sims.

She's been teasing me about what I actually do with my "best girl." Whether Alyssa is as innocent as she seems. Tonight, while

I'm accompanying Vin in one of his most dramatic numbers, "The Impossible Dream" from *Man of La Mancha*, Connie sidles next to me on the piano bench, whispering in my ear. She wants to know where Alyssa is. I tell her.

She smiles. "There's more to the show than Yiddish punchlines. You could have stepped off the stage and danced a turn or two. I do. Vin does with Beth. The guests love it. You're supposed to be such a big fan of Fred Astaire."

"I'm no Fred Astaire."

"Do you know how to dance?"

"No, not really."

"So learn."

"Learning to swim is taking up all my free time."

"I saw. We all worried that Lou was going to have to get his Speedo wet."

"Dancing will have to wait 'til next summer."

I pound out the final chords as Vin belts, *To reach the unreachable star.*

The guests shout bravos and give Vin a well-deserved standing ovation. I swear we all imagine him in costume and a white beard as Don Quixote.

Connie takes the stage. "How can I follow that?" she jokes over the applause and segues into a mock-humble version of "I Guess I'll Have to Change My Plans." Connie then introduces the comic, Morty Bierman, and the band leaves the stage. Harvey cleans out his clarinet. Benny steps outside for a smoke.

Connie pulls me aside. "Listen, what are you doing tomorrow afternoon?"

"You know—"

"*After* practicing. Why not meet me in my studio in the lodge, after lunch, and I'll give you a dance lesson."

"That's awfully kind, but—"

"Enough already. I'll teach you how to dance to 'Night and Day' so you can stop watching movies and actually take that girl in your arms."

***

Alyssa

I didn't think Sheryl and I would enjoy *True Grit*, but it's hilarious and touching. For the first time we understand why John Wayne is the biggest star in the world. It was pleasant to go to a movie without being mauled. I mean by Hank Einhorn. Leon enjoys movies too much to attack me.

Leon and I don't wind up seeing each other tonight. I'm not dressed to go to the casino and besides, it was late when Sheryl's father picked us up. Mom had returned to the hotel so she could hear Dad. He was going to do "The Impossible Dream," which she considers his best number after "Night and Day."

Instead, sitting outside our bungalow with the porch light drawing every moth between here and the Mississippi, I finally finish my short story about Howie Katz. I call him "Arthur Gowers" and he's struggling to help his father set up the movie projector at "Maltings Hotel." When the film begins he projects himself into the role of George M. Cohan in *Yankee Doodle Dandy*.

***

Leon

Thursday morning and I've finished practicing. Herman and I tell each other we'll meet up later, but I don't tell him where I'm going. While Alyssa and her girls stay inside making popsicle stick jewelry boxes because it's raining, I head to my dance lesson.

I've gone to the lodge other times when it was raining to watch the downpour under the old porch. Debussy's "Gardens in the Rain" has nothing on the real thing. I never realized that in Queens. There, rain is an annoyance as you bump into people lowering their heads and their umbrellas. Or a bus or a taxi sprays you like a fire hose. Here on the lodge porch, you can look out on Salzman's vast expanse, including the dining room, the back end of the pool, the bungalows, and the hollow with the flagpole. In the rain it's incredibly tranquil. Or exciting, if there's lightning.

I'm thinking about all this because what I'm walking into may not be pure. I may be about to make the biggest mistake of my life. I keep walking anyway.

Connie's studio opens up from her bedroom. Both rooms are enormous because Salzman's allowed its long-time entertainer to appropriate and refurbish most of the lodge basement. Her suite bears no resemblance to Sonny's cell next door. Each wall of Connie's studio has a long full-length mirror. There's also a reflecting ball.

Businesslike, with no jokes or even a hello, Connie tells me, "Shake your shoulders. Your legs, too, to loosen up." Maybe I was wrong about all this. Now it seems ludicrous. Why would she be interested in me? It's nice that she's trying to help me have a romantic time with Alyssa.

Connie's wearing black leggings with a white blouse, red belt, and low heels. Her bleached hair is pulled back in a ponytail. This is the most casual I've ever seen Connie, although she still wears her war paint.

Briskly she shows me how to hold her. "Not so close. You can't move if you're that close. Now lead me by placing your hand here, on the small of my back."

We practice a simple box step. Up to this point, there isn't any music. Now Connie places a 101 Strings album of Cole Porter on the turntable. It starts with the "beat beat beat" verse that even Fred and Ginger don't move to. Then, as the melody swells, I haltingly, clumsily begin our dance.

I'm not a dancer. I'm not even an organist who uses his legs and feet to help create music. However, I'm a musician, and I sure as hell have a feeling for "Night and Day." So before too long, things go a little more smoothly. Connie is encouraging. We make it to the end and try again, better this time. I learn to go forward, backward, turn, and promenade. It's good exercise and good clean fun.

Until Connie returns to the phonograph, places the needle back at the start of the song, unhooks her belt, and removes her blouse. She doesn't remove her bra because she isn't wearing one. I stand frozen. Grandma or not, Connie is hot. Strangely, she doesn't smile. She steps toward me, takes my hand, and leads me into her bedroom.

This makes Vanessa's room look like *Good Housekeeping*. Clothes draped everywhere or dropped on the floor. At least four ashtrays filled with stubbed-out butts. An unmade bed. I couldn't care less. A woman in black leggings, heels, and nothing else seems intent on helping me lose my virginity. I'm not going to detail every step of this seduction. It's not funny like *The Graduate*. Connie doesn't say anything witty or wry. She doesn't say anything at all. I don't express any reluctance. Quite the opposite. My only worry is whether it will be over on my end before I get my clothes off.

We'll never know, because suddenly, jarringly, someone's banging on the door. Connie seems unperturbed. I nearly have a heart attack. Who is it? Alyssa? Her father? Big Sol with his gun?

At this point, I'm prepared for the Green Berets.

Connie buttons her blouse, lights a cigarette, and opens the door. Standing on the other side…my mother.

30

Leon

My mother is glacial as ever. I'm tempted to write out how she speaks, phonetically again, because it adds an air of continental farce. We'll let that go.

"So," my mother says to Connie, not even glancing at me while, with supposed stealth, I pull on my pants. "Thank you for completing my son's education. Does he now qualify for a union card?"

Connie says nothing. Who could compete with that hauteur? I complete my toilette, consider saying something, think better of it and shuffle out, tripping on one of Connie's shoes.

I follow my mother back to our bungalow. She doesn't say a word during the endless trek or once we get inside. Finally I say, "Don't blame Connie."

"I'm not blaming her."

"Don't blame me, either. Everyone I know is screwing around up here."

"Including your girlfriend?"

"If you knew Alyssa, you wouldn't ask that."

"Is it my fault I don't know her? Everyone thinks her parents are your parents."

"Vin Lawrence has talked to me more in three weeks than my father's talked in three years."

My mother had been fussing with things on her dresser. Now she pauses. "Was that the first time you were with that woman? Who, you know, is older than I am. You know she could have a disease."

I'm humiliated. In my humiliation, I get angry. Inexcusably angry.

"A lot of people here could have a disease."

For the first time, my mother looks up at me. "What are you saying?"

"The guys I work with say the women here are sex-crazed, like Connie. At least when their husbands are away."

"What else do they say?" My mother's voice rises and trembles.

"As always, they say you're the best-looking woman here."

My mother pauses again, looks down, and slaps my face. I stand in front of her, stunned. She sits down on the bed.

"I see. I'm cheating while your father is slaving away on Seventh Avenue. I could have venereal disease."

"Mom—"

"*Quiet*. You be quiet." For the first time in my life, I see my mother cry. I want to kneel next to her. To hug her and say I'm sorry. But I can't, or won't. After a minute she stops crying and speaks.

"I only wish your father was working so hard. He's in the City, not only during the week but last weekend, and last month too, so he can be with his latest girlfriend. That's him. That's your father. Me? No, Leon, I do not 'screw around.' Not here. Not anywhere."

"Mom—"

"Mom. When was the last time you called me Mom? When was the last time you talked to me at all? I play mahjong all day until hearing those tiles cracking makes me crazy because there's nothing else to do. And the women—not that bitch Tilly Mintz, but the other women. Including your girlfriend's pal, Louise, who is a nice girl but who traipses around like we live in Tahiti. They all say, 'Your son plays so well. We hear he's going to win a competition.' Fine. Great. But who taught you to play so well? Who took you for lessons when you were five years old? Your father didn't want to pay for them, so we had to take money from Uncle Max. That piano belonged to your father's high and mighty family in Vienna, but he didn't want to pay for lessons. Who made sure you never had to miss a lesson even when I didn't know how we were going to pay the rent? Vin Lawrence? The old man?"

"Herman Pressler."

"Forgive me for not knowing his name. You never introduced me. I understand why you wouldn't introduce me to your girlfriend. I'm a slut with venereal disease. I'm not even good enough even for the old man?"

"I didn't know about Dad."

She sits on the bed and chuckles bitterly. "Yes. He was always Dad. Even though he never took you. He didn't come to your recitals. He married a Garment District model and now he's entitled to a newer model."

That's the first time I ever heard my mother crack a joke. I sense she's been working on it for a long time. But this is no joke. I don't know what to say. No. I do know what to say, but I can't or won't say it. She sits there on the bed and I stand. I'm ashamed. I'm worthless.

Finally, unforgivably, I leave.

I want to punish myself.

Instead, I go to punish Alyssa.

31

Alyssa

"If you hate this," I tell Leon, "don't pull any punches."

We're standing outside a side door to the main building, the one that leads down to the arts and crafts room. It stopped raining, but too late for swimming, so my girls worked on crafts longer than it took Michelangelo to finish the Sistine Chapel. Now they're heading back to their rooms. I hand Leon the composition book with my story about Mickey and Howie Katz, which I honestly think is pretty good.

He won't accept it.

"Can we go somewhere to talk?" Leon asks, strangely somber. Almost sullen. "Somewhere private?"

"What's the matter?"

He leads the way to our spot in the woods. It's muddy. After this I'll have to wash my sneakers. Leon doesn't seem to care about his. He rarely cares about how he looks, other than when he's wearing his tuxedo, which is always clean and pressed. Now in his rumpled chinos, he looks particularly disheveled and depressed. I'm concerned.

"Leon—"

"My mother found me with Connie Sims."

I stare at him blankly.

"I was with Connie in her room."

"What were you doing there?"

"We were about to…"

He leaves it hanging. Then I realize. He was there to sleep with her.

"You two were going to…" I can't find the words. "Make love?"

"No, not make love. That sounds ridiculous. That's not what it was."

"Okay. You went there to screw her. Does that sound better?"

He looks down at his muddy shoes.

"Did you sleep with her?"

"I was going to."

"But your mother stopped you."

That sounds more ridiculous. I look up at the overcast sky. I look at him, straight in the eyes.

"Are you telling me this to pressure me?"

"What?"

"To let me know you can have other girls. Other women?"

"No."

"Have you had other women?"

"No, of course not."

"Of course not? Why? Because your mother walked in on them too?"

"Alyssa—" He reaches for my hands. I pull them away.

"Why are you telling me this? Here? Of all places."

"I thought you deserved to know."

"I don't deserve any of this. Hank tried to make me believe I'd deserve to die alone in a nursing home if I refused to sleep with him. I thought you and I had something different."

"We do."

"Not anymore."

"Alyssa."

A tear rolls down my face.

"Not anymore."

32

Leon

The woods now loom menacingly. The casino reeks of Connie's musky perfume. The paddleball courts reproach me like a look from Vin Lawrence. He has every right to belt me, and he might. I tear away from the hotel altogether and find myself walking on the road that leads to the outskirts of town and the miniature golf course. Not to play. To get away.

I don't make it there because a half mile from the hotel is a dive that invites me to jump in. Here, nobody knows how to swim. It's called, I kid you not, the Pink Pussy Cat Lounge. Whether it ever had been pink, or whether it only looks that color to the lushes who see pink elephants, I don't know. Right now, it appears the place to be for a heartless jerk like me.

I've spent half the summer in places that are barred to minors. Luckily, as its name implies, Mount Freedom looks the other way.

It's only 5 p.m. and the sun is shining for other people, yet I carry gloom into this place. I wait for my eyes to adjust to the darkness. They don't. No surprise that the Pink Pussy Cat Lounge attracts a barfly who sleeps in the perpetual darkness of the paddleball cube—Tyrone the dishwasher.

He appears not to recognize me. Or maybe Tyrone isn't big into greetings. I climb onto a stool three down from his. He never glances up. The bartender asks what I want. I said nothing, thanks. He looks like I'd better rethink that, so I ask for a ginger ale. That grabs the attention of Tyrone and two guys at the pool table.

"Oh. The piano player," Tyrone groans.

"How are you?" I enquire.

"Well," he considers. "I'm not in the kitchen with Big Sol siccing a dog on me. I'm not hearing rubber balls pounding next to my head. So I guess I'm doing fine."

He slides back into silence. The players resume their game. The crack of the pool balls reminds me of the crack of my mother's mahjong tiles. This cracking is driving me crazy too, and I walked in only two minutes ago. Tyrone resurfaces.

"Speaking of fine. How does a four-eyed string bean like you rate the finest fox at that place even if you do dress up and play the piano."

"I don't know. Seems I don't rate her anymore."

Tyrone stares at me. "How did you screw that up?"

"Don't ask."

"I'm asking. I can't get ripped before dinner, so give me some conversation."

The bartender bangs down my ginger ale and folds his arms opposite me, glaring. He's angry about Alyssa and doesn't even know us. I thought bartenders are supposed to be sympathetic.

"I almost slept with another woman."

"Almost?" Tyrone, the bartender, and one of the pool players all exclaim together. The other pool player chokes on his drink.

"I'm not getting into that," I insist. "It's too stupid."

"So," Tyrone asks, "she caught you?"

"No, nothing like that. I told her."

The thirsty pool player spits out the rest of his drink. I'm afraid he'll ask me to pay for it.

Silence, then Tyrone asks, "Why did you tell her?"

"Because I love her."

"How old are you?"

I glance at the bartender. He shrugs, so I admit, "Sixteen."

"Well," Tyrone reflects. "I guess that is the way you love someone when you're sixteen. Stupidly."

"Okay, since everyone here is so wise. What do I do now?"

"Beg," counsel both pool players.

"Grab her and squeeze her and give her a big-ass kiss," says the bartender. He makes Johnny Cash sound like a soprano. *"With plenty of tongue."* Geez, this guy really is angry.

"Make a ton of money. That's what women want," Tyrone says sadly. "Meantime, get the hell out and go after her."

I do.

But Alyssa is nowhere to be found.

She didn't show up for the kids' early dinner. Sandi doesn't know where she is or, glowering at me, won't say.

I run to the Lawrence bungalow. Apparently, Mrs. Lawrence hasn't heard about what she'd call our "tiff." She is worried that Alyssa abandoned her group.

There's no time to search further. Thursday is Movie Night, when I'm supposed to be off, but for the first time tonight—of all nights—we're adding music to dinner. Cully's lovely wife, Donna, came up with this, and normally I'd give her credit. Donna is always striving against all odds to add class to Salzman's. What she calls International Night will have a different theme every week. Tonight it's *Vive la France.* Waiters are wearing striped sailor shirts and berets, and I have to as well. Normally I don't play at all during dinner. The dining room doesn't have a piano. But a guest who owns an electronics store brought a small version of one of the new Moog synthesizers. The idea is for me to make it sound like an accordion in songs like "Under Paris Skies," with Vin and Connie singing along.

Miserable though I am, we're all set to start when the dining room doors open at seven. But here's Vanessa rushing up, half-worried, half-smug, and bursting with the news that Alyssa has driven away with Seth, Phil, and Phyl...*and Hank Einhorn.* They're heading in Hank's Peugeot up to the Catskills.

"What's in the Catskills?" I ask, too stunned to say anything else. "That's so far away."

"Don't you follow anything?" Vanessa sneers. "It's that giant, unbelievable music thing. Everyone'll be there. The Who. Jefferson Airplane. Everyone. Alyssa left Mom and Dad a note. *A note.* Can you imagine? They've already gone after her. I'm staying with the Ginzbergs tonight. I wanted to go too. With Hank, not Mom and Dad. But..."

I'm already bolting away from Vanessa, but I don't know where to go. We all heard about this rock festival. Woodstock. Vin joked that every pothead in the country is wafting to upstate New York.

Why is Alyssa going? She's avoided Hank ever since their blow-up at Sadie Hall. She's told me again and again that Hank is arrogant, immature, subversive, and a bad influence on his teenagers—including her sister. Was Alyssa really after him all along?

Who could blame her? As everyone from Tyrone to Tilly Mintz must think, what could she ever have seen in me? Even if I'd behaved...decently.

33

Alyssa

An Hour Earlier

I left Leon and now I'm walking into Sadie Hall, my first time here since breaking up with Hank. If he's surprised, he'll never show it.

"Hi, Ally." Sure enough, he gives me a slow, knowing grin. "You've finally decided to grow up."

"What are you talking about?"

"That skinny idiot—I'm not going to even say his name—has finally bored the pants off you."

"If you mean," I reply with contempt for both of them, "that Leon has conversations instead of lunging every time he sees me—"

"Okay, let's have a conversation." Hank spreads his arms wide. "I was a schmuck. Okay? It's not like I'm some moony high school junior. Normally, believe it or not, I'm pretty restrained around women. If you haven't noticed, Alyssa, I like feasts of reason too. Instead of letting your sister and her chums spend the summer doing nothing but swimming and tanning and flirting with boys, my group's explored everything from Plato's *Republic* to Republican warmongers. So, if you've come for a conversation, darling, I'm all ears."

"I came to see Seth."

That deflates him. He is a schmuck.

First, I went to talk with Louise, but Si is up from the City a day early, and he and Louise are happily locked away in Room 115. The lovebirds didn't turn me away. They wouldn't have done that. Sonny saw me heading there and let me know they were engaged. I'm not afraid of Mr. Perlman. Seth adores him and that's all I need to know.

Out of respect for an engaged couple's privacy, I didn't go to their room.

Instead, I've come to pour my heart out to Seth. He's a wonderful listener. My Barbra Streisand-in-the-making always sympathizes, empathizes, and then orders Anthony to take us shopping. What more can a girl ask for? Seth is a wonderful person, period. For that I credit Si, and his late wife, and now, Louise. I have great parents too. Dad is too excitable to be empathetic. Mom is—she's from another place, a different time. Maybe a better time, but too remote from the way a lot of people, especially kids, act now. They're great, but I can't talk with them about this. I am going to see Seth, and I know he'll help.

There's Hank, who's older and more experienced, but...

He's handsome. I know it and he knows it. More than that, Hank's a leader. Vanessa and the other kids would follow him over a cliff. Anyone can see how he's made such a big impact at Cornell—as a freshman, no less. Hank is going to be a huge deal someday, in politics or whatever he chooses to do.

It was incredibly flattering he wanted to be with me. I still believe, because I want to believe, that it wasn't only for sex. It's a mean thought, but I have more to offer a man like Hank than Sandi Lerner can. Is it enough for a lasting relationship with a guy three years older and already a kind of celebrity? I know better than that.

I know something else too. I like Hank's looks, his intellect, and his charm, but I don't like him.

Does he like himself, I wonder. Handsome and brilliant, but always having to defy authority. Yes, Hank opposes the Vietnam War and fights for civil rights, but beyond all that, beneath the smug superiority, there's anger. He'd say righteous anger, yet it's more than that. Sheryl, who seems to know everything, says Hank hates his mother. He never talked about her with me.

You'll pull your hair out when I say this, but I knew I didn't love Hank the first time I met Leon. Insecure, fumbling, cowardly Leon. We didn't meet bowling, or on the softball field. I still can't get over what he did on the softball field. I didn't meet Leon in this awful barracks he shares with Hank and the other slobs. No, I met Leon when he played that gorgeous piece by Debussy in the playhouse, sitting remarkably still at the piano with his eyes closed, and then when he wore his tuxedo at the pool so we could listen to Beethoven under the stars, and dream about Kitty and Levin.

Kitty is real to me. Lizzy Bennet is real. They're the truest people I've ever known. I struggle to bring people to life the way Jane Austen and Tolstoy did. Don't get me wrong. I don't have a particle of their genius. Yet in my story inspired by Mickey Katz and his mentally challenged son, Howie, I believe there is one moment when they come to life, and you sense their goodness.

It's when Jimmy Cagney as George M. Cohan slows down for a moment in *Yankee Doodle Dandy* and stands with his family to reap the applause they've earned. He says for the first time, "My father thanks you, my mother thanks you, my sister thanks you, and I thank you."

My Howie Katz character—the son who's seen the movie a dozen times over the years, at all the hotels and bungalow colonies where he and his father show films—he mouths the words along with Jimmy Cagney. Sitting beside the projector for Movie Night at "Maltings" Hotel, the father in my story wraps his arm around his son, and each in his own way gives thanks for the other.

If that sounds corny, I don't care. I want to live for moments like that as a writer, and someday as a mother and a wife. It could never be with Hank.

Maybe, I used to think, I could be with someone like Leon.

There's something else I know. Something every Italian and Irish woman knows, and without doubt Jewish women too.

Leon must be punished.

I didn't do *anything* wrong. Refusing to sleep with him is not wrong. I give that jerk plenty of satisfaction without going all the way. I don't know about the sex lives of Beethoven and Debussy. Did Beethoven compose Miranda's moment of stillness in the "Tempest" Sonata and then assault women? Did Debussy conjure up "The Girl with the Flaxen Hair" to have an inflatable doll he could screw? I don't know. Levin and Darcy, and plenty of other guys who are real to me, and to Leon, managed to wait. Leon sure as hell can wait too.

"*… and they're right next to the farm where they're having it.*"

"What?"

Hank has been talking to me all this time. Now he's glaring because being ignored is not something that happens often to him.

"Did you hear a word I said?"

"No, I'm sorry."

"Well. I don't want to bore you. I'll leave that to your boyfriend." He starts to leave.

"What's at a farm?"

Hank hesitates, still nettled. Then he turns and explains, as if to one of my six-year-olds for whom he has no patience. "A frat brother, Stu Convey, called me. His parents have a cabin on a lake in Bethel, New York, near this guy Max Yasgur's farm. They know him. Stu said the farm is already a madhouse. It's hosting a once-in-a-lifetime event. They're expecting half a million people."

"Who's expecting half a million people?" Seth asks. He was floating down the stairway, from the bunkroom and overheard Hank.

"Hi, handsome," I say listlessly. "Came to talk with you about something. I'll walk you to the dining room."

"You look awful."

"Thanks. I feel better already."

"Have you been crying?"

To avoid answering in front of Hank, I return to his story. "So, you're driving all the way to Bethel to see your brother."

"I didn't know you have a brother." Seth looks affronted. "I thought you were an only child like me."

Hank squints at him. "There are no children like you. You are the one and only. I was saying"—losing patience, Hank takes a shuddering breath—"that one of my fraternity brothers has a farm next to the place where they're holding the Woodstock Festival. I'm on my way up to see it. The first day. But," Hank turns to me and tries being seductive, "I could use a little company on the drive. This will be something to tell your kids about."

"I want to come too," Seth begs like one of my future kids. He shakes my shoulders. "Honey, you can't miss this. It's going to be a-mazing."

"What is?" Phillip asks with Phyllis in tow. They're also on their way to the dining room.

"Hank is driving up to Woodstock and I'm going with him," Seth says in a whoosh.

"Hold on," Hank starts, but I cut him off.

"You have to work," I tell Seth. I'm constantly reminding Seth that he has to work. His guests usually have to remind him too, in the middle of a meal.

"I'll tell them I'm sick. *Andrew*," Seth calls to the big fella, who is something to behold lumbering past us at full tilt toward the dining room. "I'm going on a road trip with Hank and Alyssa. Tell Sol I'm too sick to work. Barry can fill in." Barry is Seth's long-suffering busboy, who was supposed to be a waiter until Mr. Perlman talked to Cully. Barry, who in effect *is* a waiter, while Seth pretends to be.

"You tell Sol," Andrew yells back.

"You tell him, Andrew, or I'll tell Sol where that lemon meringue pie went." Andrew's brow goes up. "Don't tell my father where I'm going. Do you hear me?"

"Oh, for God's sake, yes."

"Don't tell Anthony. Do you hear me?"

"Yeah, yeah." We hear Andrew pant, but faintly now, "I wish I hadn't eaten that pie." Then he's gone.

"Okay," Seth chirps. "Let's go."

"Alyssa," Hank says, ignoring Seth, but it's Seth who makes the sale.

"Sweetie," Seth reminds me, "you're off tomorrow."

"So?"

"We're coming back tomorrow?" Seth asks Hank. "Tomorrow night. You have to be back too, right?"

"I don't have to be anywhere," Hank declares.

"Well, we do, me and Alyssa. Promise you'll bring us back tomorrow night. I'll have a chance to hear…Melanie." Seth warbles her name.

"Oh, I adore Melanie," Phyllis coos. "People say she looks like me."

"What people?" Seth asks.

"Lots." Melanie and Phyllis do look alike, a little. "Let's go with them," Phyllis orders Phillip.

"I have to work."

"I'll straighten it out with Daddy." Phillip scowls. *Daddy*, you remember, is Big Sol. "I keep telling you he's a sweetheart," Phyllis insists. "He'll do anything I ask."

This is a fallacy shared by lion tamers, but Phillip had been thinking of quitting anyway. The season is almost over, his parents returned home a week ago, and he misses Brooklyn. Besides, out of our whole group, Phillip is the one who loves rock the most, for all his pantomime conducting classical music.

"Oh, what the hell." Phillip shrugs.

"What the hell?" Hank erupts. "Who the hell invited you?"

"I did. Come on," Seth wheedles. "That makes five of us, exactly the number we can squeeze into your little car."

"Oh, so we can't invite all the campers?" Hank cries in despair. Until he turns back to me. "You're joining us? Come on. It'll be amazing. I'll have you back tomorrow night."

"Come on." Phyl and Phil harmonize like Simon and Garfunkel, or Simone and Garfunkel.

"*Come on*." Seth, of course, tops them.

"Come on," Hank whispers with what sounds like real solicitude. "You need to get away from here."

What am I doing? I'm angry, humiliated, and hurt.

I need to punish Leon.

In my entire life, I've never done anything crazy.

Time to do something crazy.

34

Leon

I should have gone immediately with the Lawrences to search for Alyssa. It's not fair that I have to work this cockamamie International Night dinner on what used to be my night off. After dinner it's still Movie Night. Mickey's showing *The Eddie Cantor Story*. Eddie was another Jewish entertainer, a bug-eyed Al Jolson. Not a bad film, but—*dammit*. Why am I thinking about freaking movies? This isn't a movie. The girl I've dreamed about going to college with and marrying and having a family with—okay, it's nuts to dream that way, but I can't help it. The girl I *love* is on the road with Hank Einhorn. Who knows what else she'll agree to do once they're up there at that love-in, camping out with a half-million idiots whose idea of a love song is, "Why Don't We Do It in the Road?"

But look.

Standing here in the lobby, a second chance. Joel Salzman. Hank's friend from Cornell.

Have I mentioned Joel? I guess there's been no need until now. Joel is another oddball, like Phillip and me. He has a giraffe neck, pop eyes, and although he's skinny, a pot belly. Joel appears to be aloof, but he's shy.

He and Hank were thrown together as freshman roommates. You wouldn't think they have a lot in common. Still, Hank took Joel up on his offer to work at the hotel mostly because the work is easy and Hank could finish his book about inciting campus revolution. Joel told Hank to start the revolution without him.

Since he doesn't like hanging around the crowds at the hotel, Joel's parents found him a perfect job this summer: driving to and from the City with guests who don't have a car. At dawn, before ferrying guests, Joel also picks up fish from the Fulton Fish Market in Lower Manhattan and brings them back to Big Sol.

That means later in the day, when the guests pile into Joel's Rambler, they emerge at their destination reeking of seafood.

When Joel has to be at the hotel, he's like his father, Cully: as hard to spot as a unicorn. Yet now, when I need him more than I've ever needed anyone, here he is.

"Joel."

"What?" Joel gets startled when people talk to him.

"You've got to drive me somewhere."

"Where?"

"Woodstock."

"Woodstock? You mean upstate New York?"

"Yes."

"Why?"

"It's important. Joel, I can't tell you how important this is."

Instinctively, Joel backs away and narrows his eyes. "Why didn't you go with Hank?"

"You knew he was going up there?"

"Everyone knew. It's all he's been talking about for weeks."

Joel doesn't know that Hank and I haven't talked in weeks. Joel wouldn't know this because instead of bunking with the staff, or even hanging out with us, he goes home every night with Donna and Cully. We assume Cully goes home. Maybe he sleeps in his office.

"I would've gone with Hank," I lie, "but I forgot."

"You don't even like that music."

"I'm trying to broaden myself. Please, take me."

"You going to pay for gas?"

"Yes. Yes. And for meals."

"I like to stop at Howard Johnson's when I drive up to Cornell."

"Howard Johnson's it is. Any ice cream you like."

"You said a meal. Ice cream is not a meal."

"Let's go."

"Where are you going?" Connie walks up and butts in. She acts like nothing happened between us. For her, of course, it was nothing.

"Vin is gone," she says. "Where are you going?"

"I'm following Vin up to the Catskills."

"Why? Which hotel?"

"No hotel. It's a rock festival."

"What?" Connie flicks her cigarette onto the carpet. Joel picks it up. He doesn't like the hotel, but he protects his family's investment. Connie gets louder. "Who the hell's supposed to work this dinner?"

Hearing the commotion, Donna Salzman steps up. When she's excited—and doesn't have a microphone to make announcements— Mrs. Salzman whispers. "The guests are waiting. Where's the music?"

"Ask him." Connie points her chin at me.

I have no more time. Mrs. Salzman and I like each other. Every night at the bar, she asks me to accompany her in songs from *Finian's Rainbow*, which she starred in twenty years ago at sleepaway camp. Donna Salzman is a romantic.

"Mrs. Salzman." I pant in my anxiety. "'How are Things in Glocca Morra?' 'Look to the Rainbow.' 'Old Devil Moon.' I know you, Mrs. Salzman. They're not only songs for you. They speak to you the way music speaks to me. If you believe in those love songs—if you believe in love—you will let me skip this dinner, this one dinner, and rescue my girlfriend, Alyssa…*who's been kidnapped by Hank Einhorn*."

Donna Salzman's eyes widen as big as Eddie Cantor's. "*Kidnapped?* Have you called the police?"

"Vin and Mrs. Lawrence are already in pursuit. Now Joel and I have to go."

"Joel? My Joel? I don't like him driving at night. He gets sleepy."

"Mom, it's okay," Joel assures her. "We're going to stop frequently. At Howard Johnson's."

"You've already worked this out? Without asking me and your father?"

"Mrs. Salzman," I plead, "I'm asking you now. Every moment counts. If you believe in love and that pot of gold at the end of the rainbow, please let us go."

Donna Salzman falters. Connie looks up at the ceiling and grumbles, "I don't believe this."

Mrs. Salzman turns to Connie. "Can you sing without a piano?"

"She has a piano." We all turn and see Herman. "I can play. I lived in Paris for seven years. I know all the songs. In French."

"But," although he's a godsend, I have to warn my friend, "it's not a piano, Herman." Meaning the synthesizer.

"I saw it. It has a keyboard. A keyboard is a keyboard. Anyway, do you ever watch these people eat? Put food in front of them and they don't hear, they don't talk—the hotel could be on fire and they wouldn't notice. It'll be okay. Go."

"Go," Mrs. Salzman says squeezing my hand, "and find that pot of gold."

35

Leon

Well, there's no gold, but we've sure found a lot of pot.

By the time Joel approaches his second Howard Johnson's, in Liberty, New York, the caravan crawling to Max Yasgur's farm is at a standstill. Free spirits have parked on the side of Route 17 for the night and set up pup tents or laid out sleeping bags. Fires warm half-naked bodies, and we can smell the pot even with all the auto exhaust. You'd think we already made it to Woodstock since Janis Joplin is hollering at full blast from car radios.

"I think if we drive on the shoulder," Joel says, "we can get to that HoJo."

"Joel, you had a hamburger, fries, and a malted an hour ago. How much can you eat? It's like we're back at the hotel."

"You agreed."

"Not to the Full American Plan." Joel's gluttony makes Andrew look like Mahatma Gandhi.

We reach the Howard Johnson's without running over any flower children. They, in fact, give me a warm welcome when we slide out of the Rambler.

"*Pepe le Pew. Pepe le Pew.*"

"What are they saying?" I ask Joel.

"Pepe le Pew. You know, the cartoon. It's because you're still wearing that stupid French shirt and beret."

No one had mentioned this at the previous stop, but as we near the rock festival, people are not so polite.

"It really is pee-you," a guy as hairy as a baboon jeers. "What's in your car, man? Raw fish?"

"Hey," Joel yells. "They call it having a job. Ever hear of that?"

I stuff the beret in my pocket and would have removed the shirt—everyone else is stripping—until I'm thunderstruck to see, through the window using the restaurant's telephone booth...Vin Lawrence.

"Vin. Vin."

The hippies mimic my cry like I'm Brandon deWilde at the end of *Shane*. *"Vin. Vin."*

Swinging the door open, I run into Mrs. Lawrence. "Leon." She beams. "How nice to see you."

Only Beth Lawrence could make me believe that. Vin, still on the phone, looks harassed but then elated. He wraps up his call and joins us. Though Vin is a juicy target, wearing his tux, the tie-dyed hippies wisely leave him alone.

"Alyssa called Salzman's," he tells us. "She left a message."

"You see," Mrs. Lawrence says, smiling. "I told you she would call."

"Oh yeah. Miss Responsible. Now she wants to come home."

"Why?" I blurt out. "Has Hank done anything to her?"

"If he has, he's going to be roadkill."

"Vin," his wife soothes.

"Beth, don't start with me again. She's sixteen. He's nineteen. The switchboard operator at the hotel says she sounded okay. She wants to come home."

"Where are they?" Mrs. Lawrence asks.

"I'll check with the manager here. It sounds fairly close. They're stuck in this traffic mess, a little closer to Bethel. I'll have to walk. There's no other way to get up the road."

"I'll go with you," I say firmly.

"How did you get here?" For the first time Vin acknowledges me.

I point to the counter, where Joel is munching a club sandwich.

"Is he going to the concert?"

"No. Joel offered to give me a lift."

"Okay." Vin lets out a breath and tells Mrs. Lawrence, "Here's what we'll do. Honey, you drive back with Joel Salzman—"

"Oh no."

"I don't know how long it'll be before we find her." Vin's agitated again.

"If I'm not here," Mrs. Lawrence says softly, "you're going to lose your temper with Hank."

"I won't."

"Vin—"

"I promise. I promise, Beth. I think Alyssa...has been through a lot." Now he looks hard at me. "Is all this because of you? Did you two have a fight?"

I hesitate, ashamed to let Mrs. Lawrence know what happened.

"Sweetheart," she says to her husband. "There's plenty of time for that. Go find her. I'll go with Joel when he's finished eating."

"You could be up here longer than we are," I say, and hand Mrs. Lawrence enough money to pay for Joel's meal, as well as gas and another meal on the way back to Salzman's. She doesn't want to take it, but I insist.

Vin says, "How about paying for my gas?" He's not kidding.

That would be getting off lightly.

***

Alyssa

Did I say crazy? This is the *stupidest* thing I've ever done. The ride was bad enough. I, at least, had my own bucket seat next to Hank in the front, although the stick shift didn't stop him from sliding his hand up my thigh every five minutes. That I could control, by swatting him away with increasing ferocity. Nothing could keep Seth from whining for the whole two hours. In fairness, Seth, Phyllis, and Phillip were so smooshed in the backseat, they looked like Silly Putty. Kissing, hugging, and groping occupied the lovebirds. Seth had nothing to do but complain.

Seth: "This isn't a car, it's a trash compactor."

Hank: "What does that say about you?"

Me: Slaps Hank's hand.

And so on.

Then, as we're approaching Bethel, it finally occurs to me to ask, "How far are we from your friend's house?"

"What friend?"

"The frat brother. That's where we're staying tonight, right?"

"I haven't been able to reach him. He must be camping out already. I brought a sleeping bag."

"Did you bring one for me?"

"I thought we'd share."

I slap him even though his hand is on his thigh. "Pull over." I reach for the gear shift.

"What? Hey. You're going to strip the gears."

"Let me off at that diner."

"I'm hungry too," Seth says. "We should have brought the rest of Andrew's pie."

"He ate it all," Hank says.

"I'm not hungry. I have to make a call." I climb out of the car.

***

Leon

Into the inky blackness Vin and I stumble like Virgil and Dante, except neither of us knows where the hell we're going. Hundreds, maybe thousands of cars and vans are abandoned—along with all hope—down the middle of the road, bumper to bumper. Girls we see make us alarmed about Alyssa. Many are naked. Some are screwing. One is screaming obscenities. Rushing toward the screams, we find a crowd gathered at an open car door, helping—I swear—to deliver a baby. A brew of incense, weed, and beer mixes with BO to create the most appalling stench. On this eve of the music festival, fans are bellowing everything from Joan Baez to Joe Cocker.

Two, three, I don't know how many miles up the road to Max Yasgur's farm, we at last reach the eatery where Alyssa said she would be. She's still wearing her Salzman's t-shirt and shorts. Facing her dad, Alyssa looks mortified, then relieved, and falls into his arms. He hugs her and says nothing. Not expecting me to be here, and clearly resenting that I dogged her tracks, Alyssa ignores me. Hank does not.

"Look who's come to rescue Daddy's girl," he says to Phil and Phyl, who are kissing in a booth. "Daddy's boy."

"Hi Leon," Seth cheeps and then pouts. "Are you sure you have to go?" As much as he likes Alyssa, I can see Seth is glad to be paired off with Hank.

Vin, Alyssa, and I turn to leave. Hank knows better than to pick a fight with a beefy guy clearly seething, so he ignores Vin and vents his frustration on me. Not much to be feared from a kid in a French navy shirt looking scrawnier than ever.

"I give you credit, Leon. Usually you're at that empty playhouse with your only friend, who's what, about ninety, playing Beethoven, who's two hundred years old." Hank juts his jaw inches from mine. "Music you wouldn't have had the guts to play when it was new, and revolutionary."

I blink. For all the way he usually ignores me, Hank knows that was a smack right between my eyes.

"It's true," he smirks. "When Beethoven was blowing things up, you would have been hiding behind…who? Mozart? Bach? Whatever was old, and safe. Whatever let you hide."

Alyssa is staring at me. Vin too. They both look like they want to say something kind. Hank presses on.

"I'm a lot smarter than you are, Leon. A whole lot smarter. But I'm not hiding behind your snob culture. I've got the guts to try stopping an unjust war. A war you'd never volunteer to fight, the way Alyssa's brother did."

"Don't push your luck," Vin breaks in. "Let's go," he says to both Alyssa and me. Hank helps me leave with a dismissive shove.

"Tag along with your *ex*-girlfriend, Leon. 'Til some other guy takes her away."

I've been in only one fight in my life. In fourth grade, Dickie Haas—a kid with a glass eye who'd been held back, and who bullied all the younger kids—called my mother a whore. I didn't know exactly what that meant, and I don't remember exactly what happened next, but I found myself on top of that bum, pounding his face. Luckily for Dickie, it was winter, and I was wearing mittens. Unless he had a wool allergy, Dickie escaped serious injury.

This time I'm not a kid, and this isn't a daydream about Zorro. I know exactly what I'm doing when I haul off and sock Hank.

But I can't. He catches my wrist, wrenches my arm around my back, turns me, kicks me in the rear, and sends me hurtling headfirst into the door, right at the feet of a girl who's run into the diner, shouting, "The Beatles. *The Beatles are here.*"

***

Alyssa

Mass hysteria. Everyone crowding the diner, inside and out, like lightning bolts standing upright. Then they wave their arms, jump on tables, writhe, and squeal. Those nearest the door dive for it while Leon, lying there, curls up in a fetal position to avoid being crushed. Craning my neck and peering through the now open entryway, I behold the object of all this Beatlemania. A long black limousine. The driver's door opening. A plaid newsboy cap perched on shaggy black hair, and a bloke bellowing above the din in the most atrocious Merseybeat accent, "*Oi*. This the Dingworth Family Diner?"

Fab Four fanatics stampede the limo. Anthony stiff-arms the lot of them. Yes, of course, it's Anthony. Only a professional driver could have maneuvered through the vehicular and human traffic tonight. A professional driver, or a homicidal maniac. Anyway, he made it to the place where Sheryl, the switchboard operator, told him Seth would be. Now Anthony is swinging the passenger door open for Louise. The guys in the throng hoot and whistle. Louise is cute enough to be a groupie. She waves, completely unfazed. Next, Anthony lets out Si Perlman, and onlookers deflate faster than the Hindenburg. No Beatles. Louise takes Si's arm, Anthony makes like a one-man battering ram, enters the diner, picks up Leon with one hand and demands, "Where's the kid? Seth?"

Good question. Seth is not afraid of Anthony, much less of his own dad, but reflexively he's hiding under the table. Anthony can't see Seth, but he spots Hank and marches over.

Hank breaks the ice. "Anthony, isn't it?"

Anthony breaks Hank's jaw. This time Si Perlman lets him. The crowd quiets. Phyllis and Phillip keep kissing. I reach down to help Leon, not Hank.

Hank slowly scrapes himself off the floor and, as always, wants to protest. Si doesn't give him the chance.

"Hank," he begins.

"What the—"

"Don't make it worse with profanity, boy."

"Don't make it worse?" I think that's what Hank said. With his busted jaw, it's hard to tell.

"Not in front of Louise," Si warns.

"What the—"

"What did I tell you? The last time we talked…" Everyone in the diner inches closer to hear. This is better than Woodstock. "I told you to look out for my son. Is this what you call looking out for my son? Where is my son?"

The table next to Hank shakes. Unless Phyl and Phil are holding a séance, that's where Seth is hiding.

"C'mon out, ya little git."

"Anthony," Mr. Perlman admonishes, but Anthony is in no mood. He vents to everyone.

"I miss me dinner. I miss *The Eddie Cantor Story*, and this runaway deek's under a table, shivering like a wet mouse."

"Sethie, are you okay?" Louise joins him under the table.

"Make them go away," Seth pleads in a small voice.

"We're going away, Seth, but we're taking you with us," his father says, more sternly than I've ever heard him. This must be the voice he uses with Cully. "Seth, this was not right. You know it was not right. Your mother would be ashamed of you."

"Don't say that," Seth squeals, standing up.

"I'm sorry, but it's true. Let's go."

Anthony makes to clear a path, but everyone jumps back on their own. Mr. Perlman turns to me.

"I'm surprised at you, Alyssa. And with you," Si says, turning to Dad.

"Don't bring my daughter into this. She didn't come here on her own."

"What do you mean?" Si asks. Now I think Anthony will kill Hank, and I couldn't care less.

"I mean she—" Dad halts. He doesn't know what he means. He doesn't know why I left. I don't either, not anymore. Not with Leon lying there beaten and beaten down. "I don't know," Dad sighs. "Let's go."

"Would it be all right," Louise asks Dad timidly, "if I drive back with you and Alyssa?" Louise, who really is a darling, knows I need someone in our car to keep Dad calm.

"How are you going to drive all the way back to Salzman's with him?" Si asks. I don't think he's possessive, only worried. He asks Dad, "What kind of car do you have?"

"It's a couple miles down the road. A Riviera."

"A Buick?"

"It's a beautiful car."

Si turns to Louise. "How are you going to get to his car?"

"Cookie," Louise takes Si by the lapels and half whispers. I worry he might fall over. The poor man looks frail and tired. "You can drive us. I mean Anthony can drive us to Vin's car, which looks brand new—"

"I've got a brand-new Cadillac here to take you to Salzman's," Si wails. "And a professional driver—"

"Cookie, I need to be with Alyssa. She needs me. You need to be with Seth. Take him in the limo. Don't let Anthony give him a hard time."

"Balls up," Anthony rumbles.

"Where's your wife?" Si asks Dad. "She's with your car?"

"She went back in Joel Salzman's car."

"*Joel Salzman?*"

"It's a long story. Let's—Louise, sure, you can come with us." Dad sighs again. "Can we go?"

***

Leon

Louise spots the rest of us—Phyl, Phil, and me. Hank she has no use for. To the rest of us, she asks, "Do you all have a ride home? I mean back to the hotel?"

Phillip looks sheepish. "We're going to the festival. Phyllis and me. With…" He indicates Hank without wanting to say his name and rile up Anthony.

"How are you getting back, Leon?" Louise asks. Bless her. I figured they'd ditch me. Which would be only fair.

"Can he go with you?" Vin asks Si Perlman.

Si looks straight at me for the first time. This is no treat. He may be frail, but his stare is steely. "Did you talk my son into this?"

Seth jumps to explain, "No, he didn't, Dad. Leon drove up with Mr. Lawrence to find me." Wow, I didn't see that coming. *Good for you, Seth.*

"Yes?" Mr. Perlman says to me. "Thank you."

With that we all slink out.

But not before a girl wearing braids and beads and not much else sobs, "So, where are the Beatles?"

36

Leon

The only reason I go to the playhouse the next morning is to thank Herman and tell him my decision. With two hours to stew over it in the back of Si Perlman's limousine, that decision is final, and long overdue.

When I stumble in at 7:15, Smitty is here, Herman is here and, astonishingly, *miraculously*…Alyssa is here too. I look at her with my mouth open, exactly like the first time in the lobby. She looks at me the way you look at gum on your shoe.

"Louise says I should give you another chance. You may not want it, because Anthony says if you screw up again, you're a dead man."

"I want it."

"Don't know what this is about," Smitty says, "but, I guess, hooray." He whispers to me, "Don't screw up."

There's no cause for celebration. Alyssa looks haggard, and that's how I feel. I've put her through so much. But Herman, still sporting his beret, refuses to share the prevailing mood.

"Two hours of '*La vie en rose*' and I'm feeling in the pink," he trills. "How about some Bach?"

"Only if you play it. Thank you for filling in last night, Herman. Did it go okay?"

"Did it go okay? Next week, International Night takes us to the Argentine, and Alyssa and I are going to tango. Come on, we want Bach. Don't make us beg."

"I need to talk with you about something else," Alyssa says firmly but quietly.

"Thank you. Anything. First, though, I need to talk with Herman so he won't keep losing sleep every morning."

"Old people don't sleep," he says. "Who needs dreams when you have so many memories?"

"Well, I've been having the wrong dreams," I say, refusing to join him on the bench. "I've been kidding myself, Herman. I'm not good enough. You know it. Even if I were, even if I could win big competitions and scratch out some kind of career, I'd still be living other people's memories. Nothing that matters to anyone my age."

Herman stares at his hands. Then he stares at me. "And I was so looking forward to seeing Newark." He's joking. "You know, my friend, there's really only one memory. The shared memory that makes us human. By doing this," he gestures to the piano, "you're helping to keep it alive."

"For who? Whom." I'm going out—again—with a writer, so I have to talk correctly. "Herman, I hate to tell you, but nobody's interested. You think the people here who still like Al Jolson are old? The average person who shows up for piano recitals has one foot in the grave and the other one out the door. They go out of some sense of obligation."

"Or aspiration. That's not so terrible," Herman says, softly playing random chords. "When I started touring America in the 1920s, you know who was in the audience? Musicians and music lovers, sure. Also immigrants, like the parents and grandparents of a lot of the people here. Immigrants from all over who fled to this country because back home they were nothing. They could never get an education like the two of you are doing. Many of them couldn't read English, or even their own language, but they wanted to learn. They wanted to improve themselves." He strikes a loud chord. "Self-improvement. Such a great American slogan. They knew there was something they had missed out on, and they yearned for it. For themselves, and especially for their children. America back then made it easy. Alyssa," he says, turning to the chair she's moved next to the piano. "Leon tells me you and your mother like that marvelous Walt Disney cartoon *Fantasia*."

"I do too." I leer. "Those sexy centaur girls."

Not a good joke I realize as the words tumble out of my big mouth. Not after Connie. But, charitably, Alyssa laughs for the first time, saying, "My sister and I called out when we were little, 'That horse girl with the blonde hair, or the red hair—that's me.'"

Herman is in stitches. "Stokowski is an old friend of mine. He appeared in other movies too. Very popular movies. Also Jeanette MacDonald. Mario Lanza. They sang opera but they were big, big movie stars. Well, Lanza got too big and fat and he couldn't make movies anymore. People didn't go to their films from any sense of obligation. They wanted to learn. They loved what they learned because they had something their college-educated grandchildren don't have. Humility. The immigrants knew there was something from long ago worth learning. They didn't think if they got a diploma they knew it all."

"Like *The Wizard of Oz*," Alyssa says.

"Yes?"

"It's a line from the movie. 'When they graduate they have no more brains than you have, but they have one thing you haven't got—a diploma.'"

"Ah," Herman remembers. He plays "Over the Rainbow" and smiles. "I watch that every year on TV with my girls. Three generations. That's what I call a good movie."

While he plays, I'm thinking. "Yeah, but maybe kids my age don't want to look back. They don't want to act like aristocrats. Young people today want music for everyone that you don't have to study and dress up to enjoy."

"That's Hank talking." Herman stops playing and says, "I went to his debates. Marxists claim 'high culture' props up the white European ruling class, but Leon, great art isn't about being a snob. It speaks to everyone. It listens to everyone. It continues the dialogue that makes us human."

"What dialogue?" Alyssa asks.

"Well," Herman says, playing snatches from each composer, "take music. Bach spoke to Mozart, who spoke to Chopin, who spoke to our friend Smitty's Debussy, who spoke to—who does Sonny Jones like?"

"Duke Ellington," Alyssa and I say together.

Herman noodles a little of "It Don't Mean a Thing If It Ain't Got That Swing." I wouldn't have guessed that was his thing. "Duke Ellington," my friend adds, segueing smoothly into "Solitude," sharing almost the whole gorgeous song, "Duke Ellington is a big fan of Ravel and Debussy."

"So is Miles Davis," I note. "And Bill Evans."

"Yes? Tell Mr. Einhorn that Debussy didn't only listen to Mozart and Chopin. He loved music from as far away as Java. That's one reason Debussy strikes a chord"—Herman plays what sound like tinkling bells—"with Asians and other people all over the world."

We listen as the bells become Debussy's "*Pagodes*."

"That's the same guy who wrote my song?" Smitty asks. "That nice."

We sit thinking until Alyssa says, "I don't know much classical music, but I know my father's music. Hank ragged on me, but those old songs are beautiful. Maybe they're not Mozart—"

"Who needs to make comparisons?" Herman says. "It's all beautiful."

"I know," Alyssa adds, "that twenty-five years from now, people, some people, will still listen to those old songs when nobody's listening to Woodstock music."

Herman shakes his head slowly. "Now there, my dear, I think you might be mistaken. I think we'll still have this rock music. Or music that sounds much like it. For a sad reason. Because it's a dead end. We've turned back the clock. We've reduced music to rhythm and shouting. You'll always have it now, because there's no place else to go. Look, forget music." Herman pounds another loud chord and swivels on the bench. "People get mad if you attack their music. Do you like modern art? Paintings?"

Phillip the expert isn't here, so I say yes, and Alyssa does too.

Herman nods. "Playing in Russia after the war, the First World War, I got to know a famous artist named Malevich. He'd painted an early abstract painting. A black square. Do you know it? Well, that's what it was. Do you know what he called it? *Black Square*."

Herman guffaws so abruptly, his glasses nearly fall off.

"Now Malevich faced a problem. What can you paint after *Black Square*? Luckily, he had an inspiration. He painted a white square.

"So, Malevich was making an interesting point. Exactly as Marcel Duchamp did when he put a urinal in an art gallery. Yes, really. He called it *Fountain*. His point was that anything can be art, and there's art in everything. I understand when you reduce art to something absurd, or absurdly childish, you have nowhere to go. You silence that dialogue that makes us human. There's a bigger problem." Herman lowers his voice and takes our hands. "There are leaders, political leaders, who like this dead-end culture. Who don't want people to keep thinking and growing. The leaders want people to be children because children accept less, and they're more easily led."

"That's Orwell," I say. "Big Brother destroying history and culture."

"Also Huxley," Alyssa adds. "You know. The 'feelies' in *Brave New World*. Moronic sex and adventure movies. You're right. They keep people submissive."

We all chew on that for a moment. Then I put it to Herman. "Still, who says your culture, your high art can save anyone? Hitler loved music. The Nazis fed their people Beethoven. But," I say, taking his wrist, "you have numbers on your arm. I've never asked you about them because I know a lot of survivors don't like to talk about what happened. These numbers they branded you with, they mean you were in Auschwitz, right?"

He is silent. Then, sorrowfully he muttered, "Yes. They did this at Auschwitz." He puts down his arm. "The Nazis killed my parents and my whole family, almost. They took my darling wife from me. You love this beautiful, wonderful girl? I loved my beautiful, wonderful wife for thirty-four years. They broke my heart. They also broke my hands. I'll tell you something else, Leon, that proves your point because it's an important point. You say you won't have a big career. I was never a great soloist. Instead, I played chamber music." He turns to Alyssa. "You know what chamber music is? Music for two or three, or some small number of musicians."

"Like quartets," she says.

"Exactly. I was a member of a trio, a successful trio. The violinist was famous in Europe. No, I won't say who, Leon. He was famous for his Beethoven concerto and sonatas, and the trios we played. The most noble music. High-minded. Humane, as Beethoven is humane. But when I was arrested in Prague, and they put my wife and me on the train to Theresienstadt, a camp with a lot of musicians, my partner, my violinist friend—my fellow lover of Beethoven—did not lift a finger to help us. At least Greta and I were able to stay together there.

"We should have left Europe long before. In Heaven, I'll beg Greta's forgiveness. Then the Nazis sent us to Auschwitz, and I never saw her again. My colleague not only looked the other way, he lectured—not to me, but to others—that Jews brought the world international banking, and other Jews brought the world socialist and communist dictatorships, and all kinds of cultural depravity. Everything bad, nothing good. So, he said, Hitler was right to exterminate us.

"One of our trio's most applauded pieces was Mendelssohn's D minor piano trio. Marvelous. My partner was happy never to play it again after Hitler outlawed Jewish music. So yes, I am a survivor. Though after the war my broken hands would not let me play like before. My former friend survived too. I'm told he still teaches in Salzburg.

"More important, *kindelah*, Beethoven also survives. Mendelssohn too. Unless people like you, Leon, stop playing them."

37

Alyssa

"I want you to get a test."

We're rushing to the flagpole. Five minutes until they'll be raising the flag, and I want this settled before Neil blows his horn.

Leon stops short. "What test?"

"For venereal diseases."

"Alyssa."

"Lower your voice," I whisper fiercely, and walk even faster.

"Alyssa. I told you. We were standing in her room."

"Naked."

"Half-naked. Not the venereal half. If I could get a social disease standing in a room, maybe you got one riding in Hank's car."

I stop and stare at him, tears welling up.

"Are you going to keep bringing that up?"

"It's the first time I mentioned it."

"You should be ashamed. Why do you think I went with him?"

"For revenge."

I take a deep breath. "I was going to say, because I was so upset. But yes. Revenge is better."

"You're not Vincenzo's daughter for nothing."

"You better believe it." I'm walking again. Fast. "My mother's a tough cookie too. She doesn't show it."

"Vanessa's a terror."

"You're changing the subject. Are you going to go for that test?"

Leon stops. He's panting. "Now I'm supposed to ask Joel Salzman for another ride? I can't afford to feed him while we wait for a doctor."

"Ask your mother to take you. She ought to be concerned."

"She's concerned all right, but she doesn't have a car. Alyssa, please." Tenderly, he takes my hand. "I didn't even kiss her."

"Oh. I never thought you'd kiss her. That's so disgusting."

"Anyway," he mumbles, "it's not like you and I are having, you know. Full sex."

"Oh."

***

Leon

Thankfully, that's the end of our talk. The campers swarm. I duck behind what Alyssa told me is Albert's tree. Sure enough, here he is. I whisper to the kid, "Alyssa says you're engaged. Why aren't you with your girl?"

"Ardis is mad at me."

"Get in line. What'd you do?"

"Well, I guess I kissed Ellen Drexler."

"You guess?"

"She ran away so fast, it was hard to tell."

"Then everyone chased after you again?" I size up my chubby friend. "At least you're getting exercise."

"It's not funny."

"No, it's not. You and I better get used to begging."

38

Alyssa

I'm looking over Leon's shoulder at the last page. He holds it longer than any normal person would need to finish. I want to snatch the composition book out of his hands and hit him with it. He must think it's awful. He looks up.

"Alyssa. This… is… *amazing*."

"You don't have to say that."

"I do, but it also happens to be true. This is a fantastically well-written, funny, touching story. You've only spoken to Mickey a couple of times, for a few minutes. And Howie—"

"Do you think they'll mind? None of it is true, apart from their showing the movie. I made everything up."

"That's what makes it fantastic, in the best sense. So much imagination and heart. What are you going to do with it?"

We're back on the lodge porch, looking down at the pond.

"I don't know."

"I do." Leon smiles broadly. His electric blue eyes sparkle. "My mother knows a woman from Hunter College who's an editor at Lanning Publishing. They only exchange holiday cards, but I bet she'd read this."

"Let your mom read it first. Of course, I have to show it to Mickey Katz."

"They'll both love it."

"Did you? Really?"

"Really."

"You still have to get the test."

"Can I pass my swimming test instead?"

"You'd better pass both. Now get back to practicing. The piano. And, Leon, thank you."

He receives his first kiss since… I don't want to talk about it.

39

Leon

Two days later, Anthony drives me for the blood test in Morristown that proves I'm clean—not that it matters, because I'll be a virgin 'til my wedding night at the age of forty.

Today, Herman's granddaughter Susan is taking the two of us to Newark. We enter an area still struggling to recover from six days of race riots in the summer of '67.

After cancelling the competition that was supposed to be held a month after the riots, last year's competition went off without any problems, and now folks in Newark of all races and backgrounds are warmly welcoming twenty-three contestants from eleven countries for the World Piano Competition of 1969.

Do you know who's getting a hero's welcome?

Herman Pressler.

That imp. It's never occurred to me to do any research at the local library on this buttinski in Bermuda shorts. Turns out, Herman Pressler is a legend to insiders in the music world. He played with Casals, Huberman, and other giants. That "successful trio" of his, the Canticum, is considered one of the all-time best.

Teachers, coaches, and even judges bend down to embrace Herman. He introduces me, but of course it would be bad form to put in a good word. One person he does want me to meet is a former student of his. Herman has taught at both Julliard and the Curtis Institute in Philadelphia. This is the guy I've been arguing with every morning at Salzman's playhouse.

That student, Cate Panetti, now teaches at Yale. What a delightful woman, with a big toothy smile, and so warm. She really puts me at ease. Cate is not a judge. She's here with another contestant, a young girl from South Korea, so Herman feels he can talk me up a little. My friend tells Cate that, besides music, I read seriously—my first-grade teacher, Mrs. Stonehill, would never believe it—and that I think about "the state of the world." Out of the blue, Herman suggests that Professor Panetti might help me get into Yale.

Never, not for a moment have I aspired to an Ivy League school. Neither of my parents is a college graduate. My father went to fashion school. Mother, who had to work full-time, took night courses at Hunter, where she met that editor. One of the excellent SUNY colleges seems right up my alley. It's all we can afford. Professor Panetti says we should talk, and she and her lovely student wish me luck.

The first round begins at eleven. I leave Herman to his fans and climb up to a rehearsal area a couple of floors above the ornate and cavernous concert hall. The contestants are all dressed in suits or dresses. No formal clothes unless you make it to the finals on Saturday afternoon, so we don't need dressing rooms. There's only one piano in the rehearsal hall where we can limber up. At this moment, the music coming from that Steinway is the most astounding playing I've ever heard.

The pianist is a kid. I don't mean a teenager. A kid. The threshold age for this competition is twelve, and he can't be much older. Tall for his age and gawky, he makes me look like a muscleman. The kid sits ramrod straight. Wildly disordered hair covers his brow except when he stares at the rafters—not dreamy, but daring them not to applaud. Chopin's B minor Sonata never sounded like this before, at once stately and spiky, impossibly slow yet soaring on orchestral tone that could easily fill Symphony Hall and half of the rest of Newark. All the confidence Cate Panetti gave me trickles out of my shoes. Never having been a prodigy, never having attended a conservatory, I've never been confronted with so much raw talent.

The kid is not showing off. He soon slouches off alongside a striking woman with sable eyes who takes him in hand. They speak what sounds like Russian. A grim man accompanies them. Cate's student, Mi-hee Kim, whispers to me that the man is a Soviet "minder." Usually it's older, established performers who defect to the West. I can already tell why losing this kid would be an embarrassment.

I'm shy and at least somewhat competitive. Nevertheless, I have to go over.

"Pardon me," I say to the pianist. "Do you speak English?"

"Yes," the woman with him replies. "How can we help you?" Her English sounds English. Not like Anthony. Upper-crust English.

"Well, you could drop out of the competition. That was impressive."

The kid smiles. He scowls when he plays, but now he shares a subversive grin.

"Are you trying to psych me out?" His Russian accent is soft-pedaled because he talks softly, unlike the way he plays. I know from previous competitions that everyone the world over watches American movies, and they love to trot out the argot. "I'm Ivo." He pronounces it Eevo.

"I'm Leon."

The minder looks wary, but the woman thaws and introduces herself as Marya. She's one of Ivo's teachers. Marya politely asks if I'd like to limber up on the piano. My shyness returns, compounded by dread. She senses it and shines an understanding smile, which makes me feel worse. Ivo senses it and kindly suggests, "Maybe, Leon, we could play four-hands to relax. Do you like Rachmaninoff's second suite?"

I laugh and have to tell him, "The last time I tried that, Ivo, was with my teacher, Miss Federoff, and then I proposed."

"Proposed?"

"Marriage. She must have been twenty-five. I was ten."

"Well, I'm thirteen," Ivo laughs, "and Marya has been shooting me down for years."

"None of my students ever propose to me anymore," says Herman who, as usual, materializes out of the ether. "They may be too young for me."

Ivo has never heard of Herman Pressler, thank goodness, or I would feel like an even bigger dunce. But Marya has. They talk for a while about what Russia was like when Herman last visited, before the war. Marya is Russian, technically Georgian. Ivo is from Yugoslavia. The Soviets got a tip years ago and took him in hand. He and I share the piano bench and try playing from memory the captivating Romance from that Rachmaninoff. It would've been better with two pianos, and more accurate with the score, but playing calms me down.

When the three of them leave, Herman looks at me and says, "He won't win."

"What? Why?"

"Because I know these judges. He's not what they want. Including the one from his own Central Music School in Moscow. I hear they're actually trying to take him down a peg. So he won't be so—what would you say?"

"Brilliant? Original?"

"Unorthodox," Herman says. "Unorthodox does not play well at competitions. I'm not saying that's good. It's simply true."

"So where does that put me?"

"Someone who heard you in Cincinnati was saying good things a few minutes ago."

"Because I'm boring?"

"Because you're good. I'm not trying to psych you out." Herman loves to sound hip. "Play from the heart, *meyn khaver*." He's calling me his friend. "Play for Alyssa."

What Herman meant was that besides the Beethoven, a Bach Partita, and some Bartok, I have also worked up Robert Schumann's *Fantasie*. For a reason. The *Fantasie* was Robert's impassioned love letter to Clara Wieck. Her father was so intent on separating them that he took Schumann to court, and accused him of being a pauper, a drunk, and a libertine.

I don't drink. Thanks to bellhopping and the band I'm no longer a pauper. Since Vin mercifully doesn't know about Connie, he has no reason to think me a libertine. Still, on paternal principle, Vin objects to anyone holding hands with his daughter. Herman knows I identify with Schumann, and I play that piece beyond my own meager talent—fiercely, achingly, with Alyssa before me at every moment.

Today in Newark… it works. Alyssa can't hear it. The camp said they can spare her only on the third day of the competition, Saturday afternoon, if I made it to the finals. Today's judges seemed to respond. One even clapped. I've made the cut for round two.

Herman and I can't stay to hear the others. We apologize to Ivo, and to Cate and Mi-hee. Even if I could handle the stress, we have to get back to the hotel. This is another International Night. I'm certainly not going to let Donna Salzman down again.

As Herman said, tonight's theme is Argentina. Our gauchos and their gals eat enough steak to make cows an endangered species. When the meal winds down, Alyssa sneaks into the main dining room for a few minutes while her girls swig chocolate milk outside. I play "*La Cumparsita,*" on an upright piano Mrs. Salzman brought in, and Alyssa and Herman tango with all the sensuality of Jack Lemmon and Joe E. Brown in *Some Like It Hot.*

I wish Alyssa and I could be dancing, but I'm never going to take lessons ever again.

***

Alyssa

Could there ever be a more touching compliment than this?

Mickey Katz and Howie are back for Movie Night. It's exactly a week since I ran off with Hank to Woodstock. I don't know what he wound up thinking of the festival, and I don't want to know. Phyllis can't stop raving. Coverage has been all over the papers and TV. They'll probably make a movie.

All I care about is tonight's movie at Salzman's because I've intercepted Mickey during his set-up and handed him my short story called, "And I Thank You." Mickey raises his eyebrows, puffs on his pipe, and asks Howie to thread the first reel of *Enter Laughing.* Then Mickey reads from my composition book in a back corner of the playhouse. I should've typed it up. Marion would've let me into Cully's outer office to use the typewriter. At least my handwriting is legible, unlike Dad's and Leon's. Among other acts of contrition, Leon wrote me a letter of apology. I presume there's an apology hidden somewhere in that scribbling.

After what seems like an even longer time than it took Leon to read what really is a short story, Mickey rejoins Howie and me next to the projector. He has tears in his eyes.

"I'm honored that we inspired you to write this. Excellent, Alyssa. *Ex*-cellent. Have your parents read it?"

"Yes. Leon's mother is sending a copy to someone she knows in publishing."

"I bet a lot of magazines would be delighted to see this. *The Saturday Evening Post. Reader's Digest.* I'm not saying that because of, you know, our connection. Truly excellent. Someday, when it's in a whole collection of stories, Howie and I will say we knew you when. Did you and Leon make up?"

That non sequitur catches me off guard. "Ah, yes."

"You had everyone frantic last week. It's not for me to say, but—"

"No, you're right, Mr. Katz. I hope that didn't take away from the film."

He smiles. "They missed your father at dinner, and Connie Sims made a stink, but nobody interferes with Eddie Cantor. Those old vaudevillians were troupers. In the future, maybe you can confine your adventures to paper. Since I'm a father and a teacher, like your folks, I'm recommending."

"Thank you."

"Howie and I are more or less the stars of your story, so that gives us a little say, right Howie?"

"Right." I don't know how much of this he took in, but the projector's light is only a candle compared to Howie's megawatt smile.

40

Leon

For Friday's second round, the remaining eight contestants all have to play a Beethoven sonata of our choice. Of course, my choice is the "Tempest." Many pianists take a tempestuous approach. Mine—Herman's and mine—is agitated, but more contemplative, like the eye of the storm.

Who knows if the judges will advance me. Several other contestants, including Mi-hee, Cate's Korean student, play a favorite of young medal-seekers, Beethoven's "Appassionata." They storm like a tornado. Good thing I don't try to match their power and velocity.

Ivo could. He could blow them away. But he's going a different way. Ivo chose Beethoven's last sonata. An otherworldly piece that's considered the preserve of ripened masters, like Herman. The choice is presumptuous for a kid. Then there's the way Ivo's performing it, running with Stravinsky's idea that Beethoven got the jump on all kinds of modern things, including boogie-woogie. I don't agree with Ivo's interpretation, but he's showing that you can rethink old Ludwig and carry on Herman's dialogue.

After a smattering of applause from the small audience, three of the five judges sitting in the mezzanine put a stop to that dialogue. They tell Ivo to scram. More politely than that, but he's out. I'm at once elated and ashamed to find that, somehow, I and not he will be going on to the finals along with Mi-hee and Aleksander Merzhanov, a fifteen-year-old who was born in Russia but grew up in White Plains, New York.

Ivo doesn't seem that steamed. He and Marya feel he played well. Their confidence in their own inner compass inspires me, especially since Ivo easily could have won the whole shebang had he played it safe. I like him immensely. So does Herman, who's come up with a great idea.

"Are you doing anything tonight?" he asks.

Marya thinks my coach is being sarcastic. "We had planned on practicing," she replies dryly. "I suppose that can be postponed now. What do you have in mind?"

"Why not come back with us to Salzman's Hotel? That's where I'm staying for the summer. Leon plays piano in the band for shows and at the bar they have."

"You're going to play in a band tonight?" Ivo asked incredulously. "With the finals tomorrow?"

"Well," I say a little sheepishly, "Herman and I figure it's better not to break the routine. I'd only worry. It's still playing. The band's music is not bad."

"Where is this hotel?" Marya asks skeptically.

"About half an hour from here," Herman explains. "Maybe a little more. It's not full, and I bet they could give you rooms for the night. I'd be happy to pay if it means we could keep reminiscing about my old Russian friends." Herman indicates "the minder." "Would he mind?"

Marya confers with Grigori. That's the minder. She must be building up the show, or the bar, because Grigori nods enthusiastically.

***

Alyssa

I try not to gush too much about Leon earning his way into the finals, because he's brought along three other people from the competition. Ivo, who didn't make the cut, has a distant, wary air until he opens up. Then he's cute as can be. He and the striking Marya seem remarkably close. Not inappropriate, but intimate in a mentor-student kind of way.

While Ivo may have struck out with the judges, the teenyboppers in Salzman's coffee shop treat him like a rock star thanks to his wild hair, his exotic accent, and his immediate skill at pinball. Seth pronounces him a "one hundred percent seaworthy dreamboat."

Ivo is more taken with my sister. The little vixen can't stop giggling and placing her hand over Ivo's on the pinball flipper button. Dad walks in, sees this different kind of arms control, and pulls Vanessa aside to warn her that Ivo is a commie. Leon says he and Ivo haven't discussed politics, so he doesn't know. All I know is, to judge from his conquest of Salzman's, the Russkis have a secret weapon.

Marya is chatting with Herman and his granddaughter Susan in the playhouse, waiting for the show. Herman gets along with everyone, and the women hit it off too, especially after Marya asks to meet Susan's daughter, the infamous Ardis.

At the bar, a sinister man they came in with, Grigori, downs what must be his monthly quota of vodka, on the hotel tab. Oh yes, when Donna Salzman heard about Herman's guests, she made them her guests, which is beyond generous. However, this being a swanky Friday night, Grigori appears depressed to be the only man in the casino without a dinner jacket. With the commuting husbands back from the City, Grigori is also depressed to be the only man without a woman. He's depressed as well about Moscow being so far away, and for all I know, about the Mets starting to gain on the Cubs.

It's likely this man is naturally glum.

***

Leon

The show is a good one. Vin and Connie sing more than usual, because tonight's one of those novelty acts, a mind-reader billed as The Amazing Eduardo. Somehow, I have no idea how, he informs guests where they're from, what they do for a living—you name it. Salzman's weekday widows must worry that Eduardo knows they've been playing around, and I don't mean mahjong.

The person most worried about Eduardo is Grigori. He staggers into the playhouse from the bar, and even though Grigori doesn't say a word, Eduardo identifies him as a Russian. Grigori accuses

Eduardo of being a *shpion*—a spy, which is rich, since we all assume Grigori is a spy. What kind of report he'll send back about Salzman's, I can't imagine.

It may not reflect well on Grigori, especially after the band enlists him in the show. Vin tells me to play "*Ochi Chernye,*" and then asks Grigori to teach everyone the words. The Soviet minder grows suspicious, then sentimental, and then blubbery as Sonny plies him with more vodka. Marya shouts in Russian, presumably for encores, because Grigori climbs onstage and will not leave.

The Amazing Eduardo is happy to leave when Russian Jews in the audience grab the mic from Grigori and serenade us with their hometown hits. Ronny Mintz belts out "*Hava Nagila*" and a bar mitzvah breaks out. Sonny and the other servers shove the long tables to the walls, and the audience forms a circle to dance the *hora*. Including kids from the coffee shop who aren't supposed to be in the playhouse—Ivo and Vanessa among the most boisterous.

You wouldn't think anything could top that, until some of the Sephardic Jews ask me to play the *syrtaki* from *Zorba the Greek*. You have to see Grigori dancing himself into a frenzy and then collapsing. The guests haul him onto a chair, raise the chair over their heads, resume their dance—and I'd say that is the closest America's ever come to thawing the Cold War.

41

Leon

I've woken up from another dream. Not the old recurring one about Zorro. This dream, as you might expect, is not enjoyable—not with all the dread about today's finals. No memory lapse. No walking onstage without my pants. That would've been normal. What freaked me out in this nightmare was the piano—playing itself. Like a player piano. I was sitting in front of it afraid to put my hands on the keyboard, because every time I tried, the keys bit me like an animal. The orchestra and the audience are laughing uproariously. Here's the worst part. The piano was playing brilliantly. Finally, I slammed both my hands down on the keys, shoved back the bench, and ran off the stage, out the back door, and through the streets of Newark.

The dream ended as I jumped into a car.

It was Hank's red Peugeot.

***

Alyssa

On this Saturday morning, the morning of Leon's final round, Marya has met Ardis at breakfast and taught her a few Russian insults to hurl at her fiancé, young Albert. Susan is once again driving her grandfather and Leon to Newark, this time for the morning orchestra rehearsal. For the finals, Leon gets to play with an orchestra. I can't wait. Ivo is following with Marya, who's driving Grigori's rental car while their minder sleeps off his drunken stupor.

Amid all the ruckus and nervousness, Leon and I won't have much time alone. I hope to steal a moment before he performs this afternoon. My parents are driving me. The camp's given me the afternoon off—which I don't deserve, after all the trouble I've caused. I thanked the Goldmans and Donna Salzman.

I can't wait for Leon to see I'm wearing our lucky blue dress.

***

Leon

The finals have Mi-hee, Aleksander, and me each playing a concerto. That's a piece for piano and orchestra. Our orchestra is a group mostly recruited from the New Jersey Symphony. We also have its fine conductor, Henry Lewis. I know him from recordings of fellow Black musicians like William Grant Still and—paging Sonny Jones—Duke Ellington, who wrote a stirring, sassy ballet score called *The River*.

Aleksander is the first to rehearse. I arrive too late to hear his run-through of Liszt's first piano concerto. By all accounts, Franz Liszt was the greatest piano virtuoso ever. Princesses threw their jewelry at his feet when he played, and then fainted from ecstasy. Hopefully, Aleksander won't excite that kind of hysteria.

I'm up next. Maestro Lewis introduces me to the orchestra as the winner of last summer's Cincinnati competition. Despite my dream, they don't laugh, and the piano doesn't bite.

My piece is Beethoven's third piano concerto. It's not flashy like the Liszt, but it has everything—power, poetry, and a moment that, win or lose, I want to share with Alyssa.

She's not yet heard me play classical music in public, much less with an orchestra. I might never have another chance. To share this moment with the girl of my dreams will be the ultimate payoff for twelve years of practice.

When we finish, the string players tap their strings with their bows, and the other musicians lightly stamp their feet. They probably do that for all of us. The maestro's smile means a lot.

Aleksander did not stay to hear me, so I figure it's okay not to hang around for Mi-hee, who I like. She and Cate Panetti understand. Instead, Herman treats Ivo, Marya, and me to lunch—a light but long one.

Now we're headed back to Symphony Hall for the actual performance.

And an incredible surprise.

It seems everyone at the hotel has come to hear me. I mean everyone. Sonny got Tyrone to fill in for him bellhopping this afternoon. There's Phyllis, and also Phillip—who returned from Brooklyn to be here. Hugh, Sandi, Neil—Seth, of course. Harvey from the band—a lot of the staff are here, even people I hardly know. Si Perlman and Louise have come. Louise is giving me kisses on both cheeks. It makes me feel continental. Mr. Perlman pats me on the back, so it's okay. Anthony, thank goodness, has stayed with the limo. All I need is a bone-crushing handshake from him.

My parents arrive together. It's the first time my dad has ever heard me in a competition. Uncle Max brought him from Queens. I love my Uncle Max. He almost gets into a fight with an usher because Max wants to keep puffing his cigar. I haven't written enough here to thank Uncle Max for everything all through the years. Without him I never would have learned to play the piano. I tell him that, in his ear, and he hugs me.

Vin and Beth Lawrence give me a hug too—Vin's even bigger than his wife's.

Now get this. Donna Salzman rented a bus for the older kids and teens, so they could make this a field trip. That means Hank is here, although he doesn't come over to say hello. I'm sure he'll spend the afternoon outside, smoking and stewing far away from Anthony.

Donna has come, and you won't believe this, but she brought along Cully. He hangs back at first, afraid irate guests will jump him. Instead, most of them are delighted to say hello to this pleasant, handsome man. I shake his hand, touched that he's here.

"Mr. Salzman, I'm Leon Kraus."

"How are you? Be careful with those hands. I mean yours. Good to see you." He really is shy.

"Thanks so much," I say. "Not only for coming. For letting me work at the hotel. Especially in the band."

"Sure, sure," Cully says slipping away. "You're doing a great job."

"You do a great job," I insist, taking his elbow. "I hope you know how much Salzman's means to all these people. A lot of them tell me it's the highlight of their whole year."

"Really?" He seems amazed.

"Yes. So again, thanks, Mr. Salzman."

He smiles. "Break a leg. You have your hands, so you don't need your legs, right?"

"Well, I do use the pedals."

"Right."

"It might be embarrassing for them to have to carry me to the piano."

"True." He smiles again, warmly. "Well, Leon, knock 'em dead."

Then he glances at Si Perlman and probably wants to rephrase that.

The only person who isn't glad to see Cully is Tilly. Okay, I'm kidding. Tilly didn't come. I'm sure she's already in Salzman's card room on her second pack of cigarettes and third glass of Scotch.

Even without Tilly, even with Hank, now I really want to make good.

***

Alyssa

This must be what the Beatles go through all the time. Getting mobbed. After shaking and kissing and hugging everyone who's come to hear him play, Leon takes my hand and leads me behind a wide gilded stairway leading up to the balcony.

We've been kissing a lot since I allowed him to break the ice after Woodstock. Pretty much non-stop when we can be alone or slip behind something. For this competition, Leon has become a gold-medal kisser. At first, he was reluctant to use his tongue other than to moisten his dry lips. Then he went to the other extreme, and I thought I was kissing the Roto Rooter man.

Today… it's perfect.

***

Leon

Alyssa leaves to go to her parents. I meet Herman in a corridor. The two of us walk toward the dressing room. We've already dropped off my tuxedo. I think I look pretty snazzy, for me, until I see Aleksander in white tie and tails. He looks like Fred Astaire.

By closing the door, I can muffle the sound of his performance. But I don't. Herman and I listen as the orchestra plays the national anthem and then blares out Liszt's first theme. Aleksander follows with thunderous octaves. He's good. Not merely a pounder, but musical. At the end, Aleksander's earned a roar of applause from the audience that almost fills the hall. I have the chance to congratulate him as he returns to the dressing rooms, perspiring.

Now I'm perspiring. Until Herman pulls me down so we can look at each other eye to eye.

"You think you're trying to win a prize or a college scholarship, you're not. You're being given the chance to play a Beethoven concerto. To share it with people who care about you. Including me. Play your heart out, *meyn khaver*."

The applause that greets me is not tumultuous, but then I haven't done anything yet. I'm not wearing tails, only a slightly too small tuxedo and massive black glasses. Maestro Lewis allows me a long moment to adjust the piano bench.

There's a story about how the nutty genius Glenn Gould took half an hour to adjust his seat. Finally, the conductor George Szell suggested, "Why don't we shave half an inch off your arse?" Thinking of this on the stage, I nearly crack up. Which probably would not go over well with the judges. But it clears my head.

I nod to the maestro, and the orchestra begins.

The opening they play by themselves lasts about three and a half minutes. During the first minute, I anxiously review what I'm going to do when it's time for me to join in. Then I listen, and think only of what Beethoven is doing. By the time I enter this truly musical dialogue, I'm transfixed. Maestro Lewis and his players lift me along, back and forth, soft and loud, until it's time for my bow-wow solo at the end of the first movement, what's called the *cadenza*.

Normally a *cadenza* is my least favorite part of a concerto, and not only because I don't have big technique to show off. This *cadenza* is different. It ends with that moment I so want to share with Alyssa, and now with everyone who's come to share this privilege with me.

It ends with a trill that seems to approach the infinite, a trembling vibration that trails off into the most eloquent silence. Then the orchestra softly, ever so softly, returns, and I play a series of *arpeggios*—descending notes of an elongated chord—that is the most beautiful sound in the world.

Apart from Alyssa behind the staircase an hour ago whispering, for the first time, that she loves me.

***

Alyssa

I'm sitting with my parents in the tenth-row center, along with Seth, Cully and Donna Salzman, and Si and Louise. Mr. Perlman made a call to management. They gave him the best seats.

Newark Symphony Hall is overwhelming. More impressive than Lincoln Center because it's older and more opulent. I've never been to Carnegie Hall, but I figure it can't be much nicer.

As for the audience, few people are dressed as beautifully as Louise, Mrs. Salzman, and Mrs. Kraus, the most stunning among them. My mother looks lovely too. I was afraid that my dress might billow too much in my seat, until Mom gave me a hint about folding it under myself.

The orchestra, the conductor, and—I have to admit—the first contestant all seem to be first-rate.

Let me be honest. For weeks I've been hearing beautiful music, but also a lot of Leon's stumbling and mistakes. Followed by a lot of mild, and sometimes not so mild, cursing.

The first pianist, Aleksander, was great. He looked fabulous. What do I know, but I can't imagine anyone playing his show-stopper of a piece much better.

When Leon preceded Maestro Lewis onto the enormous stage and shook the hand of the first violinist, Seth went nuts. Everyone else was reserved. Particularly while we watched Leon fidgeting with the piano bench.

But then, when the orchestra started his Beethoven, and Leon's music thundered and sang and whispered, I swear to you I've never been so transported in my life. Leon is taking me back to the pool, under the stars, holding hands.

He's not a coward. It takes courage to get up there. It takes discipline—years and years of self-discipline. Everyone says Hank is handsome, and he is. But Leon really does look like Peter O'Toole.

Elegant, in a lanky, nonchalant kind of way. I only wish he'd shown me the tuxedo pants before. Mom would have let them down a little. Still, Leon looks wonderful. He's not gyrating and making faces like the first guy, yet you can see how moved he is.

Everyone is so quiet. Rapt. Louise is loving this, I can tell. As is Mr. Perlman. He's not pretending to conduct, like Phillip, but you can see how he almost jumps when the music does. He's letting the music fill him up.

Oh my. This must be—what does Leon call it—his long trill. Oh my God. Listen to that drum, so faint, then the *arpeggios*. Soft. Again and again. This is Jesus calming the wind and the waves, making everything pure and beautiful.

Leon, I do love you.

I can spare this ring.

***

Leon

Someone has thrown a ring onto the stage, hitting the piano. I know who it is because I told Alyssa about Franz Liszt and his delirious princesses. I wish I could tell you I bent gracefully and picked up the ring. Instead, one of the cellists is handing it to me while the audience laughs affectionately and applauds us all—Alyssa, the cellist, and me.

Herman is beaming backstage. Cate Panetti congratulates me, as does Mi-hee. She's wearing a purple gown and her hair up. Lovely. The only person Mi-hee towers over is Herman. But having heard her warm up, I already know Mi-hee is a fire-eater.

She's chosen a competition warhorse—not Beethoven's, but Prokofiev's third piano concerto. It's a great piece, climaxing in the first movement with the piano revving up like a race car at full throttle. Mi-hee rides that for all it's worth while also capturing Prokofiev's playfulness, sarcasm, and, of course, his Russian melancholy, which would have sounded a chord with Grigori—if he was awake by now.

Mi-hee is superb. The audience for the first time rises to its feet. I shout praise when Mi-hee returns backstage. She's summoned for two more ovations. One more than I got.

So that's it. She deserves to win. Aleksander was terrific too. I still envy his tails. But good as he is, Mi-hee is a future star. Maybe not a genius like Glenn Gould and Ivo, but superb.

Yet somehow—I'm not sure how, or why, or whether I should accept it—the gold medal goes...*to me*.

Or maybe not.

I believe the *real* winner of the 1969 World Piano Competition for Young People in Newark, New Jersey is Herman Pressler.

This is not false modesty. I know I didn't deserve to win that prize if the criterion was talent. Ivo is in a class of his own. Mi-hee is headed for professional success. Aleksander plays the piano better than I ever will.

I have a feeling a majority of the deeply split judges wanted to honor Herman, who is now retired, by honoring a young fellow he's been coaching. They certainly heard a lot of Herman in my Beethoven. They may also have been honoring my choice of Beethoven.

There's another story, about a visitor to Germany who heard a Mozart concerto played badly. When it ended, the visitor asked a woman next to him, "Why are you all applauding so much? The pianist was terrible." The woman replied, "We're applauding Mozart."

Mi-hee and Aleksander could not have been more generous. Ivo and Maria waited in the wings for moral support. Then, after I was given the gold medal and the check onstage—thank heaven we all won scholarship money, or I would've felt even worse—the Salzman contingent burst through the backstage door like this was the last Full American Plan meal of the season.

I won't try to describe how wonderful everyone was. Sonny gave me a sly wink and said if I wanted to make real money, I should return to bellhopping for the big Labor Day checkout. I will. Mrs. Lawrence had tears in her eyes. My mother didn't seem to resent that at all. Si Perlman took my left hand, put his other hand on my shoulder, looked me straight in the eye, and did not smile. Louise must've felt this was such a great honor, she didn't dare to approach. Instead she blew me a kiss and hugged Mother so hard I thought I'd have to break it up.

You know who did approach me from out of nowhere?

Hank Einhorn.

He strode up like he was going to deck me, and then said, "You sounded good." I was dumbfounded. Until he added, "Obviously, the Korean girl deserved to win, but that's okay. Gives me an excuse to console her."

42

Alyssa

This Saturday night before Labor Day weekend has turned into a party. For Leon. If Donna Salzman had time to arrange things, she would've dressed the band in powdered wigs with the theme, "Classical Music, Can You Dig It?" As it is, the audience in the playhouse has given him an ovation, and Leon's mother, of all people, requested the beginning of the Schumann *Fantasie*. By now she knows it's our not-so-secret declaration.

The act tonight is a big one. Morey Amsterdam. He used to be on *The Dick Van Dyke Show*. Mr. Amsterdam is too mainstream to tell jokes in Yiddish. Finally, I understand them.

The great moment of the night, of the whole day—of the whole summer—is Dad announcing that he and Herman Pressler have a special award of their own. Dad asks me to join Leon on the dance floor while Herman takes his place at the piano.

Do I have to tell you what my father sang? It's transporting Leon and me to Fred and Ginger's gazebo by the sea, under the moonlight, where we hold each other and gaze into each other's eyes and hardly notice that my father is wincing a little when he croons about Leon wanting to spend his life making love to me day and night... "Night and Day."

__Epilogue__

Alyssa and Leon

Where to begin?

Albert, the kissing bandit, took over his father's Cadillac dealership. He wound up with three wives. Not, we trust, simultaneously. Although with Albert, we couldn't be certain.

Ardis was not one of them.

Hank gained national notoriety along with his friends Abbie Hoffman and Jerry Rubin. The latter famously declared, "All money represents theft." Later, like Rubin, Hank landed a corner office on Wall Street.

Hugh became a chiropractor. His office is off the green in his beloved Morristown, which since 1969 has erected skyscrapers yet retains its charm. He married a lovely girl. She was never a centerfold, but he can look at her without a flashlight.

Phillip also moved beyond centerfolds. In a way. He went to Princeton and stayed there, running its prestigious art museum, which he turned into his personal pornography collection. Phillip's first acquisitions included a bare-breasted Minoan snake goddess and a Bouguereau nude that would have made Mae West blush.

Do men ever outgrow their boyhood fetishes? A lucky few are allowed to indulge them while donors stand around sipping sherry.

Someone who didn't outgrow anything is Andrew. On the contrary, Andrew is now slim. He has to be since his heart attack. We lost touch, but Sheryl—the former switchboard operator who's still plugged in to everyone—tells us he's okay.

Seth is more than okay. He runs Page Five of the *New York World* and has entrée to every party and show on both coasts. You might suppose Seth's writing is bitchy, but long ago Louise convinced him that compassion counts for more than clout. There's plenty Seth could write that never gets into print, or onto the *World*'s website. We know, because he gossips with us all the time.

Our group includes Seth's husband, Arthur. They've now been married for thirty-one years. We introduced them when Arthur was our college classmate. Up until graduation, Arthur never came out of the closet. He didn't want to upset his family, so he led a celibate life. When he did come out, Arthur became one of the pioneering attorneys and law professors in the country advocating gay rights. He also loves classical music, and occasionally takes Seth to concerts, which Seth hates.

Si Perlman was always proud that the bar he partly owned, The Stonewall Inn, played a historic role in the gay rights struggle. Si died in 1989, after twenty years of wedded bliss with Louise. He never went to prison. Anthony did—for a bar fight, of all things. He dropped the accent in 1980 after John Lennon was killed.

Louise lives in the City and she also has a place back home near her family in Ohio. She remained an observant Jew.

We don't know what happened to Tilly Mintz—and we don't want to know. The woman was mean to the bone.

We both went to Yale. While there, Duke Ellington was an artist in residence. We reacquainted the great man with his biggest fan when Sonny Jones came to visit. The Duke graciously claimed he remembered Libby Jones's little boy from the Howard Theater in Washington. Sonny became Ellington's driver.

About ten years later, Sonny started his own limo service for celebrities and hired Tyrone as a driver. One celebrity who never rode with Sonny was Frank Sinatra. Which was lucky for Frank because he would've gotten an earful. In fairness, Sinatra, like Sonny, idolized Billie Holiday, so they could've talked about that.

Classical music lovers will have guessed that Ivo is Ivo Kuljerić. Six years after Newark, Ivo rocketed to classical superstardom by losing another competition. That's because one of the judges, the great Martha Argerich, stormed out in protest. Ivo married Marya, and we all remained close. Our friend won't mind us telling you that he went to pieces when Marya died four years ago.

As we'd go to pieces if anything ever happened to either of us. We married not long after graduating from college. Louise, Seth, Sonny—a lot of the people in these pages, including Joanie Caffiero from first grade—came to our wedding.

We have three daughters. Maggie is named after Magda, who divorced Fredi after Leon graduated from high school. Maggie and Magda love shopping together, and Magda taught Maggie mahjong. We also have twin girls who don't want us even to write their first names, now that they've read too much about our embarrassing youth.

"You were at Woodstock?"

Well...almost.

Leon became music director for WQCN radio in New York. Please keep sending your donations. With Harvey Shapiro's help, Leon has his own long-running show, interviewing pianists and playing historic recordings. Brahms made one for Thomas Edison in 1889. It's unlistenable, but don't tell Harvey.

Herman helped too, until our dearest friend passed away at the age of 101. God bless him. The Canticum Trio figures high on Leon's playlist. Leon also plays in a trio, but he insists it's not nearly as good.

Alyssa, as you know, is Alyssa Lawrence. You may not have known that her first published story was the one about Mickey and Howie Katz, and she's still friends with them. *The New Yorker* didn't get the chance to publish that story, but it's taken almost all the others since, with Lanning Publishers bringing out Alyssa's collections and novels. Beth still proofreads them.

Vin passed away two years ago. We miss him every day.

Salzman's Hotel declared bankruptcy in 1975. Izzy's boys fought valiantly to keep it afloat, and 'til the end they had help from Si Perlman, but vacation patterns changed.

As Andrew the busboy predicted, more and more guests moved out of Brooklyn and the other boroughs and bought homes on Long Island. That meant husbands could see their wives every night. Whether this prevented or hastened divorces is hard to say.

You can find a website Phyllis started where guests and staff stay in touch, and the Salzman family gets to see how much their summer resort meant to us all.

More than the walk on the moon and Woodstock, it changed our lives.

ABOUT THE AUTHOR

Jack Atherton's family owned a Mount Freedom summer resort called Ackerman's Hotel where he worked as a bellhop. Jack went to Yale, wrote music reviews, practiced law, and then anchored and reported for television stations in San Antonio, Miami, Cincinnati, and Dayton. His first novel, *Falling for Miami*, is published by Boroughs Publishing Group.

Jack and his dream girl, Aymsley, have been married for thirty-eight years. Their two remarkable daughters don't want Dad to write about them either.

CONNECT WITH JACK:
website: RealJackAtherton.com
facebook: facebook.com/jack.atherton.9480
twitter: @jackatherton111
instagram: @Anchormanjack

www.BOROUGHSPUBLISHINGGROUP.com

If you enjoyed this book, please write a review. Our authors appreciate the feedback, and it helps future readers find books they love. We welcome your comments and invite you to send them to info@boroughspublishinggroup.com. Follow us on Facebook, Twitter and Instagram, and be sure to sign up for our newsletter for surprises and new releases from your favorite authors.

Are you an aspiring writer? Check out www.boroughspublishinggroup.com/submit and see if we can help you make your dreams come true.